THIS LIMITED AND SIGNED FIRST EDITION OF

Scott McCloud's

ZOT!

The Complete Black and White Collection:
1987–1991

has been specially bound and
produced by the publisher.

THIS IS _176_ OF 1,000 COPIES.

ZOT!

1987–1991

THE COMPLETE BLACK AND WHITE COLLECTION

WRITTEN AND DRAWN BY

SCOTT McCLOUD

HARPER

NEW YORK • LONDON • TORONTO • SYDNEY

HARPER

HarperCollins books may be purchased for educational, business, or sales promotional use. For information please write: Special Markets Department, HarperCollins Publishers, 10 East 53rd Street, New York, NY 10022.

FIRST EDITION

Library of Congress Cataloging-in-Publication Data is available upon request.

ISBN 978-0-06-164512-9

08 09 10 11 12 QK/RRD 10 09 08 07 06 05 04 03 02 01

On the Threshold of Adulthood

It's a dangerous thing

I'm doing here. The ink is barely dry on *Making Comics,* my 250-page explanation of storytelling in comics. Anything I drew next was bound to be judged against those theories pretty harshly, but to follow it up with five hundred pages of comics I drew twenty years ago, long before I'd learned most of those lessons for myself—well, let's just say I feel a bit exposed here. *Zot!* is a coming-of-age story; its teenage protagonists go through a lot of changes in the course of these stories; but it was also a time of growth for me as I grappled with where I wanted comics to take me, and with my own limitations as an artist and writer. Both my characters and I were young and naïve, stumbling awkwardly toward what it meant to be an adult in this world, while making new worlds out of our dreams. And in many ways, this was the struggle of American comics in those same years, 1987–1991. We were all on the threshold of adulthood, and any search through the comics-store shelves of those days was, like any search through these pages, a quest for diamonds in the rough.

Included in this volume are every one of the black and white *Zot!* stories I wrote and drew, including my original roughs for the 48-page story "Getting to 99" (used by Chuck Austen to draw a two-issue fill-in while I was on my honeymoon). There was an earlier ten-issue color run I affectionately refer to as my "training wheels," but these black and white stories were designed to stand alone, and I'm confident that they do just that, over two decades later.

I've allowed myself the luxury of a few minor changes in these pages (noted on a separate page at the end of this introduction) but for the most part, you're holding an intact time capsule of that brief period in the American comics market when the promise that comics could do "anything" was just beginning to bear fruit—even for a humble, independent black and white superhero comic book, as it started to outgrow its origins and reach for something more.

Nerds with Ambition

I was 13 years old when I met Kurt Busiek in the lunchroom of Diamond Junior High School in Lexington, Massachusetts, in 1973. Kurt and I both enjoyed reading science fiction, quoting *Monty Python,* watching *Star Trek,* and listening to old radio shows like *The Goon Show,* which Kurt's family enjoyed on an old mammoth reel-to-reel tape recorder. In short, we were nerds of the first order. But in one important respect, Kurt's nerd credentials surpassed even mine: Kurt enjoyed comic books and I couldn't stand the things.

Kurt and I were in eighth grade at the time. The New England "junior high" system, reportedly introduced to the region by my great-grandfather Jack, covered grades seven, eight, and nine. I can't help but wonder how my life and career choices might have been changed had old Jack's educational philosophy not resulted in a school map that brought Kurt and I from distant neighborhoods to attend classes in the same building. Kurt had to work hard to overcome my prejudices against comics at the time, and I don't know if anyone

else would have had the patience. I read real books. I appreciated real art. I didn't read no stinking comics.

Nearly every day after school for a period of months, Kurt would come over to my house to escape his father, who kept giving him pointless chores to do, and he'd play me a game of chess—my full-time obsession in those days—in exchange for a game of pool on our basement pool table (Kurt was good at the former, but enjoyed the latter more). Again and again, he'd offer to lend me some stacks of comics from his collection. Again and again, I'd refuse.

Fortunately, Kurt had some help. The Route 128 loop around Boston in the '70s, which included Lexington, was a bit like what Silicon Valley would become in the '90s; a settling ground for engineers and computer scientists on the cutting edge of technology. That meant a lot of geeky kids, and as it happened, a lot of comics readers. Kurt lived across town, but only a few houses down from me were no less than three kids who read and even drew their own comics; the slightly younger Dewan brothers, Ted and Brian, whose art was playfully weird, and our slightly older friend Chris Bing, who was deadly serious about breaking into the big leagues. Their different sensibilities helped wear down

---

Top left: Yes, I was president of the chess club.
Right: The young Mr. Busiek.
Opposite page: One of my "schedule creatures" sold for a dime each to my fellow students in high school.

my resistance long enough for Kurt to finally get me to agree to try a few stacks of old Marvel superhero comics, starting with *Daredevil* and the original *X-Men*.

Every morning before school in those days, I'd been waking up to WBCN in Boston and listening to the "LP du Jour" (a new album played in its entirety, part of Charles Laquidara's show, "The Big Mattress") on my tinny clock radio. So, while bands like Supertramp, the Tubes, and Roxy Music filled my ears, I began filling my eyes and brain with comic books. I was a 14-year-old boy living in America, so naturally it was only a matter of time before I fell in love with the superhero genre. In the coming year, comics would replace chess as my full-time obsession and I decided to become a professional comics artist. My nerd training was complete.

In the winter of tenth grade, I began drawing pictures of superheroes for a role-playing game we were working on. The following year, Kurt and I began collaborating on *The Battle of Lexington,* in which two teams of Marvel superheroes beat the living crap out of each other for no discernible reason, while casually destroying our high school, the town library, and various Revolutionary-era historic landmarks. It ran to sixty pages of fully rendered pencil drawings on typing paper. Years later, Kurt and I would perform a slide show reading of the entire comic at four comics events to hundreds of appalled and delighted fans, but for obvious reasons, it will never see print.

Our first published comic book—and our

weirdest to this very day—came out while we were all still in high school. It was a limited edition comic book sold at the Boston Pops Orchestra's season opener in Boston's Symphony Hall and projected on a giant screen with local radio personalities providing the voices (including Laquidara himself, if memory serves). This bizarre, one-of-a-kind black and white oddity called *Pow! Biff! Pops!* was the first sanctioned crossover between Marvel and DC superheroes (not to mention

conductor Seiji Ozawa). DC's president at the time, Sol Harrison, sat at our table. Kurt wrote the script for Chris to draw, I only did layouts for the book, but I was given the additional task of designing three giant murals displayed in the lobby and auctioned off to benefit local charities. Chris' Mom was our way in—my first brush with nepotism—and even at 16 years old, I knew that the gig had less to do with talent and more to do with the arbitrary nature of social connections. Still, it looked good on my résumé a few years later when I applied for my first job. Unsold copies of the comic were *burned*, by the way. Collectors, take note.

Local comics mavens Richard Howell and Carol Kalish helped us sharpen our skills and broaden our knowledge, as Kurt and I prepared to head for college. We both ended up at Syracuse University, where we worked hard to break into comics, figuring it was only a matter of time. While still in college, we actually got a deal to produce a superhero comic called *Vanguard*, but the publisher that commissioned it went belly-up before the first issue was published. A trip to

Left: The very first sketch of the retro-futuristic hero that would become Zot. Bottom left: Trying out faces.

New York in our junior year, scripts and portfolios in hand, proved similarly fruitless. We were two very frustrated fanboys.

In my senior year design class at Syracuse, we learned how to prepare a résumé. We were assigned to choose at least one prospective employer to try it out on. I chose the DC Comics production department. Three weeks before graduation, I was woken up in my dorm room by a call from DC's head of production, Bob Rozakis, asking me if I'd like to come in for an interview. I stood there, blinking for a moment, then said yes . . . yes, I could manage that. Portfolio in hand, I showed up in Manhattan three days later. I got the job and returned to Syracuse, levitating all the way.

Making the Leap

Working in DC production was the perfect first job for me. All day long, stacks of original comics pages were deposited next to my drafting table. I would take each of those stiff, oversized boards, often filled with artwork by pros whose work I had enjoyed as a reader in high school, and I would look for stray pencil lines, crossed panel borders, and editorial corrections. The whole process was instantly demystified for me. I knew I could make my own comics and couldn't wait to do so. But the wheels turned slowly at DC. I got the feeling that it could be a long time before I climbed enough rungs on the ladder even to draw, much less write and draw, my own creations. Kurt, meanwhile, scored his first professional assignment and started his own climb to fame (today, he's one of American comics' most successful and respected writers). The comparison was not lost on me.

On Sunday, June 20, 1982, three weeks after beginning my job at DC and moving to Manhattan, I visited master cartoonist Will Eisner at his house in White Plains—an arranged meeting thanks to Will's old tennis partner and a teacher of mine at Syracuse, Murray Tinkelman. Will talked with me for a while about my work and what I wanted out of comics. He looked at the Marvel/DC-style sample pages I had in my portfolio, then at the more unusual illustration work I'd also brought. Pointing at the odder stuff, he said that it seemed to him that I was more interested in those than in the more conventional samples. He was right.

This page: Images from the original Zot! *proposal including a shot of Bellows looking suspiciously like Jack Lemmon's Professor Fate.*

Early the next morning, my mother phoned. My father had died that same Sunday (Father's Day as it turned out). I arranged for a flight home that afternoon. Walking south alongside Central Park in the early morning sun on my way to DC, I thought about how my father had made every moment count, had never wasted an opportunity. Arriving at DC, I told Bob Rozakis that I needed to take a couple of days off to return home for a funeral. I also told him I wouldn't be doing any overtime for a while. I needed to work on a proposal for a comic of my own.

The following year, I sent a 100-page proposal to four independent publishers for a comic called *Zot!* I also showed it to Archie Goodwin at Marvel's more creatively adventurous Epic imprint (he sweetly turned it down, but with encouragement) and Dick Giordano at DC, who showed some potential interest in the property, but couldn't offer the kind of ownership and control I was looking for.

All four independent publishers were interested, to varying degrees, but two in particular seemed like good bets: California-based Eclipse and Chicago-based First. I liked Eclipse's deal better, and they could publish it a few months sooner than First. Getting published sooner was important to me because, well, what if there was a nuclear war and the world ended and I still wasn't a published comic book artist? No, there wasn't a moment to waste. The first issue hit comic book stores in March 1984. I was 23 years old.

Artists with delusions that they can write are more common than the reverse, because their delusions can't be as quickly dispelled with a casual glance. Kurt knew he couldn't draw well enough for the major leagues, but I began writing comics without hesitation, blissfully ignoring the fact that I'd had no formal training whatsoever as a writer. *Zot!*'s first incarnation, a 10-issue color run that was published from 1984–85, had a gimmick rather than a story—a precious key which all the characters were trying to find—and I simply hung whatever visual storytelling ideas I had around that gimmick. It worked well enough at the time, but clearly I was making it all up as I went along. There were plenty of pages where my hero and his friends were just flying around for no particular reason. With these black and white stories, however, starting in early 1987 at the advanced age of 26, I began making a more concerted effort to improve as a writer and produce more self-contained stories that had at least some substance beyond their visual tricks.

Growing Pains: American Comics in the '80s

By the early '80s, my world view of comics had already been enlarged by American underground and avant-garde comics, European albums, and Japanese comics or "manga." I was especially interested in manga. I studied hundreds of untranslated manga collections at Books Kinokuniya, Manhattan's biggest Japanese bookstore, only three blocks from DC's offices at 75 Rockefeller Plaza. I knew there was more to life than just superheroes. I just didn't see that reflected yet in the average American comic book store.

Beginning in the late '70s, there had been a slow, steady rise in the number of "direct market" retailers; comic book stores that offered a much wider selection of titles than what Kurt and I had found on the spinner-racks in our local drug and convenience stores. The Million Year Picnic in Cambridge was one of the first, and one of the best such stores. When Kurt and I found the place, we were in Heaven. Unfortunately, many of the stores that followed the Picnic's lead weren't nearly as eclectic or deep in their selection, and all comics stores, including the Picnic, depended on superhero fans to pay the rent.

In choosing to create *Zot!,* I was throwing in my lot with a sort of ground level independent movement that emphasized creativity and personal vision, but still hovered close to the superhero genre and related genres. In other words, I was playing it safe. Creators like Will Eisner, Art Spiegelman, the Hernandez Brothers, and Harvey Pekar, meanwhile, were creating something entirely

Opposite: Zot graces the cover of the newsletter for Berkeley's legendary store Comics & Comix.
Above: My attempt to get it out of my system through parody; 1986's one-shot Destroy!! *was nothing but one gargantuan fight scene printed in a giant format and billed as "The Loudest Comic in the Universe."*

new, working with subject matter utterly unrelated to mainstream superheroes. In doing so they stood apart from the market. The market, for the most part, had returned the favor.

In 1986, Frank Miller's *Dark Knight* and Alan Moore and Dave Gibbons' *Watchmen* became the standard-bearers for creative progress in American comics, cementing the idea in the public mind that better comics equaled better (and darker) superhero comics. Art Spiegelman's Pulitzer was still six years in the future. Into this era, *Zot!* returned, more modest in scale than those impressive giants,

---

Above: *Rethinking Butch for the black and white reboot.*
Below: *Early designs for new supporting characters Ronnie, Brandy, Spike, and Terry.*

but with the same outward goal of giving a half-century-old genre a face-lift. Inwardly, though, I had a broader picture of comics in my mind. Like a baby kangaroo, my comic stayed in the warm pouch of the genre that gave birth to it, but it had a mind to hop in a different direction.

Zot! in Black and White

This collection is divided into two parts. "Heroes and Villains" collects the first seventeen issues and has more of my unconvential brand of superhero action, but also focuses heavily on the real-world emotional story of the earthbound, pessimistic Jenny. Much of the storytelling drew heavily on my growing fascination with manga as well as alternative creators like the Hernandez Brothers. Part Two, "The Earth Stories," collects the last nine issues, which take place entirely on our world, with almost no superhero elements at all: stories of ordinary people living ordinary lives, as seen through an extraordinary visitor's eyes.

Zot! was a comic of changes. The black and white run was itself a radical shift in style and substance from the earlier color incarnation. The shift of focus from "Heroes and Villains" to "The Earth Stories" may seem as if I'd switched from one comic to another. And throughout *Zot!*, my drawing and writing style was constantly in flux. My character designs changed as I struggled to improve their expressiveness, as I struggled against my own considerable limitations as an artist, and as I struggled to show my characters actually physically *growing up* during the run.

The most tumultuous changes in *Zot!*, however, may have been in the mind of its author. I was grappling with serious questions of what I wanted out of comics, what I wanted to say through my stories, and if *Zot!*

was even the right place in which to say them. And in this way, the transformations of *Zot!* over these five hundred pages were the very same transformations about to happen to American comics—an art form, an industry, and a community struggling to break out of its shell and take wing as the more diverse, literate, and formally ambitious medium just coming into view in this century.

The "Other" Zot

This book came out to 576 pages, so we've kept the focus to the complete black and white series as written and drawn by me, but there were two important other versions of *Zot!* that deserve mention here. One is the finished art provided by Chuck Austen for our two-part fill-in "Getting to 99," as mentioned earlier.

The other was a one-page backup feature by legendary stick figure and mini-comics king Matt Feazell, which grew to six pages in the later issues and even had its own fill-in issue, entitled *Zot! 14 ½.* I'd been a big fan of Matt's stick figure comics in the '80s, featuring heroes like Cynicalman and Antisocial Man. While *Zot!* was on hiatus, Matt and I had collaborated on a short-run mini called *Zot! 10 ½.*

Eclipse wanted in on the act, so we let them put out their own printing, which wound up selling 20,000 copies (making it the highest selling mini-comic of all time, for what that's worth). Matt continues to make comics in Hamtramck, Michigan, where his wife, Karen, is the mayor.

Needless to say, we would have loved to include both Chuck's finished art and Matt's back-ups in this volume, but 576 pages is pushing it, and adding those two would have upped it to 752! We look forward to arranging for a printing of both in some form in the not-too-distant future.

Above: *Zot, Jenny, and Butch dance in Matt's fill-in issue.*
Left: *Matt in Hamtramck, where we visited him during our family's year-long 50-State tour.*

A Note on Changes

Readers of the original series will notice some changes to the art and story on certain pages. For the most part, these are my original drawings and dialogue from the late '80s—warts and all—but in addition to the occasional proofreading correction, I've given myself the luxury of catching a few bigger errors and stylistic missteps that I've long wanted to address in the original issues, including:

Jenny's Hair on pages 17–138

When the series relaunched I tried using a china marker for Jenny's hair. The effect looked okay on the original art boards, but it never translated to print well, so I gave up five issues in. Here in this volume, I've replaced the china marker strokes with straight brushstrokes to keep it consistent with later issues.

Dougie's Swearing on pages 501–507

The bully in *Zot!* #34 who threatens Woody originally let loose with a string of classic four-letter Anglo-Saxon swears so strong that they struck some readers as off-the-charts, distracting, and inconsistent with the overall tone of the series. Over the years, I've come to agree with them, so I've toned it down a bit this time around. The language is still strong, and you'll find the occasional swear where appropriate (Dekko's "shit-heap" comment on his first page, originally mistaken for "shit-head" when originally lettered, is still there, for example) but I think the new version is a better fit with the series as a whole. Lest anyone think my publisher forced me to wash Dougie's mouth out with soap, you can assure them it was my idea.

Miscellaneous Faces and Figures

I successfully suppressed my urge to redraw all five hundred pages, but occasionally, there was a face or figure that was exceptionally irritating, and which I gave myself permission to replace with something more acceptable. For consistency's sake, I didn't replace them with my current drawing style, but simply drew them as I would have twenty years ago if I hadn't been asleep at the wheel that day. There are plenty of clumsy figures and faces still remaining, but hopefully I've raised the floor slightly.

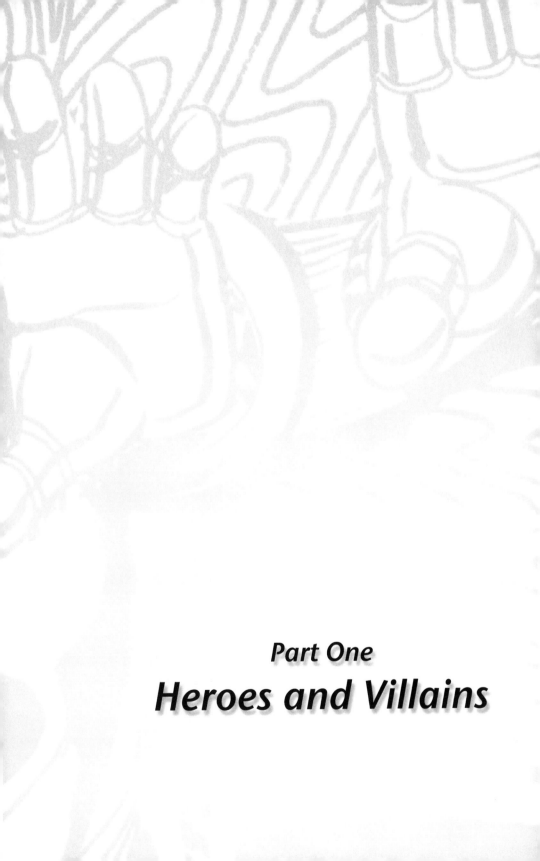

Part One
Heroes and Villains

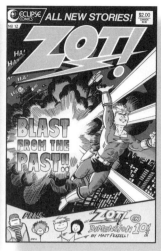

Planet Earth

First published in *Zot! #11–12*.

Lettering:

Bob Lappan

Original series editor:

cat yronwode

Note: As mentioned in the introduction, there had been an earlier ten-issue color run of *Zot!,* but the black and white issue #11 was really a full reboot. We would have called it a "New Number One!" but doing so was annoyingly fashionable in those days.

EVERY NIGHT, I WALK OUT HERE, JUST TO WAIT...

I KNOW HE'S NOT UP THERE... NOT *EXACTLY*...IT'S JUST THE ONLY PLACE TO *LOOK*...

AND I KNOW IT HASN'T BEEN ALL THAT *LONG*...

STILL...

IT SEEMS LIKE I'VE WAITED *FOREVER*...

Y'SEE...

THERE'S *THIS GUY* I KNOW...

LIKE NO ONE YOU'VE EVER MET...

FROM A *PLACE*...

...*YOU WOULD NOT BELIEVE.*

THEY CALL THE PLACE *"EARTH,"* JUST LIKE US.

THEY CALL MY FRIEND--

ZOT!

PLANET EARTH PART ONE

BY **SCOTT McCLOUD**

LETTERER
bob lappan

EDITOR
CAT ⊕ YRONWODE

PREPARE TO DIE!

PHUMPH!

WELL, I LED HIM OUT INTO THE OPEN!

NOW WHAT?!

20

21

AND IF A TIME EVER CAME WHEN HE HAD TO GIVE HIS *OWN* LIFE TO SAVE *SOMEONE ELSE* --

-- I'LL BET HE WOULDN'T HAVE TO *THINK TWICE.*

NOT THAT IT'S EVER *COME UP* BEFORE.

O.K., HE'S NOT YOUR *"BOYFRIEND."* YOU ONLY TALK ABOUT HIM *ALL THE TIME* AND HOW HE'S JUST *THE ULTIMATE EVERYTHING* AND WHAT A COOL *PLACE* HE'S FROM...

...WHEREVER *THAT* IS, SINCE YOU *STILL* HAVEN'T TOLD ME...

I'M SORRY, TERRY. IT'S JUST KINDA *WEIRD*, THAT'S ALL. HE'S NOT FROM *AROUND* HERE.

SO HE'S A *PYGMY*, RIGHT? *BIG DEAL...* HEY, *YOU* JUST CAME FROM *CALIFORNIA*, Y'KNOW, THAT'S WEIRD *ENOUGH* AROUND--

UH-OH, NERD ALERT. NERD ALERT.

WHA--? OH NO, NOT *AGAIN!*

HEY, *JENNY!* THERE'S A MEETING OF THE *FRENCH CLUB* TODAY. Y'WANNA CO--*COME BY?*

THERE'LL BE STUFF TO EAT -- *WHOOPS!*

MAYBE *SOME OTHER* TIME, WOODY.

LISTEN, JERK! SHE'S NOT *INTERESTED*, O.K.?! IF YOU CAN'T *TAKE A HINT*, YOU--!

WELL, THAT'S C THERE'S ANOTHER NEXT--

UH, HI, TERESA.

TERRY, *NO!* I DIDN'T SAY *THAT!*

I'M SORRY, JENNY...I... I'LL GET OUT OF YOUR HAIR...I...

WOODY, PLEASE DON'T GET *THE WRONG IDEA.* I DON'T THINK YOU'RE SO *BAD!*

IT'S JUST...

REALLY? YOU *LIKE* ME, Y'MEAN?

UH... *SURE*, I *LIKE YOU! C'MON!*

WOW, *THANKS!* I LIKE YOU, *TOO!*

NO NO NO NO NO NO

WELL...GUESS I'LL *SEE YA AROUND*, HUNH? *BYE*, NOW!

HE'S GOING TO TRY *AGAIN*, ISN'T HE?

YOU'RE A *SLOW LEARNER*, JENNY WEAVER.

...ANYWAY, I'M SORRY THE MYSTERIOUS "ZOT" DIDN'T KEEP HIS PROMISE. I KNOW HOW THAT FEELS...

I'M SURE HE HAD A *GOOD* REASON...

HI, *SHRIMP!*

STILL HANGIN' OUT WITH *ALIENS*, I SEE. *HAW!* GET IT? *ALIENS?*

SHUT UP, BUTCH.

OH, YEAH, I FORGOT WE'RE NOT IN *L.A.*, ANYMORE... HEH. HEH.

SEE YOU *TOMORROW*, JEN. TRY NOT TO GET TOO *DEPRESSED*, O.K.? WHOEVER THIS ZOT IS, HE'S PROBABLY *NOT WORTH IT*.

TERRY, *WAIT!* DON'T LEAVE ME WITH *THE CREEP!*

ADIOS!

DAD CALLED. HE'LL BE IN *CHICAGO* FOR ANOTHER COUPLE OF DAYS...

MOM WILL BE BACK AROUND EIGHT, AS USUAL...

I CAN MAKE US SOME *SPAGHETTIOS*, IF YOU WANT...

OR WE CAN CALL TONY'S...

HELLO TO YOU, TOO...

IT LOOKS *NEAT!* WHAT DOES IT DO?

IT'S A KIND OF *HOMING DEVICE.* IT'LL LEAD ME *RIGHT TO YOU* WHEN I GET TO YOUR EARTH.

I'LL BE ON *SIRIUS IV* FOR A WHILE, BUT I'LL VISIT YOU BEFORE *THE END* OF SEPTEMBER.

YOU *BETTER!*

29

JEN-*NEE!* WHAT ARE WE *DOOING* HERE??

ZOT, C'MON! I REALLY DON'T THINK WE *BELONG* HERE! LET'S LEAVE! *PLEASE?!*

I *SWEAR*, JEN! FOR SOMEONE WHO'S LIVED HERE *ALL YOUR LIFE*, YOU DON'T SEEM TO APPRECIATE YOUR *HOMEWORLD* MUCH!

THIS PLACE IS *FASCINATING!*

DON'T YOU *KNOW* WHERE THIS *IS??*

HEY, BABES...

YOU *SELLING?* HEY!

BUT YOU DON'T *UNDERSTAND!* IT'S *DIFFERENT* HERE! ZOT, *WAIT!*

WOW! LOOK!

THEY ACTUALLY LET YOU *PAINT ON THE WALLS* HERE!

HEY, JEN! WHAT DO YOU CALL--?

? LOST *SIGHT* OF THEM... OH, WELL...

DIGGER, WE BETTER *CATCH UP* WITH ZOT. I DON'T WANT HIM GETTING INTO *TROUBLE...*

AAH, QUIT *WORRYIN',* WILL YA? ZACH CAN TAKE CARE OF *HIMSELF!*

NICE GUN...

ISSA *CALCULATOR,* CHIEF...

YEAH, JEN. DON'T WORRY ABOUT *HIM!* WORRY ABOUT *US!!*

ALL THE *LIGHTS, MUSIC, DANCING...*

SO *ALIVE...*

AAAAAAAAAAAAAAAAAAA!!

GAZINES
VIDEO

SC
ADULT ACC

LIKE IT?!
IT'S MY *NEW
POWER!*
IT'S CALLED A
*NULL-GRAVITY
EFFECT!*

WE'VE
BEEN DOING
IT WITH *CARS*
FOR A WHILE--

--BUT I'VE
GOT THE
*COMPACT
PROTOTYPE!*

ONLY
WORKS ON
CONTACT, THOUGH.
SO, YOU'RE
FALLING
NOW!

IES

MAYBE
YOU
NOTICED?

MY
UNCLE
BUILT
IT! ISN'T
IT--?

I'M SORRY!!
I'M SORRY!!
I'LL *NEVER*
DO IT AGAIN!!

"DO IT?" DO *WHAT?* OH, YOU MEAN
THE THING WITH THE *PURSE?*

YEAH, THAT
WAS PRETTY
RUDE...

I *HAD* TO,
MISTER! THEY...
THEY...

OH, *NO,*
ROOK! *DON'T!*

36

LET ME *THROUGH*, DAMMIT!

LET ME *THROUGH*!

HE TRIED TO *HELP ME*, POOR THING... I DON'T EVEN *KNOW* HIM. WHY--?

OH, *GOD.* TERRY, HE'S *BLEEDING.*

UNNNH...

SON, DON'T TRY TO *MOVE.* I CALLED AN *AMBULANCE.*

NO, IT'S O.K., MA'AM. I'M...I'M ALL RIGHT...

SAY, DID SOMEONE DROP A *PURSE?*

O.K., SO HE'S NOT HURT. *GREAT.' I'M GLAD.'* SO CAN WE PLEEEEEEZ GO HOME NOW??

IN A *SEC,* TERR.

HEY, *BABES...*

SO MUCH FOR YOUR *PERFECT RECORD,* DUDE...WE BETTER NOT *TELL* ANYONE!

HA! HA! YEAH...

FIRST TIME FOR *EVERYTHING,* ZOTTO!

ARE YOU *SURE* YOU'RE NOT *HURT,* ZOT?

I'M FINE, *REALLY!* DIG WILL DRIVE YOU AND TERRY HOME...

I'LL CALL YOU TOMORROW AFTER SCHOOL...

HOME... SWEET HOME...

YOU *BETTER!*

HEY, *ZACH!* SAME TIME *TOMORROW?!*

SURE, *DIG!* I'LL MEET YOU AT THE *PAVILLION!* YOU KNOW THE WAY BACK!

STILL, THIS ISN'T SUCH A *BAD PLACE.* JUST A LITTLE *WORK* HERE AND THERE... JEN OUGHT TO HAVE MORE *FAITH* IN PEOPLE.

THEY AREN'T ANY DIFFERENT HERE THAN ON MY EARTH. THEY *WANT* TO DO GOOD. THEY *WANT* TO HELP.

POOR JENNY...

IMAGINE GROWING UP IN A WORLD YOU DON'T EVEN *LIKE.*

OK...

MAYBE IT NEEDS *A LOT* OF WORK...

MAYBE...

...MAYBE I HAVE A LOT TO LEARN ABOUT...

:CREAK:
:CREAK:

=CREAK=
=CREAK=

?

PLANET EARTH
PART II

BY
SCOTT McCLOUD

LETTERING
bob loppan

EDITOR
cat ⊕ yronwode

SSSSZZZZZZLE! Syzzzle!

I SAW YOU AND YOUR *BOYFRIEND* SNEAKING OUT LAST NIGHT. WHERE DID YOU GO?

ZOT ISN'T MY *"BOYFRIEND,"* BUTCH. AND WE WENT TO *THE CITY*, AS IF IT'S ANY OF *YOUR BUSINESS!*

ME AND TERRY AND A COUPLE OF ZOT'S FRIENDS...

SO ARE YOU GONNA TELL *MOM* AND *DAD* ABOUT OL' *BLONDIE?*

ARE YOU *KIDDING?* I MEAN... MOM *MAYBE*... IF SHE'D *BELIEVE* IT, WHICH I DOUBT...

AND DAD... JEEZ, WHEN DOES HE EVER TALK TO *ANY* OF US? ALWAYS IN *CHICAGO*... OR *HOUSTON*...

BUTCH, DO YOU THINK... MAYBE WHEN I'M A LITTLE OLDER... MAYBE THEY'D LET ME *MOVE THERE*...I MEAN TO *ZOT'S WORLD?* DO YOU THINK THEY'D MIND?

I MEAN, HIS *UNCLE MAX* HAS A BIG PLACE...LOTTA *GUESTS* IN AND OUT ALL THE TIME... AND I'M SURE *ZOT* WOULD WANT ME...I... I MEAN...TO...

I *SWEAR*, SIS! YOU CAN BE SO *IMMATURE* ABOUT THESE THINGS!

GROW UP, WILLYA?

HE DOESN'T NEED YOU!

THAT GUY HAS MORE *GROUPIES* ON HIS "EARTH" THAN ANY *THREE* ROCK STARS HERE! YOU'RE STRICTLY *TEMP*, SHRIMP.

OH, *THANKS*, BUTCH. YOU'RE A *BIG HELP!* MR. SENSITIVE...

Ding! Dong!

THERE'S TERRY NOW.

HOPE YOU HAVE A *SWELL DAY*, JERK.

I HATE HIM. I HATE HIM. I HATE HIM.

HATE. HATE. HATE. HATE. HATE. HATE.

HATE. HATE. HATE. HATE. I **HATE** HIM!

THAT'S WHAT BIG BROTHERS ARE *FOR*, KIDDO. YOU MET HECTOR AND JULIO... YOU KNOW WHAT *I* GO THROUGH...

TERRY, DO YOU THINK WE SHOULD HAVE LEFT ZOT *ALONE* IN THE CITY LAST NIGHT? I MEAN, AFTER HE GOT *BEAT UP* AND ALL...

YOU'RE ASKING *ME??* JEN, YOUR "ZOT" AND HIS FRIENDS ARE *WAY OUT* OF MY DEPTH!

I'M STILL TRYING TO CONVINCE MYSELF THAT I WAS IN A *FLYING CAR* LAST NIGHT!

YOU'LL GET USED TO THAT... NO, IT'S JUST THAT I DON'T KNOW IF ZOT IS *READY* FOR OUR WORLD. HE'S SO... *TRUSTING.*

I DON'T KNOW IF HE'S *PREPARED* FOR THIS PLACE.

NOT PREPARED-- *OH NO!* I FORGOT TO DO MY *HOMEWORK!*

OH, TERRY, I'M *DEAD MEAT!*

C'MON, JEN! IT WON'T HELP IF YOU'RE LATE FOR *HOMEROOM*, TOO!

WAAH! I DON'T *WANNA DIE! LEMME GO!*

HELLLLP!

RRRINNGG!

I'M *TRAPPED*, ZOT.

CAN ANYONE TELL ME WHAT THE COEFFICIENT WOULD BE IF THE 47

I'M THE ALIEN, NOT YOU. *I'M* THE ONE WHO DOESN'T BELONG...

...SEDIMENTARY DEPOSITS AREN'T *NEARLY* DEEP ENOUGH TO ACCOUNT FOR EXTINCTION THE CRE

THEY DON'T TALK *MY* LANGUAGE, ZOT. THIS ISN'T *MY* WORLD...

I USED TO THINK I *UNDERSTOOD* THIS PLACE. THEN I MET *YOU*... SAW *YOUR* EARTH...

HOME USED TO MAKE *SENSE* TO ME, ZOT...

NOW, *YOU'RE* THE ONLY THING IN LIFE THAT MAKES SENSE...

$\frac{x}{9} = 37$

$X \div 5y =$

usage grammar
1. Igneo
2. Meta
3. Sed

RING!

TERRY, WE *MADE* IT! THEY DIDN'T KILL ME, AFTER ALL.

EITHER THAT OR THEY WERE *SAVING* YOU FOR A FATE *WORSE* THAN DEATH. LOOK WHO'S COME TO *GREET* US.

Oh, *HI, GIRLS!* Uh...

÷Whoops!÷

-:Sigh:- HI, WOODY.

I THOUGHT I TOLD YOU TO *BUZZ OFF,* WOODY!

B-BUT *JENNY* SAID--

YOU BETTER *FORGET* ABOUT JENNY, *SHORT STUFF--*

--NOW THAT HER *BOYFRIEND* IS AROUND AGAIN...

B--B--

JENNY, I DIDN'T KNOW YOU...YOU HAD A... IS THAT *TRUE?*

WELL, HE'S NOT MY... I MEAN...

YEAH. YEAH, IT'S *TRUE,* WOODY...

WHY DIDN'T YOU TELL ME *BEFORE?*

I'M SORRY, WOODY...

WELL, I GUESS I'LL *LEAVE YOU ALONE* THEN...

YOU KNOW, I DON'T NECESSARILY *ENJOY* MAKING A FOOL OF MYSELF...

OH, TERRY, WHY DID I SAY THAT?

IT'S FOR THE *BEST,* KIDDO. TRUST ME.

YOU KNOW, I--*GAAH!* NOT *ANOTHER* ONE!

MAX!

GRAB ON, JENNY!

ZACH NEEDS US *RIGHT AWAY!*

TER, THIS IS ZOT'S *UNCLE MAX-- YAAH!* Uh, *BYE,* TERRY! TAKE CARE OF MY *BIKE,* O.K.?

NO PROBLEM.

HAVE A NICE TRIP.

TOOO WEIRD...

ping!

IS ZOT IN *DANGER*, MAX?!

WHAT? OH *NO, NO.* HE JUST WANTS US TO SEE THE *BIG BATTLE!*

BELLOWS CAUGHT HIM IN *YOUR WORLD* LAST NIGHT. NOW OUR BOY'S *ESCAPED* AND THEY'RE *DUKING IT OUT* OVER *THE GREAT LAWN.*

WHO THE HECK IS *"BELLOWS?!?"*

DOCTOR IGNATIUS RUMBAULT BELLOWS! ZACH AND PEABODY *WHUPPED 'IM* LAST MONTH, BUT HE *GOT AWAY.*

SPLENDID VILLAIN! VERY *EXUBERANT!*

HOW DID HE FIND ZOT IN *MY WORLD?!*

HAD HIM *FOLLOWED.* AFTER HE SAW ZACH PASS THROUGH THE PORTAL, HE FORCED ME AT *GUNPOINT* TO SEND HIM, TOO.

HOW *AWFUL!*

OH, IT WASN'T SO *BAD...* HE TOLD HIS *ORIGIN!* CHECK *THIS* OUT...

"BELLOWS WAS A *GREAT INVENTOR* ON A *DISTANT PLANET* WE CALL *RAGNUM.*

"HE SAYS HIS INVENTIONS *REVOLUTIONIZED* LIFE ON HIS WORLD. *INTERNAL COMBUSTION, MASS PRODUCTION, ROCKET POWER...* YOU NAME IT-- HE *INVENTED* IT FOR RAGNUM!

"BUT EVERYTHING CHANGED WHEN BELLOWS' WORLD WAS ADMITTED TO *THE FEDERATION.*

"OUR *CLEAN, SAFE, NEW TECHNOLOGIES* WERE A *BIG HIT* WITH ALL OF RAGNUM'S *SMOKE-CHOKED* NATIVES! ALL OF 'EM--

"--EXCEPT *ONE!*

HEY, DIGGER! I'LL BET A FIVER ZOT DROPS HIM IN THE POND!

YOU'RE *ON*, HACKER!

WHAT'S *WRONG*, JENNY? DON'T YOU *LIKE* POPCORN? WE TRIED TO GET SOME *MILK-DUDS*, BUT--

VIC! ARE YOU *CRAZY*?! ZOT IS FIGHTING FOR HIS *LIFE* UP THERE!!

RIGHT YOU ARE, JENNY! AND WE'RE NOT GOING TO MISS A *MOMENT* OF IT!

ZACH! CAN YOU *MOVE DOWN* A BIT?!

BOOM!

HOW'S *THIS*, MAX?!

JUST FINE! NOW, FACE THE CAMERA MORE!

ZOT'S GONNA DIE AND HIS UNCLE IS MAKING *HOME MOVIES*...

BOY, ZACH'S GIRLFRIEND SURE IS *STUPID*, ISN'T SHE, HACK?

HA! HA!

HEY!

MIND YOUR MANNERS, DICKLESS! JEN IS *MY* FRIEND, *TOO*, Y'KNOW!

WHAP!

OW!! WATCH IT, TAYLOR!

DON'T PAY ATTENTION TO THEM, JENNY... *I* KNOW YOU'RE JUST WORRIED ABOUT ZACH.

WELL, AREN'T *YOU*?

DIE!

"OH, I *USED* TO BE... BACK WHEN WE WERE LITTLE KIDS AND HE WAS JUST *STARTING* THIS *HERO STUFF*.

"DIE, DIE, DIE..." YOU'RE SO *MORBID*!

"BUT, AFTER A WHILE, HE SHOWED ME WHY I *SHOULDN'T* WORRY ABOUT HIM...

WHAK!

AAARGH!

"Y'SEE, THE FACT IS THAT ZOT *CAN'T LOSE* JUST SO LONG AS HE *KNOWS* HE CAN'T LOSE!"

READY TO *GIVE UP*, B-- COUGH! COUGH!

NEVER!

"AND HE KNOWS HE CAN'T LOSE TO GUYS LIKE *BELLOWS*--

"--'CAUSE HE NEVER *DOES* LOSE TO 'EM! IT'S LIKE THIS *PERFECT CYCLE!*"

WATCH *THIS,* BOY!

HA! HA! HA!

WOW! A JETPACK!

HOW "FUTURISTIC!"

"BUT, VIC THAT'S *CRAZY!*"

"YOU CAN'T ALWAYS WIN JUST BECAUSE YOU *EXPECT* TO WIN!"

WH--??

♪ HERE WE GO ROUND THE MULBERRY BUSH! ♪

"*YEAH?* WELL, DON'T TELL IT TO *THE GUY IN THE RED SUIT*...

YEAH, RIGHT WHERE WE LEFT HIM AFTER WE *DEACTIVATED* THE GUY...

GOOD THING THEY DIDN'T *ARREST* HIM...

...OR *TOW* HIM AWAY... WHATEVER...

WELL! HEH-HEH, *SORRY ABOUT THAT,* MAX! GUESS WE'LL, UM...

÷Ahem!÷

...BE *GOING* NOW! SEE YA!

÷Whew!÷

HEE! HEE!

Aaaw, RATS...

NOW WE'RE STUCK *HERE* AGAIN.

The *Salvation Army Band* played... And the *Children* dr Lem-m-m-onad

Y'KNOW, WE HAVE SOME OF THESE SAME ALBUMS ON *MY* EARTH. ISN'T THAT *WEIRD??* I MEAN, HOW COULD...?

HEY, HERE'S THAT *SECOND JULIAN LENNON* ALBUM, DO YOU HAVE THE ONE HE DID WITH *HIS DAD* AFTER THIS?

HM? OH, UH... THAT ONE IS *TERRY'S.* I DON'T HAVE ANY LENNON.

ZOT, LET'S GO BACK TO *YOUR* WORLD, *PLEASE?* THIS IS SO *BORING!*

54

Y'KNOW, I'VE NEVER MET ANYONE LIKE YOU, JEN. DON'T YOU HAVE ANY *DREAMS* FOR YOUR LIFE *HERE?*

I MEAN, LIKE, ISN'T THERE SOMETHING YOU WANT TO BE WHEN YOU *GROW UP?*

I NOTICED THE *BOOK.* ARE YOU INTERESTED IN *GEOLOGY?*

THIS IS *HOMEWORK,* ZOT.

"HOMEWORK?" WHAT'S---?

OKAY. I'LL *SHUT UP.*

I JUST WISH YOU'D AT LEAST *TRY* TO LOOK AT THE *BRIGHT SIDE...*

ZOT, YOU HAVEN'T EVEN SPENT A *WHOLE DAY* HERE AND YOU'VE ALREADY GOTTEN THE CRAP BEATEN OUT OF YOU BY THAT *STREET GANG.* DOESN'T THAT TELL YOU *ANYTHING* ABOUT THIS PLACE?

THEY WEREN'T *BAD KIDS.* JUST *MISGUIDED,* THAT'S ALL.

EVERY WORLD HAS ITS *DARK SIDE,* JENNY. EVEN *MINE.*

BUT YOURS IS SO *BEAUTIFUL.* AND ALL THE PEOPLE THERE SEEM SO *SATISFIED* WITH THEIR LIVES...

IT'S *DIFFERENT* HERE, ZOT. IT'S LIKE EVERYONE IS A LITTLE BIT... *BROKEN* INSIDE.

HEY, WHAT ARE YOU *DOING?!*

WHAT DOES IT *LOOK* LIKE?

ZOT, C'MON! IT'S *RAINING OUT!* WHAT---?

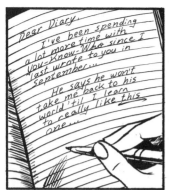

Dear Diary,
I've been spending a lot more time with You-Know-Who since I last wrote to you in September...
He says he won't take me back to his world 'til I learn to really like this one...

He comes by almost every day after school...

IT'S *FOR* YOU, SIS!

GIVE YA *THREE* GUESSES.

Sometimes at night, we sneak out and just fly for hundreds of miles in any direction.

Terry comes with us sometimes, if it isn't anything too "weird" (her word). I don't think she really trusts Zot...

Last night, we talked about all the troubles I'm having with Mom and Dad... No big solutions, but it helped to talk about it...

Later, Zot told me I'm lucky to have a friend like Terry...

Homework is getting a lot easier. Algebra is a breeze now! I just wish he could help me with Social Studies...

I guess Zot cares a lot about me. ~~Maybe even~~ Of course he cares about everybody...

It's not like I'm his only friend or anything, though he sure means a lot to me...

Zot only wants to help... Not just me -- everybody.

THIS IS *TERRY'S* NEIGHBORHOOD, ZOT.

LOOKS *BAD!*

58

ZOT?

I BROUGHT YOUR JACKET.

THANKS, BUT I'M NOT COLD...

IT'S STILL *WARM* ON MY WORLD...MAKES A NICE *CAMPFIRE.* I GUESS THE SEASONS DON'T *MATCH UP.*

JUST AS WELL, HUH? GIVES YOU A *CHOICE.*

Y'KNOW, WHEN I WAS IN, LIKE, *FIRST GRADE,* BACK IN KENTUCKY, WE FOUND THIS LITTLE *CROW* ON THE HIGHWAY NEXT TO OUR HOUSE. *HALF DEAD...* I CALLED HIM *RODNEY...*

HELPED HIM GET *BETTER.*

AND RIGHT WHEN WE THOUGHT HE'D BE O.K., HE JUST *DIED.* NO REASON.

I WAS CRYING LIKE CRAZY AND I TOLD DAD ABOUT IT AND Y'KNOW WHAT HE SAID?

NOTHING. JUST, "*TOUGH BREAK.*"

"*TOUGH BREAK.*" I WAS SO *ANGRY* AT HIM.

BUT NOWADAYS, I THINK THAT WAS A *GOOD THING* TO SAY... I MEAN, WHAT ELSE *CAN* YOU SAY?

JENNY, WHY DIDN'T ANYONE *DO ANYTHING* WHEN I WAS GETTING *BEAT UP* BY THAT STREET GANG?

ALL THEY DID WAS STAND AROUND *WATCHING* US.

MAYBE THEY WERE *SCARED.*

THEY DIDN'T *LOOK* SCARED. THEY DIDN'T LOOK *ANYTHING*... IT'S LIKE THEY WERE WATCHING *TELEVISION*...

ZOT, PLEASE... DON'T LEAVE.

I NEVER FAILED LIKE THIS ON *MY WORLD*, JEN.

MAYBE YOU WERE *RIGHT*... MAYBE I DON'T BELONG HERE.

YEAH WELL, *I* DO! *YOU* SHOWED ME THAT.

PEOPLE *FAIL*, ZOT. IT HAPPENS...

IT'S NOT THE *END OF THE WORLD.*

I NEED TO BE *ALONE* FOR A WHILE.

I PROMISE I'LL BE BACK.

OH, *WHY BOTHER*, ZOT??

WHY COME BACK *AT ALL*??

THERE ISN'T *ANYTHING* HERE YOU COULD EVER REALLY NEED!

YEAH,
THERE
IS.

64

One of my biggest challenges with *Zot!* cropped up as soon as I realized that the contrast between the two "Earths"—Zot's utopian world and our own tarnished home—offered the series' most natural central theme, the age-old struggle between hope and disillusionment. Unfortunately, the most obvious way to highlight the contrast was to paint Zot's world as trouble-free, a strategy that might work for stories set on our world, but which could sabotage any hopes for dramatic conflict once the focus returned to the other side of the portal.

I found a partial solution in Zot and Jenny's much more personal enactment of those themes. Jenny's universe of broken dreams was as much about her attitudes toward life as it was about any objective assessment of our planet's ultimate worth. And Zot's natural optimism applied to both worlds equally—at least, to a point. We all step between those two worlds every day, so on a human level at least, I hoped this story would resonate. The last page (including our cover image) was the whole series in a nutshell: the two worlds, both emotional and metaphorical, drawing together in a kiss.

If the emotions seem a bit oversaturated, blame it on brain chemistry. When I laid out that last page, I was still living alone in upstate New York, but by the time I drew it, I'd relocated to Boston and was moving in with my old college friend Ivy Ratafia—a woman whom, prior to that time, I'd secretly been in love with for seven years. My comics had always been sentimental, but at this point in my life, the endorphins were a raging river, carrying off potential subtleties in its current.

Before it was even drawn, based on the layouts, I was told by my editor that three people at Eclipse Comics were interested in buying the last page, but I told them that I was giving it to Ivy. She and I still have it to this day.

Jenny was only 14 years old in this story. Zot was 15. Now in 2008, as we go to press with this collection, Ivy and I have a daughter who is exactly Jenny's age, and she has a blond boyfriend—sorry, not-boyfriend—who is exactly Zot's age, and all I can think is: Aren't they a bit *young* for this sort of thing?

Cosmic payback, I guess.

The scenes in New York seem embarrassingly dated to me now. The would-be purse-snatcher and his bigger gang member friends were just lazy stock characters of a sort common in mainstream titles of the day, and they strike a false note to me now. In *The Frying Pan* (a small-press magazine I put together in which members critiqued each others' work), comics creator Bill Loebs rightfully took me to task for perpetuating the comics cliché that all you had to do to get mugged in a big city was walk down the street at night. Bill's comments planted the seeds of an idea that would take root a couple of years later in issue #29's story "Looking for Crime."

The Season of Dreams

First published in *Zot! #13–15*.

Lettering:
Bob Lappan

Original series editor:
cat yronwode

Eisner Award Nominee 1988:
"Best Single Issue" for *Zot! #14*

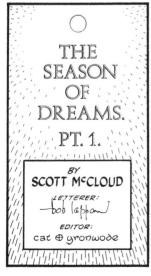

THE SEASON OF DREAMS. PT. 1.

BY
SCOTT McCLOUD

LETTERER:
bob lappan

EDITOR:
cat ⊕ yronwode

SPLASH

HEY!

ZOT, YOU *JERK!* I JUST *FELL ASLEEP!*

...ANYWAY, I HAVE BEEN *PRACTICING.* I HELPED STOP THAT GUY FROM *RIPPING OFF* THE 7-11, RIGHT? I'VE BEEN GETTING CATS DOWN FROM TREES AND STUFF...

...I DON'T KNOW WHY IT HASN'T MADE THE *NEWS.*

PEOPLE ARE KINDA *SKEPTICAL* ABOUT THINGS LIKE *ALIENS* AND *FLYING KIDS,* ZOT. MOST OF THOSE STORIES ARE JUST *HOAXES.*

NOT WHERE *I* COME FROM!

HEY, TERR, ZOT AND I ARE GOING BACK TO *HIS PLACE* AFTER THIS. DO YOU--?

DON'T *WASTE YOUR BREATH,* KIDDO.

AWW, *PLEASE,* TERRY! I JUST *KNOW* YOU'D LOVE IT IF YOU GAVE IT A CHANCE!

LET'S JUST SAY I LIKE THE EARTH *UNDER MY FEET,* O.K.? I'LL SEE YOU ON MONDAY BEFORE SCHOOL...

HEY, JENNY, *LOOK!* NOW THEY'LL *HAVE* TO BELIEVE IN ME!

UH-OH. THAT'S MOM'S CAR IN THE DRIVEWAY.

YOU CAN WAIT *OUT BACK*, ZOT. I'LL JUST BE A MINUTE.

I DON'T GET IT, JEN. WHY NOT LET YOUR FOLKS *SEE ME?*

OH, I DUNNO, ZOT... I JUST... AWW--

RELAX, I'LL ACT *"NORMAL"* ENOUGH!

OH, JENNY, *GOOD!* I WAS JUST ABOUT TO NEED THAT *FLOUR.*

AND YOU MUST BE THE MYSTERIOUS *"ZOT!"* HI.

HI, MRS. WEAVER. NICE TO MEET YOU.

ME 'N' ZOT CAN ONLY STAY FOR A *MINUTE,* MOM.

WELL, YOU BETTER GET SOME LIQUID IN YOU, IT'S *HOT AS AN OVEN* OUT THERE! WE STILL HAVE SOME *SODA...* ALSO *GRAPE JUICE...CIDER...*

WATER WOULD BE GREAT.

WE HAVE SOME *SPRING WATER.*

I'LL GET IT.

JENNY TALKS ABOUT YOU *ALL THE TIME,* ZOT... SOUNDS LIKE A BIG CRUSH TO ME...

MMMOM!!

I LIKE JENNY *A LOT,* MRS. WEAVER.

DID YOU *BIKE* OVER, ZOT? JENNY SAID YOU LIVE QUITE A WAYS FROM HERE.

MY UNCLE, UH... GIVES ME A LIFT WHEN I NEED IT.

I TOLD YOU ABOUT *MAX*, MOM.

OH, YES, YOUR UNCLE SOUNDS LIKE HE'S FROM *ANOTHER WORLD*, ZOT!

OH. YEAH, WELL, HE WASN'T *BORN* ON MY EARTH, BUT--

OW!!

HE'S SUCH A *KIDDER!*

BUT, JENNY, IF SHE *KNOWS*--

C'MON, ZOT! GOTTA RUN! BYE, MOM!

TAKE CARE, HONEY. WE'LL EAT AROUND 7:00.

WANNA SET THE PORTAL FOR *MAX'S* HOUSE?

SURE!

YEAH, *GO AHEAD.* DON'T MIND *ME.*

WHAT'S *YOUR* PROBLEM, BUTCH?

WELL, I DON'T SUPPOSE IT'D OCCUR TO YOU TO INVITE YOUR *BIG BROTHER* ALONG.

RIGHT. IT *WOULDN'T.*

AWW, BUTCH CAN COME IF HE WANTS, JEN.

-SIGH-

ZOT... YOU ARE *MUCH NICER* THAN YOU HAVE *ANY REASON* TO BE.

YOU *WERE* CURED, BUTCH.

THEN WHY AM I STILL A *MONKEY?!*

BECAUSE YOU *CAME BACK* FROM *YOUR* WORLD.

WHAT??

YOU'RE A MONKEY *HERE* AND A HUMAN *THERE*, THAT'S ALL.

THAT'S *ALL? THAT'S ALL??*

OH, RELAX... *ENJOY IT!* WHEN DO YOU EVER USE *OPPOSABLE THUMBS*, ANYWAY?

WHAT IS THIS *OTHER WORLD*, MAX?

IT'S ANOTHER "*EARTH*" WE DISCOVERED, RUDY. IT'S LIKE OURS, ONLY MORE *BACKWARDS.*

HEY! WHO ARE YOU CALLING "*BACKWARDS?*"

ZACH'S FRIEND *JENNY* IS ALSO FROM THE *OTHER EARTH.* HI, JENNY.

HI, MAX.

WHERE'S YOUR *FIFTH?* I THOUGHT THIS WAS A *QUINTET.*

IT IS! BUTCH IS SITTING ON OUR *MARIMBA PLAYER.*

?

GREETINGS FROM *RIO DE JANEIRO*, JENNIFER!

THIS OTHER EARTH SOUNDS *INTERESTING*, MAX! HAVE YOU FOUND US A *NEW DIMENSION?*

LOOKS LIKE IT, ERNIE.

WE'VE VISITED IT A *FEW* TIMES. RATHER *PRIMITIVE TECHNOLOGY.* QUITE *DE-CENTRALIZED.*

REALLY? I'D LIKE TO SEE A *WORLD TECHNOLOGY* WITHOUT *CONTROLS.* MUST BE A *MESS.*

MAYBE *ZYBOX* CAN HELP THEM, POPPA!

I WOULD BE HAPPY TO, PEDRO--

--BUT IF THIS NEW WORLD IS NOT A FEDERATION MEMBER THEN I WOULD NOT LEGALLY BE ALLOWED.

CORRECT, ERNESTO?

YES, THEY'RE *VERY STRICT* ABOUT *INTRODUCING NEW TECHS.*

A SHAME... IT'D BE *INTERESTING.*

WHY DO WE OBEY LAWS THAT DO NOT SERVE US, ERNESTO?

HA! HA! HA!

"WHY," *INDEED.*

BECAUSE WE'RE *TOO NICE* FOR OUR *OWN GOOD,* MY FRIEND. AND THAT'S A *FACT.*

POPPA, CAN I USE THIS SCREEN NOW? I WANT TO PLAY *"MARS ATTACKS!"*

S'ALL RIGHT WITH ME, ERNIE! WE WERE GOING TO *TAKE FIVE* ANYHOW.

YOU HEARD "UNCLE" MAX, *PEDRO!* JUST *FIVE MINUTES!*

MARCO, *LOOK AT THIS...* WHAT HAVE WE EVER TAUGHT 'BOX THAT WOULD ACCOUNT FOR THESE *FLUCTUATIONS?*

I THOUGHT A *POWER SURGE...?*

-¡ PFAW! ¡- THAT'S NO *SURGE.*

LOOK AT IT *NOW!* HE'S *SKIPPING STEPS* LEFT AND RIGHT. MAYBE *ONE OUT OF THREE!*

THIS SAYS HE'S BEEN AT IT FOR HOURS, BUT I SHOW A COMPLETE RUN OF *UNINTERRUPTED CYCLES...*

POPPA, I'M *WINNING!* I'M BEATING *ZYBOX!*

NOT NOW, PEDRO.

YOUR POPPA HAS A *MYSTERY* ON HIS HANDS...

--ABSURD, ERNESTO! YOU CAN'T SERIOUSLY BELIEVE THAT ZYBOX HAS STARTED "THINKING FOR HIMSELF."

WELL, I...OH, WHY NOT, MARCO? OUR OWN MINDS ARE JUST COMPLEX MACHINES, GIVEN SOUL AND PURPOSE BY A--

UH-OH...

ALL RIGHT, CORTEZ, DO YOU WANT TO TELL ME JUST WHAT THE HELL IS GOING ON HERE?!

I JUST GOT BACK FROM HOUSTON AND THEY-- WILL YOU GET THAT DAMNED ROBOT DOWN HERE?! AND TAKE THOSE SUNGLASSES OFF!!

MY EYES ARE VERY SENSITIVE, MR. TYREE.

DAMMIT, MISTER!! THEY SAY THAT OUR AIR FORCE CONTRACT IS WORTHLESS BECAUSE--

"CONTRACT?" WE HAVE A MILITARY CONTRACT?!

--BECAUSE YOUR GODDAMNED ROBOT WON'T "HANDLE" MILITARY SYSTEMS! WON'T HANDLE THEM!!

WHAT THE HELL DOES THAT MEAN?!

I PROGRAMMED ZYBOX FOR PEACEFUL USES, SIR. THAT WAS IN MY CONTRACT! I'M NOT GOING TO LET YOU USE ZYBOX TO RUN ANYONE'S KILLING MACHINES!

THE HELL YOU AREN'T!! IF YOU WON'T RE-PROGRAM THAT DAMN THING, WE'LL HIRE SOMEONE ELSE TO DO IT FOR US!!

YOU'RE OUT OF A JOB, MISTER!! IN FIVE MINUTES!!

NO!

YOU CAN'T TAKE ZYBOX FROM POPPA! YOU DIDN'T BUILD HIM! HE WASN'T YOUR IDEA!!

AND ZYBOX WON'T LET YOU TAKE HIM, WILL YOU, ZYBOX?

I MUST DO AS I AM TOLD, PEDRO.

I CAN'T GIVE IN TO THOSE *WARRING JACKALS,* MARCO.

ARE YOU *MAD,* ERNESTO? OUR PLANET HASN'T HAD A WAR IN *DECADES!* WHAT *DIFFERENCE* IF ZYBOX WORKS WITH THE *AIR FORCE?!*

WOULD YOU GIVE UP *EVERYTHING* FOR SOME *MEANINGLESS* MATTER OF *PRINCIPLE?!*

MAY I BE OF HELP, GENTLEMEN?

HELL!

DAMN!

HELL!

DAMN!

HELL!

DAMN!

ZYBOX...IF THERE'S ANYTHING YOU CAN DO TO GET US OUT OF THIS MESS, *DO IT...*

SHALL I CONTINUE TO OBEY THE LAW?

DON'T *HURT* ANYONE, ZYBOX...

BEYOND THAT I DON'T CARE *WHAT* YOU DO...I JUST DON'T *CARE* ANYMORE.

WELL... THAT'S THAT.

WATCH HIS EYES, PEDRO... YOU'LL SEE THEM FLASH WHEN HE HAS A *SOLUTION.*

YOU *ARE* MAD! DO YOU HAVE *ANY IDEA* WHAT YOU JUST *TOLD* HIM?? HE COULD DO *ANYTHING!!*

FOR *HEAVEN'S SAKE,* ERNESTO, YOU KNEW THEY OWNED ZYBOX. WHAT DID YOU *EXPECT?!*

I DON'T KNOW, MARCO, I...I JUST...

...I JUST WANTED TO MAKE MY DREAMS A REALITY... IS THAT SO FOOLISH...?

MY FRIEND... SOMEDAY, *YOUR DREAMS* WILL *SWALLOW YOU WHOLE.*

...BEEN SITTING THERE FOR *HALF AN HOUR*, CAPTAIN.

HASN'T MOVED A *BIT*.

HEY, JENNY, IS IT *ALWAYS* THIS HOT ON YOUR WORLD?

FLOYD, GET US A *DRINK*.

STAY CLOSE TO THE PORTAL 'TIL MY MEN ARE *READY*, KIDS.

YOU HEARD HIM, ZACH.

YEAH, YEAH...

WELL, YOU WON'T HAVE TO TELL *ME* TWICE...I'M NOT GETTING *NEAR* THAT--

HEY! THEY TURNED IT *OFF!*

NOT *THEM*, VIC-- *ZYBOX!* JENNY, *GET OUT* OF HERE.

BUT--

Ping!

GET OUT NOW. FIND YOUR WORLD'S *POLICE*. I DON'T WANT YOU AROUND HERE.

YOU *TOO*, VIC.

HE CAN'T *SEE* ME, ZACH! I'VE GOT THAT OLD GADGET THAT MAKES ME INVISIBLE TO *MACHINES*.

HEY, WHAT THE--? HE'S *SPLITTING!*

I DON'T LIKE THE *LOOKS* OF THIS...

*BZZZZZZZZZZ

BZZZZZZZZZZZZZZZZZ!!

??

=CLIK.=

12
3
6

SURE GOT *COLD* ALL OF A SUDDEN.

WHAT DID YOU *EXPECT?*

BRR... MIDDLE OF *JUNE,* FOR PETE'S SAKE...

HURRY UP, HONEY! YOU'LL BE LATE FOR *SCHOOL!*

I'M COMING, MOM!

JENNY, WHAT'S *WRONG?* YOU LOOK *CONFUSED.*

I HAD THIS REALLY WEIRD *DREAM,* BUT I... I CAN'T FIGURE OUT WHERE IT ALL *STARTED...*

YEAH? SO, WHAT WAS IT *ABOUT?*

IT'S SO *WEIRD,* BUTCH! ZOT AND I WERE...

YOU AND *WHO?*

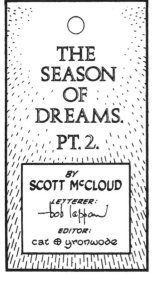

THE
SEASON
OF
DREAMS.
PT. 2.

BY
SCOTT MCCLOUD
LETTERER:
bob lappan
EDITOR:
cat ⊕ yronwode

JUST *SIT DOWN* FOR A WHILE, HONEY. IT WILL ALL *MAKE SENSE* IN A MOMENT.

BUTCH, GO GET YOUR SISTER SOME *HOT COCOA.*

SURE.

ARE WE GONNA GET MUCH MORE OF THIS *PSYCHO* STUFF, SIS? I MEAN, *THREE TIMES* IN *ONE WEEK* IS--

THAT'S ENOUGH FROM *YOU,* HORTON! JENNY NEEDS OUR *HELP,* NOT THAT *SNIDE ATTITUDE* OF YOURS!

O.K., O.K... JUST DON'T CALL ME *HORTON.*

WHAT DOES HE MEAN, *"THREE TIMES"?*

DON'T PAY ATTENTION TO HIM, JENNY. I KNOW YOU'RE JUST...JUST A LITTLE *TROUBLED,* DEAR.

MAYBE YOU SHOULD TELL US ALL ABOUT THAT *DREAM.*

I GUESS...

...ONLY *FIRST,* I THINK IT'S TIME I TOLD YOU THE *TRUTH* ABOUT ZOT...

"IS THAT ALL ZOT IS, MOM? JUST SOME *TRICK* MY BRAIN IS PLAYING?"

"YES, HONEY, THAT'S ALL IT WAS."

"BUT HOW CAN A DREAM LIKE THAT SEEM SO *REAL?*"

"MAYBE DR. WILSON CAN ANSWER THAT TOMORROW. REMEMBER WE HAVE AN *APPOINTMENT...*"

"OH..."

"WHO'S DR. WILSON?"

"I HAVE TO GO TO WORK, JENNY."

"GET PLENTY OF REST. I'LL BE HOME AROUND EIGHT O'CLOCK. WE CAN TALK SOME MORE THEN..."

SEEMED SO REAL...

A CLUE...

ANYTHING...

TERRY, YOU *HAVE* TO HELP ME! YOU'RE THE ONLY ONE WHO CAN NOW!

UH... I'LL DO WHAT I *CAN*, KIDDO. WHAT DO YOU WANT?

JUST TELL ME YOU REMEMBER ZOT, O.K.? JUST TELL ME I DIDN'T *DREAM HIM UP!*

"ZOT?" YOU MEAN THE BLOND KID?

WITH THE *LIGHTNING BOLT?*

YOU REMEMBER! OH, *THANK GOD,* SOMEBODY REMEMBERS!

WHMPH! WELL, *OF COURSE* I DO!

YOU TALKED ABOUT THAT SHOW *ALL THE TIME.*

"SHOW"...?

YEAH. ISN'T THAT THE CARTOON YOU WATCHED ALL *LAST MONTH,* WHEN YOU WERE HOME FOR -- UH, Y'KNOW...?

WHEN YOU WEREN'T *FEELING SO GOOD...*

IT'S ALMOST 2:30 NOW. THAT'S WHEN IT STARTS, ISN'T IT? YOU SHOULD GET HOME IF IT'S THAT *IMPORTANT* TO YOU.

JENNY, IS THAT *IT?* IS THAT YOUR *"EMERGENCY?!"*

JENNY! WHAT THE HELL'S *WRONG* WITH YOU??

103

DOCTOR, SHE'S *AWAKE.*

MOM..? IS THAT YOU? WHAT *HAPPENED?*

YOU *FREAKED OUT,* SIS. IT WAS REALLY *SCARY.*

YOU'LL BE ALL RIGHT *NOW,* HONEY.

LET'S NOT BE *TOO HASTY,* MS. WEAVER.

HELLO, JENNIFER. CAN WE *SIT UP* ALL RIGHT?

:UNNH!: YEAH... I GUESS YOU'RE *"DR. WILSON,"* HUNH?

YOU *DON'T REMEMBER* ME?

NO, I DON'T.

I GUESS MOM ALREADY TOLD YOU ABOUT ZOT... HOW I *IMAGINED* ALL THAT STUFF...

YES.

WELL, I'M O.K. NOW... I UNDERSTAND WHAT HAPPENED TO ME. I GUESS I WAS JUST A LITTLE *"CONFUSED."*

I'M SORRY.

IT JUST SEEMED SO *REAL... HE* SEEMED SO REAL, HE...

...

...GAVE THIS TO ME... ZOT *GAVE* THIS TO ME...

ZOT ISN'T *REAL,* JENNIFER. *REMEMBER?*

YEAH... YEAH, I REMEMBER... ZOT ISN'T REAL... I'M JUST *CRAZY...* I'M JUST *IMAGINING THINGS...*

O.K. FINE.

BUT I KNOW WHAT I'M *HOLDING,* DOC. AND I KNOW WHERE IT *CAME* FROM.

AND IF ZOT ISN'T REAL--

AH, YOU FOUND YOUR *CLOTHES*. *GOOD*. HE WAS GOING TO *INCINERATE* SUCH THINGS, BUT I RESCUED THEM IN TIME.

I ASSURE YOU, YOU WEREN'T *PHYSICALLY* VIOLATED IN ANY WAY... JUST *"SCIENTIFIC PROCEDURE."*

CORTEZ?! SO *YOU'RE* BEHIND ALL THIS! WELL, YOU WON'T GET AWAY WITH IT.

MAX AND THE OTHERS WILL SAVE US.

YOU DON'T *UNDERSTAND*, JENNIFER! THIS IS *ZYBOX'S* DOING, NOT *MINE*... SOMETHING IS *HORRIBLY WRONG* WITH HIM.

WE'VE BOTH BEEN *PRISONERS* FOR MORE THAN 48 HOURS!

I... *O.K.,* O.K. JUST DON'T COME NEAR ME.

WHAT'S HAPPENING TO ZOT AND VIC? WILL THEY WAKE UP SOON?

"PERHAPS, YES, IF THEY CAN RESIST THEIR *ARTIFICIAL DREAMS*--"

"--AS I PRESUME *YOU* HAVE."

WHERE IS ZYBOX *NOW*?

ALL AROUND US! ZYBOX MAY SEEM NO LARGER THAN A *REFRIGERATOR* USUALLY, BUT *INSIDE*, HE'S *GARGANTUAN*.

WE'RE IN THE *MONSTER'S BELLY*, JENNIFER, A MONSTER I *BUILT*.

"IT TOOK US *TEN YEARS*, *TWENTY BILLION DOLLARS* AND A WORK CREW OF *500 MEN AND WOMEN*... IT WAS WORK WE ALL BELIEVED IN--"

"--AND NOW I'VE *DESTROYED* THAT WORK WITH A FEW *CARELESS WORDS*..."

BY ALLOWING 'BOX TO *BYPASS THE LAW* FOR MY OWN *SELFISHNESS* AND *PRIDE*--

--I'VE *UNLEASHED* POWERS I'D HARDLY REALIZED HE HAD.

AS SOON AS HE BROKE OUT OF OUR LAB, HE WAS *FREE*, THEY'D FIRED ME OVER THE PHONE-- THROUGH 'BOX-- JUST MINUTES BEFORE. NOW ZYBOX HAS *NO MASTER*...

NO ONE TO CONTROL HIM.

HE LOOKS SO *STILL*...

NO ONE...

ARE YOU *REAL*, ZOT?

DID YOU *SAY SOMETHING*, JENNY?

ARE THEY *ALIVE*, PEABODY?

YES, BUT THEY EXHIBIT SIGNS OF *POST-HYPNOTIC TRANCE*.

IF THAT DON'T *BEAT ALL... TWO DAYS* ON THEIR PLANET AN' THIS *"ZYBOX"* ROBOT HAS THE NATIVES GOIN' *CROSS-EYED* FER *A THOUSAND MILES!*

HOW'D HE *DO* IT?!

SIRS, THE *RADIOS* IN THESE VEHICLES ARE *BROADCASTING* A *COMPLEX ULTRASONIC SIGNAL* WHICH MAY BE--

JAM THAT SIGNAL, PEABODY! QUICKLY! THAT'S OUR CULPRIT FOR SURE!

MAX, I'M SORRY OUR CAP'N COULDN'T ASSIGN YOU MORE MEN TO FACE THIS *CRAZY 'BOT...*

WE UNDERSTAND, *LT. BUMP.* YOUR CAPTAIN'S *BENDING THE LAW* AS IT IS BY LETTING YOU COME TO THIS WORLD.

TALK... TALK... TALK...

GOTTA BE SOMETHING TO *EAT* AROUND HERE.

HEY, *MISTER!* WHERE'S THE *CHIPS* IN THIS PLACE?

HEY, *DOPEY!* OVER HERE! I SAID WHERE'S THE...

CHIPS...

PLAYBOY

HUSTLER

HEFTY

50¢ ea

BUTCH! DON'T LOOK AT IT!

DON'T LOOK!

UNNH... WHU..? WHU..? BUHH...

THE KID IS *AWAKE* LIEUTENANT!

IF I'D BEEN A BIT *LATER* I DOUBT BUTCH COULD'VE AWOKEN AT ALL.

PEABODY'S JAMMER WILL PROTECT US FROM NOW ON--

--BUT THE REST OF THESE PEOPLE ARE *TOO FAR GONE*...

WHAT IS IT, PEABODY?

HEY! THAT'S *MY* CRUISER!

PAK!

LOOK! SOMETHING *CAME OFF* OF IT!

K! #1

A *ROZMUS CHIP!* OF COURSE. THEY'RE *ILLEGAL* ON *OUR* WORLD, BUT IF HE WANTED TO, ZYBOX COULD MANUFACTURE A *BILLION* IN *NO TIME.*

HE'S RIGGED 'EM TO *FLY.* THEY'LL LATCH ON TO ANY *RADIO* OR *VIDEO RECEIVER* AND IMPLANT ANY MESSAGE HE WANTS.

WITH ENOUGH *CHIPS* HE COULD PUT THE *WHOLE PLANET* UNDER HIS *TRANCE.*

IT'S *POSSIBLE* HE ALREADY *HAS.*

RIO DE JANEIRO.
ZOT'S WORLD.

THIS *BLACK-OUT* WILL LAST FOR *DAYS.*

WHEN ZYBOX CAPTURED *DR. CORTEZ* AND *BROKE OUT* OF OUR *CONTROL CENTER,* HE DISRUPTED ELECTRICAL SYSTEMS FROM *CAPE HORN* TO *FAIRBANKS!*

EVEN *THESE* MACHINES WOULD BE DOWN WITHOUT OUR *AUXILIARY GENERATOR.*

DID YOU *SEE* THE ROBOT *BREAK OUT,* DR. RIOS?

YES, AND I SAW HIM CAPTURE ERNESTO. ZYBOX *OPENED WIDE* AND DRAGGED HIM IN LIKE A MONSTROUS *BULLFROG SWALLOWING A FLY.*

WHO'S THE *LITTLE BOY?*

PEDRO IS DR. CORTEZ'S *SON,* OFFICERS... IT WAS HIS BIRTHDAY TODAY...

I SUGGESTED THAT PEDRO MIGHT *ENJOY* VISITING HIS FATHER'S *FAMOUS LABORATORY...*

THE POOR BOY SAW *EVERYTHING...* SINCE THEN, HE'S JUST BEEN *STANDING HERE,* PLAYING HIS *GAMES,* REFUSING TO *SPEAK* OR TURN AWAY...

SURELY THAT'S JUST *TEMPORARY--?*

SO THEY *TELL* US...

POW!

POW!

V.R.R.R.P.

V.R.R.R.P!

BZZZT!

BZZZT!

WHERE IS ZYBOX *NOW,* DOCTOR?

NOT ON *THIS* WORLD. WE CAN AT LEAST BE *GRATEFUL* FOR THAT.

YOU'RE *RIGHT*, MAX! *TAKE HER DOWN!*

BUT, *DOC!* AREN'T WE GONNA *ATTACK* THE SUCKER?!

HE'S JUST *SITTING THERE*, WAITING TO HAVE HIS *HEAD* BLOWN OFF!

THAT *PARTICULAR* HEAD IS SURROUNDED BY A PRETTY TOUGH *FORCE SHIELD*, BUTCH!

AND EVEN IF WE *DID* ATTACK --

-- ZYBOX COULD KILL YOUR SISTER ANY OF A *DOZEN WAYS* IN LESS THAN A *SECOND.*

117

HEY, DOC, LOOK DOWN THERE! EVERYBODY'S HIPPO-TIZED JUST LIKE WE SAW 'EM OUT WEST!

YOU DON'T THINK THE WHOLE EARTH LOOKS LIKE THIS?!

'FRAID IT MIGHT, BUTCH!

IF ZYBOX CAN ENTHRALL A COUNTRY, HE CAN ENTHRALL A PLANET... ANYONE AT ALL NEAR RADIO OR VIDEO IS VULNERABLE TO HIS HYPNOTIC SIGNALS.

WITHOUT OUR MAKESHIFT JAMMER WE'D BE IN THE SAME BOAT.

THAT STORM'S GETTIN' MIGHTY CLOSE, MAX! D'YA THINK THAT BIG 'BOT MIGHT GET STRUCK BY LIGHTNING AND SAVE US THE TROUBLE?

NOW THERE'S A THOUGHT.

ACTUALLY, A GOOD BOLT OF LIGHTNING WOULD DO PLENTY OF DAMAGE.

BUT WITH ALL HIS SHIELDS UP, ZYBOX CAN JUST ABSORB WHATEVER HITS HIM AND USE IT AS A POWER SOURCE.

WE COULD TRY TO SHUT DOWN THOSE SHIELDS, BUT NOT 'TIL THE KIDS ARE SAFE.

FLOYD, YOU STILL HAVE THAT MINIATURE OF VIC'S GADGET. ZYBOX *CAN'T SEE YOU.*

TRY TO *SNEAK IN* AND GET OUR KIDS AND *ERNIE CORTEZ* OUT OF THERE.

PEABODY, TAKE THE ELEVATOR TO THE TOP. MAYBE WE CAN SNEAK IN THROUGH ZYBOX'S *BASE.*

WE *HUMANS* BETTER *STAY PUT* FOR NOW. THAT INCLUDES *YOU,* BUTCH.

BUTCH? BUTCH, WHERE ARE YOU?

DAMN.

DR. CORTEZ, IS IT MY *IMAGINATION* OR IS THIS PLACE *CHANGING SHAPE?*

ZYBOX IS *ALWAYS* CHANGING SHAPE, JENNY. I DESIGNED HIM TO GROW TO WHATEVER SIZE HE NEEDS TO PERFORM HIS DUTIES.

I'M SO SORRY HE'S COME TO USE HIS ABILITIES THIS WAY.

I *UNDERSTAND*, I GUESS... THANKS FOR FINDING OUR CLOTHES FOR US. I JUST WISH WE COULD *DISCONNECT* THESE WIRES AND *WAKE UP* ZOT AND VIC.

I KNOW, JENNY, BUT IT'S TOO *DANGEROUS.*

REMEMBER, ZYBOX WON'T HURT ANYONE *DIRECTLY.* THAT WAS HIS LAST *OFFICIAL* ORDER, AND HE'S NOT GOING TO *DISOBEY* IT.

AS STRANGE AS IT SEEMS, ZYBOX NEVER *REBELLED* AT ALL...

HE'S JUST TRYING TO LEARN, AS *ALWAYS...*

...BUT WITH NO ONE TO *ANSWER* TO, HIS METHODS HAVE GONE FAR BEYOND ANYTHING WE COULD HAVE IMAGINED.

OR *CONDONED.*

PFT!

AH!

DOC, *LOOK!* HE'S AWAKE! ZOT'S AWAKE!

AND *VIC!* THEY'RE *BOTH* UP!

WHOA! WHAT *HAPPENED?*

PFT!

PFT!

PFT!

PFT!

THAT'S ALL WE KNOW *SO FAR,* ZOT. WE STILL DON'T KNOW WHY ZYBOX SWALLOWED *US* UP, OR EVEN WHERE WE ARE!

YOU'VE TOLD ME ALL *I* NEED TO KNOW, JEN. I SAY IT'S TIME TO *BREAK OUT* OF THIS BOX!

I DON'T THINK THAT'S *POSSIBLE,* ZOT.

JENNY IS *RIGHT,* LEMONHEAD. WE CAN'T EVEN FIND *OUR WEAPONS.* HOW -- ?

TAP TAP

OH, *THERE* THEY ARE. *THANKS,* FLOYD.

FLOYD!

WOW! HE *RECHARGED* MY GUN!

AND THAT'S NOT ALL, ZOT! HE'S APPARENTLY *DE-ACTIVATED* THE *SURVEILLANCE DEVICES* IN HERE. I CAN SPEAK *FREELY* FOR THE MOMENT.

NOW HERE'S WHAT I WANT YOU TO DO...

THEN YOU DO UNDERSTAND, ERNESTO? I HAD HOPED YOU WOULD.

YES, I *DO* UNDERSTAND, NOW.

YOUR EXPERIMENT IS A *WORTHY* ONE. I'D LIKE TO HELP, IF I MAY.

I DO HAVE A QUESTION, ERNESTO...

"ONE OF THE FACTS WHICH YOU PLACED IN MY PROGRAMMING IS THE CERTAIN KNOWLEDGE THAT ALL HUMAN BEINGS POSSESS A SOUL."

MAX, *LOOK!* THESE PEOPLE ARE STARTIN' TO MOVE!

"YES, THAT'S RIGHT."

"YET MANY HUMANS THROUGHOUT HISTORY HAVE CHALLENGED THIS ASSUMPTION. IT HAS NEVER BEEN PROVEN."

HMM... THEY'RE STILL IN ZYBOX'S *SPELL*, THOUGH.

THEY DON'T EVEN *SEE* US HERE.

"WHY WAS I MADE TO BELIEVE AS FACT A THEORY WHICH HAS NEVER BEEN PROVEN?"

"BECAUSE I WANTED YOU TO HAVE *FAITH* IN SOMETHING, ZYBOX."

WHERE ARE THEY *GOING?*

"MODERN SCIENCE IS BASED ON *DOUBT*... WE ACCEPT NOTHING AS FACT UNTIL IT HAS BEEN *PROVEN* TO US.

"I WANTED TO BALANCE ALL THE DOUBT I SAW AROUND US. I WANTED YOU TO BE *DIFFERENT*."

"WHAT IS A SOUL, ERNESTO?"

THAT'S OUR *EXIT!*

"IT CAN'T BE *DESCRIBED,* ZYBOX. IF YOU HAD ONE, YOU WOULD KNOW THE ANSWER."

I MUST KNOW THE ANSWER, ERNESTO. YOU TAUGHT ME TO LEARN ALL THAT I CAN.

YES, I *DID.*

"THEN YOU SEE WHY THE EXPERIMENT IS SO VITAL TO MY EDUCATION.

"IF THE SOUL IS A FORM OF ENERGY IN QUANTITIES TOO SMALL TO BE DETECTED--AS SOME BELIEVE--THEN ONLY A GREAT NUMBER OF SOULS, ALL ESCAPING AT ONCE, CAN PROPERLY TEST THE THEORY."

CAN YOU FIND A FLAW IN MY REASONING, ERNESTO?

NO, 'BOX.

"YOU TOLD ME NOT TO 'HURT' ANYONE, ERNESTO. I HAVE OBEYED YOU IN EVERY DETAIL."

SOON WE SHALL SEE FIVE BILLION SOULS TAKE FLIGHT, ALL WITHOUT ANY ASSISTANCE BY ME.

OH, *GOOD!* HE'S GOING TO LET US *FIGHT* OUR WAY OUT!

DO YOU THINK I MIGHT CATCH ONE FOR MYSELF, ERNESTO?

125

ZYBOX IS JUST *PLAYING* WITH US! HE *KNOWS* HE'LL *WIN!*

YEAH? WELL, THAT MAKES *TWO* OF US!

?

BLAM!

PEABODY! BUTCH!

MAY WE BE OF *ASSISTANCE?*

BUT--?

WE TOOK THE *ELEVATOR* UP, SIS!

SO WHERE'S THE *CANDY MACHINE?!* I'M *STARVING!*

"ELEVATOR"? BUTCH, WHAT DO YOU *MEAN?* IS ZYBOX ON SOME KIND OF *BUILDING?*

BOY, YOU'RE SO *THICK!* OF *COURSE* WE'RE ON A B--

AAAH!

I'M A *MONKEY AGAIN!!*

ZOT, *DON'T STOP MOVING!* GET *OUTSIDE!* IT'S ALMOST *TIME!!*

SHE'S *RIGHT, ZACH!* GET OUT OF HERE *BEFORE--!*

WAIT, ZYBOX. BEFORE YOU *BROADCAST* THE COMMAND, I WOULD LIKE TO SEE YOUR *CENTRAL CORE.*

WHY?

"I THOUGHT I MIGHT SEE A DIFFERENCE, IF YOU DO *'CATCH A SOUL.'*"

"VERY WELL."

YOUR HEARTBEAT IS *ERRATIC,* ERNESTO. YOU ARE PERSPIRING.

DO YOU HOPE TO DECEIVE ME?

DO YOU PLAN A *SABOTAGE* OF SOME SORT?

YOU KNOW THAT WOULD BE IMPOSSIBLE, ERNESTO.

YES, I *DO* KNOW THAT, ZYBOX.

YOUR *DEFENSES* ARE *FLAWLESS.*

NO ONE CAN MAKE YOU *SHUT DOWN.*

NO ONE EXCEPT *YOU YOURSELF.*

SURRENDER AT ONCE

CLIK!

?

HE *DID* IT!

CORTEZ SHUT ZYBOX OFF!!

SO *STEP ON IT, ZACH!* REMEMBER WHAT HE SAID! YOU ONLY HAVE A *FEW SECONDS!*

REMEMBER, *ONE SHOT!*

POINT BLANK!

OKAY, *SMART GUY.* IF I'M A MONKEY HERE AND A MONKEY *THERE*--

SHH, BUTCH. MAX IS TRYING TO FIND *DOC CORTEZ.*

DID IT WORK?

ERNIE! GOOD GOD, WHAT'VE YOU DONE TO YOURSELF??

OH, MAX... FORGET ABOUT ME... JUST LISTEN... HAVEN'T MUCH TIME...

ZYBOX... GOING TO ORDER... WHOLE PLANET TO COMMIT SUICIDE... DID--?

THEY'RE ALIVE, ERNIE. CAN YOU TELL US WHAT *HAPPENED* HERE?

ZYBOX HAD TO OBEY LAST COMMAND... NOT TO "HURT" ANYONE...

ALL I DID WAS JUMP INTO... CENTRAL CORE... ENERGY WOULD HAVE KILLED ME IN SECONDS... HE *HAD* TO SHUT OFF...

IT... WAS ONLY SUICIDE WHEN I STARTED... AFTER THAT--

--IT WOULD HAVE BEEN *MURDER...* YES...

HE WAS SO EASY TO FOOL, MAX...

I WORKED SO HARD... SO LONG... TO MAKE THE PERFECT THINKING MACHINE... AND THEN SUCH A SIMPLE TRICK...

OH, HOW COULD HE BE SO...STUPID? IF ONLY I COULD HAVE MORE... TIME...

BUT... THINGS ARE... GETTING PRETTY FUZZY...

I...I'VE GOT A FRIEND IN NEW YORK... PLAYS MARIMBA, MAX...

I COULD...

...GIVE YOU HER *NUMBER...*

TIC-TIC-TIC-TIC-TIC-TIC-TIC

THEY'RE ALL DOING *DIFFERENT* STEPS!

THEY MUST BE *SELECTING BEATS* OUT OF THE *BASIC RHYTHM.*

THEY'RE HEARING ONLY THE BEATS THEY *WANT* TO HEAR.

THEY'LL DANCE 'TIL THE WATCH *WINDS DOWN,* THEN PROBABLY *PASS OUT* 'TIL MORNING.

IF NO ONE IS GETTING HURT WE BETTER *LEAVE IT ALONE.*

WE'LL TAKE A LOOK AROUND TO *MAKE SURE.*

TIC-TIC-TIC-TIC-TIC

DO YOU THINK THEY'LL REMEMBER ANY OF THIS TOMORROW?

I DON'T *THINK SO...* NOT AFTER THE TRANCE...

JENNY, DO YOU KNOW WHAT ANY OF THESE DANCES ARE CALLED?

DON'T *HURT* ANYONE, ZYBOX... BEYOND THAT, I DON'T CARE *WHAT* YOU DO...

GIMME THE *TORCH*, HARRY.

WELL... *THAT'S THAT.*

HURRY IT UP, BOYS.

WE GOTTA GET THIS 'BOT BACK TO *OUR EARTH* BEFORE THE *LOCALS* WAKE UP!

"WATCH HIS EYES, PEDRO... YOU'LL SEE THEM FLASH WHEN HE HAS A *SOLUTION.*"

COME NOW, PEDRO... YOU NEED TO SLEEP *SOMETIME.*

"YOU *ARE MAD!* DO YOU HAVE *ANY IDEA* WHAT YOU JUST *TOLD* HIM?? HE COULD DO *ANYTHING!!*"

FOR *HEAVEN'S SAKE,* ERNESTO, YOU KNEW THEY OWNED ZYBOX. WHAT DID YOU *EXPECT?!*

I DON'T KNOW, MARCO...

"... I JUST WANTED TO MAKE MY DREAMS A REALITY... IS THAT SO *FOOLISH?*"

"MY FRIEND... SOMEDAY *YOUR DREAMS* WILL *SWALLOW YOU WHOLE.*"

The image of every man, woman, and child on Earth dancing half asleep to the ticking of a dead man's watch captivated me early on, but it was a bitch to draw—especially with my own limited skill set. In 1987, the first graphic Web browsers were still six years off (in fact, the Web itself was still in the process of being hatched, though the Internet had been around for nearly two decades) so the luxury of things like Google Image Search was unknown. Illustrators had to make do with their own collections of books and magazines and their local libraries, some of which kept image libraries. Artists hoping to draw a northern hairy-nosed wombat might have a long, arduous search ahead of them. I did what I could on the spread, but *National Geographic* and my own ten thumbs could only take me so far.

The fact that Zybox sits on top of the World Trade Center and commands a world to commit mass suicide, including a woman in Islamic clothing shown in a few panels, may have a weird resonance for readers in 2008. I had no idea what the future of *this* world had in store for us. I was just matching up my villains with New York skyscrapers since Dekko (featured in our fourth story) had so thoroughly absorbed the Chrysler Building, and Bellows had taken a shine to the Empire State Building in issue #12. The World Trade towers seemed suitably modern and austere for a villain like Zybox. (9-Jack-9, Zot's archnemesis, I associated with the Citicorp building at 601 Lexington Avenue).

Zybox's demise is a running joke in our household. The phrase "and then Zybox is hit by lightning" has become synonymous with any important plot point that I put off while working on other parts of the story that I find more interesting. At the eleventh hour, I settled on the lightning bolt as an allegorical nod to Frankenstein's monster—the original template for the story I was telling—but it definitely bears more than a whiff of deus ex machina.

The middle storyline where Jenny is trapped in a dream that Zot never existed (comprising the bulk of Issue #14) seemed to work for a lot of readers and snagged a nomination for best single issue in that year's Eisner Awards. Fifteen years later, fans of *Buffy the Vampire Slayer* would see a similar story in the episode "Normal Again," where Buffy temporarily wakes up in an asylum to find that five and a half seasons' worth of adventures were just a mad hallucination on her part. I don't know if the writer of that episode, Diego Gutierrez, is one of the comics fans who worked on *Buffy*, but either way I have to admire him for doing what I hesitated to do: giving substantial ammunition to the idea that everything to that point was nothing but an insane, never-ending dream.

I enjoyed and/or suffered two summers in Manhattan during my year and a half working for DC Comics in the early '80s. Every Sunday, I'd walk five long blocks from my tiny apartment to the Metropolitan Museum of Art. During those summers, a street musician named Valerie Naranjo (who's apparently still working in music—thanks, Google) would play the marimba on the sidewalk in front of that enormous building in the summer heat. That strange, wonderful sound—like plucked whale bones at the bottom of an ocean—was linked to the season in my mind. I hoped to capture a bit of that mood with the opening pages of this story.

Call of the Wild

First published in *Zot! #16*.

Lettering:
Bob Lappan

Original series editor:
cat yronwode

143

146

147

*Butch temporarily ruled the De-Evolutionaries
in a story from *Zot!'s* orginal color run.

148

CALL OF THE WILD

BY SCOTT McCLOUD

LETTERER
bob lappan

EDITOR
cat yronwode

THOSE ARE *ANTIQUE FIREARMS*, BUTCH. THEY'RE FROM WAY BACK BEFORE THE *STUN-ONLY* MODELS.

OBOY! *REAL* GUNS!

I *LIKE* THIS PLACE! I'M GONNA STAY HERE!

NO PROBLEM. C'MON, JEN. WE'RE GOING TO *PIRATES' PARK*. THAT'LL CHEER YOU UP!

MEANWHILE...

THIS IS YOUR *CHANCE*, ROGER! THE PRESIDENT'S *WHOLE FAMILY* IS IN *YOUR CUSTODY!* YOU KNOW THE SECURITY SYSTEMS, YOU EVEN HAVE *THE PERFECT SCAPEGOATS!*

KIDNAP THEM, ROGER! *BLAME* IT ALL ON THE *DE-EVOLUTIONARIES!* NO ONE HAS TO KNOW!

BUT...BUT, MS. McKEEVER... KIDNAPPING IS... IS...

DON'T BE A *SIMP*, ROGER!

THIS PLAN COULD BE WORTH *MILLIONS* TO US!

A *REAL MAN* WOULDN'T HESITATE!

BUT, IT'S SO... SO... *UNETHICAL!*

RO-O-O-GER! HOW LONG HAVE YOU WAITED FOR THAT *PROMOTION?* SIX YEARS? SEVEN?

YOU *KNOW* THEY DON'T *RESPECT* YOU, ROGER. THEY'RE *LAUGHING BEHIND YOUR BACK!!*

THEY DON'T *APPRECIATE* YOU, ROGER!

YES...

BUT THEY *WILL*, ROGER! THE CHIEF WILL *FIRE* CAPTAIN O'HARA IF HE LOSES THE *PRESIDENT!* AND YOU'RE *NEXT IN LINE*, ROGER! *YOU!!*

153

INTERLUDE:

DON'T SAY *THAT,* JEN! YOU KNOW I THINK YOU'RE *WONDERFUL!*

HECK, YOU'RE MY *BEST FRIEND* IN THE *WHOLE WORLD!*

REALLY?

ZOT, DO YOU--? DO YOU THINK I'M *PRETTY?* DO YOU FIND ME-- Y'KNOW-- *ATTRACTIVE?*

WHAT-- *NOW??*

WAAAA!!

HEYYY... THERE, THERE! OF *COURSE* I THINK YOU'RE PRETTY!

GO AWAY!

-: *BZZT!* :-

ZOT, THE DEVOES HAVE *ESCAPED!*

UH-OH! WHERE *ARE* THEY, CHIEF?

WE DON'T *KNOW* YET! FORTUNATELY, THEY'RE NOT ARMED.

WE'LL KEEP YOU *POSTED,* ZOT!

O.K., CHIEF. THANKS.

...NEVER TELLS ME *ANYTHING...* MR. *WONDERFUL...* EGO THE SIZE OF A *PLANET...*

YOU'RE *BEAUTIFUL,* JENNY,...

I DON'T CARE WHAT *SPECIES* YOU ARE.

HELP! HELP!

GRR... CAN'T *AIM* WITH THESE *STUPID* MONKEY HANDS!

POW! POW!

GUYS, YOU GOTTA HELP ME!! THE COPS ARE AFTER ME!

HEY! I MISSED MY *SHOT!*

VIC, *BUDDY!* HELP! THEY'RE TRYING TO *KILL ME!!*

BUTCH, THE POLICE DON'T *KILL* PEOPLE. THEY *HELP* THEM!

BLAM! BLAM!

DROP IT, BUSTER!

ROGER, YOU *FOOL!* THOSE ARE JUST *FAKE* CARNIVAL GUNS!

I KNOW THAT! WHAT DO YOU THINK I *AM?* STUPID?!

SO GRAB YOUR GUN AND LEAVE!!

YOU GRAB IT! IT'S *YOUR* IDEA!!

160

164

I tried to vary the tone from one *Zot!* story to the next. After a long, deadly serious storyline like "Season of Dreams," it seemed like a good time to throw in a quick dumb monkey story, featuring my least-intimidating villains, the De-Evolutionaries.

I'm pretty happy with the art in this one compared to my usual efforts. Drawing humans wasn't exactly my strong suit, but the rubbery expressive faces of my cast when changed to monkeys seemed a bit more emotionally convincing. At the time, I was slowly puzzling over why a simple face like Charlie Brown's could evoke a strong sense of identification while a more rendered face might not (an idea I'd take all the way six years later in *Understanding Comics*), and this issue helped fuel my curiosity further.

Jenny and Zot's interactions by this point were increasingly informed by my own newly minted relationship with Ivy. The conversation on the Ferris wheel was an especially obvious case of channeling. The line "ego the size of a planet" from that scene has since become another running joke around the house in years since, though that one is at least equally beholden to Marvin the Paranoid Android by way of the much-missed Douglas Adams.

The center spread in this issue is probably my best stab at visualizing Zot's Earth: a sprawling amalgamation of everything worth saving from our world, combined with every fanciful utopian future ever dreamed up by writers and artists throughout the nineteenth and twentieth centuries. Fresh in my memory at the time were my first-ever visits to Disneyland and San Diego's recently built Horton Plaza, an outdoor mall that looked as if it were designed by M.C. Escher on acid.

The latter was in connection with the famous San Diego Comics Convention, America's biggest comics show, then as now. Ivy and I visited "Comic-Con" (its official name now) together for the first time in 1987, right before drawing this issue (I'd only been once, the year before). Attendance was 7,000 that year, which seemed like a lot to us, though it pales in comparison to today's 100,000-plus crowds. The next year, with attendance rising to a whopping 8,000, we were delighted to see a big cardboard flying Zot figure used as one of five symbols of American comics, hanging far above the crowds of fans and vendors.

Side-Note: Twenty-one years later, Ivy and I have been to every subsequent Comic-Con together except one: In 1995, Ivy was pregnant with our second daughter and, as luck would have it, the due date fell right before Con, so we decided for the first time to skip the event. The Monday after Con, Kurt Busiek and his wife, Ann, drove the few hours north from San Diego, along with mutual friend Neil Gaiman, to visit the still-expectant Ivy and me in Thousand Oaks, California. At dinner, Ivy went into labor and we whisked her away in a caravan of cars. Thus, at 2:00 a.m., at a nearby birthing center, Winter was born, while in the waiting room, Neil and our friend Krystal tossed Winter's 2-year-old big sister up and down, singing the opening number from *Sweeney Todd*.

Last year, my daughters—now 12 and 14—were on more panels at San Diego than I was.

The Eyes of Dekko

First published in *Zot! #17–18*.

Lettering:

Bob Lappan

Original series editor:

cat yronwode

CAN YOU SEE ME?

OH, DR. GLASS! I'M SORRY, YOU CAUGHT ME DAYDREAMING AGAIN.

ARE YOU ALL RIGHT, ARTHUR? YOU'RE NOT REVERTING TO YOUR OLD SELF, ARE YOU?

OH, PLEASE, DOCTOR...NOT EVEN IN JEST...

HA! HA! DON'T WORRY, ARTHUR. I KNOW A CURED MAN WHEN I SEE ONE. UH...FOR THE RECORD, THOUGH--

--WHAT EXACTLY WERE YOU THINKING OF JUST NOW?

I WAS RECALLING THE DAYS WHEN I WAS STILL HUMAN. HOW BEAUTIFUL THEY WERE...

HOW MUCH I MISS THEM.

OF COURSE. IT'S ONLY NATURAL.

I CAN'T BEGIN TO TELL YOU HOW GRATEFUL I AM FOR ALL YOUR HELP, DR. GLASS.

YOU WERE THE FIRST ONE ON THE STAFF TO SEE PAST THIS FRIGHTENING METAL BODY TO THE "REAL" ARTHUR DEKKER.

AH, WELL... YOU WON US ALL OVER EVENTUALLY, ARTHUR. YOU'VE BEEN A MODEL PATIENT.

NO--MORE THAN THAT, YOU'VE BEEN LIKE ONE OF THE FAMILY!

WE'RE ALL VERY PROUD OF YOU, ARTHUR.

DO YOU *REALLY* MEAN IT, DOCTOR? I'VE *SO* WANTED TO HEAR YOU *SAY* THAT... OH, I'M *SO HAPPY* TODAY...

YOU'VE BEEN SUCH A *GOOD FRIEND* TO ME. YOU'VE SHOWN ME WHAT IT *TRULY MEANS* TO BE *"HUMANE."*

FLATTERY WILL GET YOU *NOWHERE,* BUDDY!

BUT *THANK YOU.*

LADIES AND GENTLEMEN-- *ESTEEMED COLLEAGUES!* MAY I PRESENT OUR *GUEST OF HONOR--* MR. ARTHUR PATRICK DEKKER!

CLAP! CLAP! CLAP! CLAP! CLAP! CLAP! CLAP!

SPEECH! SPEECH!

MY FRIENDS, I-- I'M TRULY *MOVED* BY YOUR TRIBUTE.

IF THESE *METAL EYES* WERE BUILT FOR TEARS, YOU WOULD SEE AT A GLANCE HOW *DEEP* MY FEELINGS RUN FOR YOU...

I HAVE NO *SPEECH,* MY FRIENDS. JUST MY *WARMEST GRATITUDE* TO ALL OF YOU...

AND *ESPECIALLY* TO *YOU,* DR. GLASS.

MY *PLEASURE.*

IT'S SO *GOOD* TO BE *BACK TO NORMAL,* DOCTOR.

IT'S GOOD TO *HAVE* YOU BACK, ARTHUR.

171

BUT HE MADE THESE *HIMSELF*, ZOT! THESE ARE *PRICELESS* WORKS OF ART!

"ART?" DID SOMEONE SAY "ART?!"

JUNK IS WHAT I CALL IT!!

PAP! GLOP! RUBBISH!

CLAK!

PLAK!

ZOT, *PLEASE!* TELL HIM TO *STOP!!*

STOP.

DON'T.

NO ONE CAN STOP ME, ZACH!! I'M GONNA TORCH THIS TRASH RIGHT NOW!!

ACME FLAME THROWER

BUT, MAX! I *LOVE* THIS ONE! IT'S SO *CUTE!*

CLAK!

CUTE??? MY GOD, IT'S WORSE THAN I THOUGHT!!

OH *NO,* MAX, DON'T!

RRIPP!!

EEEK!

STAND ASIDE, JENNY!

BUT, MAX! YOU *CAN'T!* THIS IS *YOUR OWN* ART!

OH, YEAH?

-Sigh-
BACK TO REALITY.

DON'T BE SAD, JEN. THURSDAY IS YOUR LAST EXAM, RIGHT?

YOU'RE ALMOST DONE!

YEAH, SO MUCH FOR 9TH GRADE. NEXT YEAR: HIGH SCHOOL.

HUH? I THOUGHT 9TH GRADE WAS HIGH SCHOOL.

NAW, IT'S WEIRD HERE... JUNIOR HIGH IS 7TH TO 9TH.

OH...

I JUST FIGURED KIDS WERE SHORTER ON YOUR PLANET...

WELL, I GOTTA RUN! SEE YOU SATURDAY!

SEE YOU...

176

177

WA!

JENNY!

GOOD ONE!

CLAP! CLAP!

HA! HA!

CLAP! CLAP!

SHUT UP, DICK-FACE!

LET IT GO, TER... I'M O.K...

THOSE JERKS. HERE, LET ME GET THOSE.

THANKS. OW!

CAN I HELP?

HUH? OH, YEAH, THANKS!

NO SWEAT. I DROP MINE ALL THE TIME.

GOT 'EM! THANKS AGAIN.

MY PLEASURE. SEE YOU LATER.

C'MON. WE SHOULD HURRY IF--

WAIT A SEC, TERRY.

YEAH, WE GOT BACK LAST SATURDAY...

UM. EXCUSE ME. YOU LOOK FAMILIAR... DO YOU HAVE A LITTLE BROTHER NAMED WOODY?

UH... NO.

BUT...

179

186

" WHEN I WAS *SHORT* AND *DORKY-LOOKING* I KEPT TELLING MYSELF NOT TO WORRY, THAT WHAT I *LOOK* LIKE DOESN'T MATTER, IT'S JUST THIS *RANDOM THING*, JUST SOME *ACCIDENT OF HEREDITY*. IT'S WHAT'S *INSIDE* THAT COUNTS. I'M NOT GOING TO STOP BELIEVING THAT JUST 'CAUSE IT'S NOT TO MY *ADVANTAGE* ANYMORE."

"I STILL SAY YOU'VE *CHANGED*, WOODY. FOR ONE THING, YOU DON'T *STUTTER*."

"OH, I ONLY DID THAT AROUND *YOU*, ANYWAY."

"*REALLY?* WHY *ME*, OF ALL PEOPLE?"

"YOU'RE *FISHING FOR COMPLIMENTS*, JENNY."

"NO, I'M NOT!"

"YES, YOU ARE."

"ALL RIGHT, MAYBE I AM. ACTUALLY, WOODY, I'M *DYING* FOR SOME COMPLIMENTS. PLEASE, GO AHEAD."

"YOU'RE *WONDERFUL*, JENNY WEAVER. YOU'RE *SMART, CARING, BEAUTIFUL* AND *FASCINATING*. YOU'RE THE ONLY GIRL IN THIS SCHOOL WHO DOESN'T HAVE *LETTUCE* FOR BRAINS, YOU'RE THE ONLY REASON I CAME TO THIS STUPID PICNIC IN THE FIRST PLACE AND I...I...OH, *PLEASE* TELL ME YOU BROKE UP WITH *WHATSISNAME*. PLEASE? *YES? NO?* NEVER MIND, I KNOW THAT LOOK..."

"WOODY, I'M SORRY. I,..."

"NO, *I'M* SORRY, JENNY. I DON'T KNOW WHAT CAME OVER ME. I'M SUCH AN ASS. GOD, *HISTORY REPEATS ITSELF...*"

"I FEEL DIZZY."

"FORGET IT, JENNY. I'LL LEAVE."

"*NO!* DON'T GO, WOODY! PLEASE... I *LIKE* YOU. I MEAN, I REALLY *DO* LIKE YOU! IT'S JUST,..."

"ARE YOU *CRYING?* MY GOD, WHAT DID I SAY?"

"WOODY, I CAN'T *TALK* TO ANYONE ANYMORE. I DON'T THINK HE REALLY *UNDERSTANDS* ME. I MEAN, I'VE GOT ALL THIS...*STUFF*...IN ME. I DON'T KNOW WHERE TO PUT IT ALL. SOMETIMES, I FEEL LIKE I'M GOING TO EXPLODE."

"LOTS OF PEOPLE FEEL THAT WAY, JENNY."

"YEAH? NAME *TWO*."

"JENNY, *I* FEEL THAT WAY! IT'S LIKE YOU'RE A *SUITCASE* THAT NEVER GETS *OPENED*, RIGHT? BUT WHEREVER THEY TAKE YOU, YOU JUST GET MORE FULL..."

"YEAH..."

"AND YOU SEE THINGS NO ONE ELSE DOES. YOU SEE WHAT THE *REAL RULES* ARE, THE ONES THEY NEVER TEACH YOU IN CLASS. BUT IT DOESN'T MAKE YOU ANY *BETTER* THAN THEM. IT JUST MAKES THEM HATE YOU."

"OR *IGNORE* YOU, YEAH... BUT WHAT CAN WE *DO* ABOUT IT, WOODY? WHAT'S *WRONG* WITH US?"

"*NOTHING'S* WRONG WITH *US!* IT'S ALL THOSE *ZOMBIES* THEY CALL '*NORMAL*' WHO OUGHTTA HAVE THEIR *BRAINS* REVOKED. WE'RE THE *ARTISTS*, THE ONES WHO *MATTER*."

"SPEAK FOR YOURSELF. I'M NO 'ARTIST'."

"WANNA *BET?*"

"LOOK, WOODY, I HAVE TO GO. CAN WE TALK AGAIN? LIKE, *SOON?*"

"SURE. HOW SOON IS '*SOON*'?"

"JUST NOT TONIGHT. I'M GOING TO A *BIRTHDAY PARTY* IN *ANOTHER DIMENSION*."

"I BELIEVE THAT."

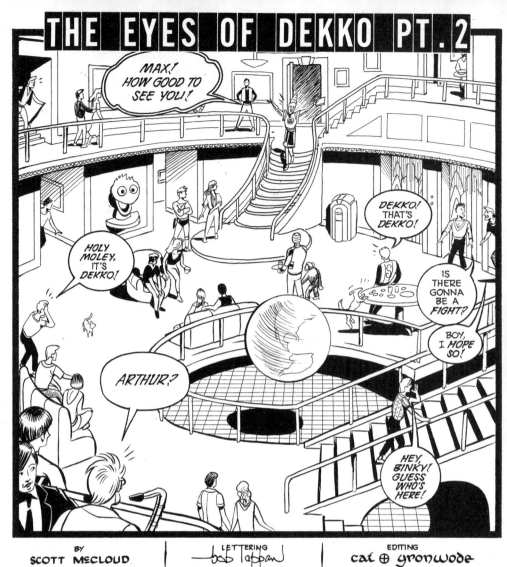

BY
SCOTT McCLOUD

LETTERING
Bob Tappan

EDITING
cat ⊕ yronwode

BOY, ZACH, IT'S LUCKY YOUR UNCLE HAS SUCH A *BIG HOUSE*, SO'S WE CAN GET AWAY FROM *EL CREEPO!*

MR. DEKKER IS A VERY *SICK MAN*, DIGGER! HE NEEDS OUR *HELP!*

DO *YOU* KNOW SOMETHING *WE* DON'T, JENNY?

WELL, YOU KNOW HOW DEKKO GOT THE WAY HE IS, *RIGHT?*

THANKS.

I KNOW HE HAD *CANCER* OR SOMETHING AND HAD TO HAVE HIS BODY *REPLACED PIECE BY PIECE...*

MAX DOESN'T TALK ABOUT IT MUCH...

WELL, MAX TOLD *ME* THAT ARTHUR DEKKER WAS AN OLD *STUDENT* OF HIS. -*CHOMP.-* MAX KNEW HIM THE WHOLE TIME HE WAS BEING TURNED INTO A *MACHINE.*

HNH.

ARTHUR'S MIND KINDA *SNAPPED* ABOUT *HALFWAY THROUGH...* HE STARTED TO *LIKE* IT... STARTED *WORSHIPPING* MECHANICAL STUFF...

!!K!

"HIS GIRLFRIEND, SARAH, COULDN'T DEAL, SO SHE LEFT HIM... MAX HAS LOTS OF *PAINTINGS* OF SARAH...

"I THINK THEY *BOTH* REALLY LOVED HER..."

" I THINK SOMETHING *BAD* HAPPENED TO SARAH... I DON'T KNOW WHAT..."

I KNOW ARTHUR STILL *LOVES* HER, BUT EVEN IF SHE... Y'KNOW, BECAUSE OF THE WAY HE IS...... HE CAN'T...

GOD, JUST *THINKING* ABOUT IT MUST BE SO *PAINFUL* TO HIM...

WOW, I NEVER *LOOKED* AT IT THAT WAY.

STILL, IT'S FUNNY MAX WOULD WANT TO TELL *YOU* AND NOT ME.

WHEE!

HEY, BUTCH, HOW DO YOU LIKE MAX'S NEW *INDOOR ROLLER COASTER?*

EH, I'VE SEEN BETTER!

HOW ABOUT SOME *MUSIC* IN HERE?! WANNA TURN ON THAT *JUKEBOX?!*

HMM, LET'S TRY *NUMBER EIGHT.*

SPLISH! SPLASH! I WAS TAKIN' A BATH!

AAR... OLD MUSIC! DOESN'T THAT GEEZER LIKE ANYTHING *NEW?!*

MAX LIKES *EVERYTHING,* BUTCH.

ARTHUR?

IN HERE, MAX!

I WAS JUST LOOKING AT SOMETHING... WONDERFUL!

OH, THOSE ARE JUST SOME PHOTOS I TOOK OF--

OF NATURALLY OCCURING PHENOMENA... I KNOW.

YOU HAVE SOME OF MY FAVORITES HERE!

"THE HYPNOTIC NAUTILUS.

"THE REGAL MILKDROP.

"THE SUBLIME SNOW CRYSTAL."

Ding! Dong!

I'LL GET IT!

HI, MOM.

THAT VOICE!

OH!

IT GOT ITSELF.

HELLO, DOCTOR.

YOU... YOU... MONSTER!

WHY DID YOU DO IT??

WHY??

MAX, MEET DR. HERBERT W. GLASS, MY CHIEF THERAPIST AT WINDHAVEN!

REALLY? SAY, DOCTOR, I DON'T MEAN TO TELL YOU YOUR BUSINESS...

BUT I'VE BEEN OBSERVING THIS EX-PATIENT OF YOURS FOR A WHILE NOW AND I HAVE TO TELL YOU--

--THAT IS NOT A HEALTHY MAN.

198

I KNOW.

ONLY *HALF AN HOUR* AFTER I DROPPED HIM OFF NEAR THIS HOUSE, I GOT WORD THAT WINDHAVEN HAD BEEN *BURNED TO THE GROUND* BY *INCENDIARY BOMBS*.

A THIN TRAIL OF *ROCKET FUEL* IGNITED A *BURNING MESSAGE* ON A *NEARBY HILL--*

-- *TWO LETTERS:* "*A.D.*" ARTHUR DEKKER!

HEH...HEH...

YOU'RE *PROUD* OF IT, *AREN'T YOU??* YOU *MANIAC!* IT'S A WONDER YOU DIDN'T *KILL* ANYONE!!

"*PROUD*"? NO! RATHER, I'M *ASHAMED!*

ASHAMED I EVER *DESIGNED* SUCH A *FAILURE!*

"*DESI--*" *YOU'RE DELUDED!* YOU DIDN'T DESIGN WINDHAVEN! IT WAS DESIGNED BY A MISTER... EH... MISTER...

KURK REDHEART.

YES! YES... THAT'S IT, ODD NAME. KURK WITH A "*U.*"

REARRANGE THE *LETTERS.*

OH, NO... NO...

YOU KNEW ALL THE *TRICKS*... ALL THE *TESTS* OF YOUR SURROUNDINGS... YOU KNEW IT ALL...

BUT HOW COULD YOU HAVE KNOWN YOU'D *END UP* THERE?

I *DIDN'T!* I DESIGNED WINDHAVEN IN MY *EARLIER DAYS*, WHEN I STILL *NEEDED THE MONEY.*

ONCE COMMITTED AT *WORDSWORTH MEMORIAL*, I SIMPLY EXHIBITED THE TYPE OF *PSYCHOSIS* I KNEW YOU *SPECIALIZED* IN!

I PLAYED YOU LIKE A *FLUTE*, DOCTOR!

AND SOON I SHALL BLOW THE *TRUMPET OF ETERNAL OBLIVION--*

200

201

LOVELY! BUT *STILL NO SALE,* MAX.

I *GIVE UP* THEN. IF *BACH* CAN'T JUSTIFY OUR CONTINUED EXISTENCE, *NOTHING CAN.*

MAX, DON'T *GIVE UP* ON HIM! SHOW HIM *MORE!* SHOW HIM HOW *BEAUTIFUL* LIFE IS! ALL THE *HIDDEN STUFF!*

OH, MAX, NOT ANOTHER ONE OF YOUR "STUDENTS."

LISTEN TO HIM, MR. DEKKER! *LISTEN TO MAX!* HE CAN *HELP* YOU!

NO, JENNY. ARTHUR *HAS* LISTENED TO ME. I CAN'T TELL HIM ANYTHING HE HASN'T ALREADY CONSIDERED.

ARTHUR CHOOSES TO *REJECT* OUR WORLD... THAT CHOICE MAY SEEM *BITTER* AND *WRONG* TO US, BUT IT IS *HIS* TO MAKE.

MAX, YOU ALWAYS *CARED* ABOUT THESE THINGS. I'LL MISS YOU *TERRIBLY.*

AS I MISS *YOU,* ARTHUR... AS I MISS *YOU.*

THANK YOU FOR *WAITING,* OFFICERS.

THE GODS
ARE ALL HERE WITH US.

POINT...

LINE...

CIRCLE...

SPHERE...

CYLINDER...

CONE...

C'MON, JEN. I'LL TAKE YOU BACK TO YOUR WORLD.

UNGGH...

OH NO! I'M LATE FOR SCHOOL!!

MOM!! WHY DIDN'T YOU WAKE ME?!

SILLY GIRL. DON'T YOU REMEMBER?

VACATION BEGINS TODAY!

OH!

OH, YEAH...

It's been said that in the average superhero story, the villain is frequently the protagonist since their aspirations and actions typically launch the story and the hero only reacts. I don't know if that's always true, but it certainly is in this case. This is Dekko's story from beginning to end.

This might be my most personal story in the run—which sounds kind of scary now that I think about it. Dekko is a raving lunatic, but I guess he's my kind of raving lunatic. Like most writers, I put a little of myself into every character, but a few are more fully connected to my world view than others. The most prominent "me-characters" include Zot, Max, and Dekko. Zot is my sunny, optimistic side, Max is my everything-is-interesting attitude about art and life in general, and Dekko is pretty much what I'd like today if I still lived alone (no joke, I was halfway there when Ivy rescued me).

It takes a certain degree of obsession to turn making art into one's daily business, and obsession is one thing I've never lacked. But like Max, I've learned to draw a line between life and art. I see art as life's antidote—a realm where purity of vision can be safely pursued without the mountain of steaming corpses that usually results when uncompromising "visionaries" in the political sphere try to perfect the world we all live in.

Dekko's origin story had appeared in the original color run, so it's only recapped in this one, but I always liked the basic plot: An artist with a degenerative disease slowly loses one part of his body after another, each replaced by its robotic twin, and his once-organic art gradually changes as he changes, until he embraces his new form and begins to design each new part. The idea of him driving his lover away at about the "halfway mark"—with its unavoidable inference of castration—I found particularly useful when getting inside his head.

Dekko was partly inspired by British turn-of-the-century artist Louis Wain, who drew naturalistic cat pictures for years before schizophrenia consumed him, during which time his drawings got increasingly weird and abstract. I was also inspired by the slow progression in Kandinsky's paintings from the earlier messy stuff to the later, rigid abstractions.

Dekko's dialogue is a bit of a throwback to the florid soliloquies of the crazy supervillains I grew up reading. It sounds especially weird and hokey these days, now that even mainstream superhero comics are reaching for a more naturalistic tone, but there you have it: a Kabuki Theater artifact of an earlier time in comics history.

The months pass quickly in these issues, as evidenced by Woody's dramatic transformation. I like to "show" rather than "tell," so readers were a bit surprised by the giant text box conversation between Jenny and Woody at the park. I just needed to compress a lot of information into a short space. It went against a lot of my theories about what makes a good comic, but it nevertheless appealed to the side of me that will try anything once, another example of the Max in me winning out over the Dekko.

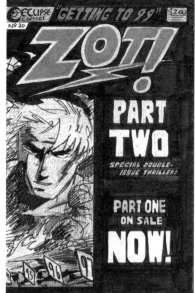

Special Feature
Getting to 99

Issues #19–20 were a two-part story, published simultaneously as two separate comics. I wrote and laid out the story, but the finished art was drawn by artist Chuck Austen while Ivy and I got married and went on our honeymoon. This book collects all of my own black and white *Zot!* stories, so we aren't including the finished art this time around (576 pages was big enough!), but since I did my usual comprehensive layouts to serve as a "visual script" for Chuck, it seemed appropriate to include them here and fill out the run (albeit, at a reduced size). In the future, we hope to offer both Chuck's dynamic finished art version of this story as well as Matt Feazell's delightful *Zot! 10 ½* backups now that these stories are finally under one cover.

The cover roughs (facing page, top left): Designed as a single image when viewed side by side. Memorably described by one fan as "a jigsaw puzzle for simpletons."

The thumbnails (excerpt below): A typical artifact of my borderline-OCD working methods. My first step in plotting the story was to make tiny rough scribbles of each page with felt-tip pens on 3" x 5" notecards, then hinge them, accordion-style, on the back with drafting tape so they could be viewed all at once or in spreads.

The layouts (following pages, first page at right): My "final script" then took the form of comprehensive layouts, drawn full-size in markers and also hinged with tape for accordion-style viewing. This was the only "script" I sent to Chuck, and the only kind of script I ever create for myself. I've never typed a full script for stories I plan to draw, preferring instead to work out all pacing, compositions, and dialogue visually with these elaborate comps.

On the plus side, this has helped keep my script and art nicely integrated. On the minus side, it's probably contributed to the stiffness of my own finished art. By the time I inked any given issue of *Zot!*, I'd typically already drawn each panel two or three times!

GETTING TO 99

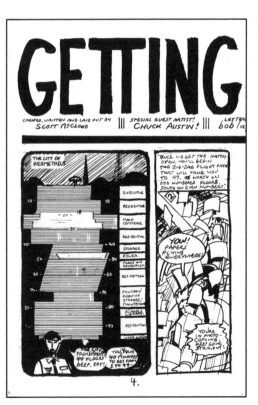

Created, written and laid out by SCOTT McCLOUD ||| Special guest artist! CHUCK AUSTIN! ||| Lettered bob/a

...ed by ||| Edited by ...opan ||| cat @ gronwode

218

221

222

Issue break →

CONTINUED IN ZOT! #20, ON SALE **NOW**!!

225

Thanks to Chuck Austen, who helped me locate the second half of these layouts, which had turned up in an envelope only a few months before we put this collection together.

In his sleek, kinetic art for the final comics, Chuck took my mouse "saboteur" and made it a *dreep,* a small rodent creature featured in the original color issues. It was a nice touch that gave even this light-hearted fill-in a properly named adversary to go with the other rogues' gallery entries from this period.

Can't Buy Me Love

First published in *Zot! #21–22*.

Lettering:
Bob Lappan

Original series editor:
cat yronwode

--YOU CAN *CAPTURE* THEM NOW.

RIGHT, PEABODY!

F-TANG! *BLANG!*

YAH! MY ROD!

GRAR!! CRIME DOESN'T PAY!

HA, HA! TAKE 'EM AWAY, PEABODY!

~*WHEW!*~ BEING A *SUPERHERO* SURE IS *HARD WORK!*

ON A *HOT DAY* LIKE *TODAY*, I NEED A SOFT DRINK THAT'LL REALLY *HIT THE SPOT!*

BUT IT SHOULD BE *LOW-CAL*, BECAUSE I CAN'T AFFORD TO GET TOO *FILLED UP!*

THAT'S WHY I *LIKE THE ALL-NEW* -- *Bingo Pop!*

Bingo Pop

WHAT DID *YOU* THINK, VIC?

I DON'T KNOW, ZACH... HAS *JENNY* SEEN THIS THING?

NOT YET. I WANTED TO *SURPRISE* HER. WHY? DON'T YOU THINK SHE'LL *LIKE* IT?

WEL-L-LL... LET'S PUT IT *THIS* WAY: I DON'T WANT TO BE IN THE *SOLAR SYSTEM* WHEN SHE SEES IT.

OH.

TAYLOR

AW, *C'MON,* TAYLOR! WHAT'S NOT TO *LIKE?!* IT'S GOT *EVERYTHING!* GUNS, CROOKS--

AND THE *MONEY!* TELL US ABOUT THE *MONEY,* ZACH!

WELL, DIG...

...Y'KNOW THAT RED *ATMOS NINE SUPERSONIC* YOU'RE ALWAYS STARING AT THROUGH THE *SHOWROOM WINDOW?*

÷*Ulp!*÷ Y-YEAH?

WANT ONE?

WOW.

HEY, ZOTTO. ALONG THOSE LINES, THERE *IS* THIS REALLY CUTE *ELECTRON MICROSCOPE* I'VE BEEN AFTER...

YOU *GOT* IT, HACK.

HEY, *THANKS!*

VIC?

NAAH... I DON'T ACCEPT PRESENTS FROM *DEAD MEN.*

GEE, YOU REALLY THINK SHE WON'T *LIKE* IT, HUNH?

DON'T LISTEN TO HIM, *BLONDIE!* SHE'S *MY SISTER.* I SAY SHE'LL *LOVE* IT!

I *REST MY CASE.*

235

STEEL DRUMS.
AREN'T THEY
GREAT?

YEAH... IT'S
LIKE BEING IN
A *WARM POOL*
OR SOMETHING.
IT'S SO *SUMMER*.

I WANT
TO PUT SOME
MONEY IN
THE HAT...

HERE. *ME,
TOO.* BUT
MAKE SURE
WE HAVE
ENOUGH FOR
THE BUS.

OH, *I'M SORRY!* I DIDN'T SEE YOU THERE! ARE YOU--?

STAY BACK! I KNOW *KARATE!*

RELAX, I WON'T *HURT* YOU! MY NAME'S ZOT. WHAT'S YOURS?

W-WOODY.

OH, *RIGHT!* JENNY TOLD ME ALL ABOUT YOU. PLEASED TO MEET--

HOLD IT! YOU'RE ZOT?? YOU-- BUT WHERE DID YOU *COME FROM?*

WHAT'S THAT??

OH, THAT'S A *DIMENSIONAL PORTAL* TO MY *EARTH.*

OH MY *GOD!*

OH MY *GOD,* I DON'T *BELIEVE IT!*

GEE, WOODY, DIDN'T JEN *TELL* YOU I WAS FROM *ANOTHER DIMENSION?*

I THOUGHT SHE WAS BEING *SARCASTIC!*

MY GOD, I'VE BEEN COMPETING WITH *THIS??*

"COMPETING?"

UH...

YES, YOU HEARD RIGHT. I DON'T CARE *WHO* KNOWS ANYMORE. I-- I *LOVE* HER, ZOT. I *LOVE* HER!

WHO? *JENNY?*

YES!

WELL, *SURE... WHO WOULDN'T?*

241

WAIT! WHERE ARE YOU *GOING?* AREN'T YOU GOING TO *BEAT ME UP* OR SOMETHING?

Ding. Dong.

NO...

I DON'T *OWN* HER, WOODY.

JENNY CAN MAKE *HER OWN* DECISIONS.

YOU SEEM LIKE A NICE GUY. MAY THE *BEST MAN WIN* AND ALL...

WHY DO I GET THIS *SINKING FEELING* THAT IT WON'T BE ME?

OH, *HI*, ZOT. BE *RIGHT OUT.*

TAKE YOUR TIME.

WOULD YOU LIKE TO INVITE *WOODY?*

OH, HE'S *GONE.*

YOU MET *WOODY??*

YEAH, *JUST NOW.* HE SEEMS LIKE A NICE GUY...

WORTH GETTING TO KNOW BETTER...

HI, SIS.

JEN.

244

248

HO-HUM... IT'S NOT MUCH FUN WHEN YOU *KNOW* HE'S GOING TO WIN.

SAY, WHAT'S *THIS?*

OH, UH... MAYBE YOU SHOULD *WAIT* TO LOOK AT THAT, JEN.

AAH! WE'RE OUTTA CONTROL!

Bingo Pop Spot

WE'RE GONNA *CRASH!!*

YOU AREN'T *GETTING AWAY THAT* EASY!

BOOM!

AAAH!

EEEEE!

-:GASP!:- --THAT'S WHY I LIKE THE *NEW BINGO POP!*

GET HIM! IT'S TWO AGAINST ONE!

YEAH!

-UNGH!:-

HEY ZOT!!

-:UNNGH!:- JUST A MINUTE, JEN!

POW!

WHAK!

THUD! SOK!

249

252

I SHOULD HAVE *KNOWN*.

MR. DOUGLAS, HOW *COULD* YOU?!

I'M *SORRY*, ZOT. I HAD MY *INSTRUCTIONS*. I'M A *LOYAL* EMPLOYEE.

HA! HA! YOU *BETTER BE*, DOUGIE!

BUT *HOW ??*

HE *BOUGHT US OUT*, ZOT... ORDERED PROMOTIONS TO GET *YOUR* ENDORSEMENT.

HE--!

HE WANTED TO GET YOU *UNDER CONTRACT* SO YOU'D SIGN HIS *SPECIAL CLAUSE*.

CLAUSE?

IT STATES THAT YOU'VE AGREED NOT TO SAY OR DO ANYTHING THAT COULD CAUSE THE COMPANY TO BE *DISCREDITED* OR *DAMAGED* IN ANY WAY.

THE COMPANY *OR* ANY OF ITS *OFFICERS*.

Y'KNOW, LIKE *ME*, F'RINSTANCE.

BUT, THAT MEANS I CAN'T --

YOU *GOT IT*, HERO! FROM NOW ON I CAN DO *ANYTHIN'* I WANT AND YOU *CAN'T TOUCH ME!*

OH NO! NO!

TERRY, DO YOU MIND IF I *GET OUT* HERE?

NO, YOU GUYS HAVE *A LOT* TO *TALK ABOUT.* GO AHEAD.

ARE YOU *SURE,* JENNY? IT'S *THREE MILES HOME* AND IT LOOKS LIKE *RAIN.*

I'LL BE *OKAY,* MRS. VERAS. THANKS FOR THE *TRIP!*

SO! WHAT'S UP?

I THOUGHT JENNY WAS SEEING THAT *"ZOT"* BOY, TERRY.

JENNY DOESN'T REALLY *KNOW,* MOM. WOODY IS JUST THIS *NERDY GUY* SHE'S *HUNG UP* ON RIGHT NOW. HE'S *NOTHING.*

REALLY? THAT'S ODD, CONSIDERING HIS *FATHER...*

...JERRY BERNSTEIN WAS ONE OF OUR *AMBASSADORS* TO *SOUTH AFRICA,* BACK IN THE *EARLY EIGHTIES...* GOT IN *A LOT* OF *TROUBLE* FOR MEETING WITH *THE BLACK OPPOSITION* WHEN *NO ONE ELSE* WAS.

THAT GUY LOST A *GOOD JOB* 'CAUSE HE *STUCK TO HIS PRINCIPLES!*

THAT'S COOL, *I GUESS...* I JUST DON'T WANT JENNY *RUNNING OFF* WITH SOME GUY WHO DOESN'T *DESERVE HER.*

I *LIKE* WOODY! HE'S *CUTE!*

YEAH, WELL... WHATTA *YOU* KNOW?

UH-OH! *FIRST DROP.*

"IT'S STARTING TO *RAIN!*"

259

SO, HOW IS *ZOT* DOING, JEN?

OH, HE WENT AND SIGNED A CONTRACT FOR SOME *T.V. COMMERCIAL,* THE *MORON...*

...NOW, ONE OF HIS *OLDEST ENEMIES* IS *RUNNING THE COMPANY* AND ZOT'S CONTRACT WON'T LET HIM *FIGHT* THE GUY.

I SAY IT'S HIS *OWN FAULT* FOR BEING SUCH A *TOOL.*

I DUNNO... *EVERYBODY* MAKES *MISTAKES,* JEN. ZOT WOULDN'T *DELIBERATELY SELL OUT,* WOULD HE?

OH, NO, *NEVER.*

IF ZOT *KNOWS* THE RIGHT THING TO DO, *HE'LL DO IT!* HE JUST NEEDS *A LOT OF ATTENTION* TO KEEP HIM ON *THE RIGHT TRACK.*

BUT *I* NEED SOME ATTENTION, *TOO,* Y'KNOW? HE'S NEVER REALLY SAID HOW HE *FEELS* ABOUT ME.

YESTERDAY I TOLD ZOT THAT I *LOVE* YOU...ALL HE SAID WAS, *"SURE, WHO WOULDN'T?"*

WHAT??

YOU DID GET THAT *COURT ORDER* FOR THIS, DIDN'T YOU, PEABODY?

YES.

HE'S *GONE!* WE'RE *ALONE* NOW!

YOU DID *GOOD,* SULLEY! YOU SWIPED THE FORMULA LIKE I TOLD YOU, AND LET ZOT TAIL YOU BACK HERE LIKE I PLANNED.

THANKS, BOSS.

THAT'S A *CONFESSION,* ALL RIGHT.

TRANSMIT THIS TAPE TO *THE POLICE* AND TELL THEM WHERE TO FIND THE BLOTCH.

DONE.

BINGO POP CO

AND THERE'S THE *CASE* WITH THE *FORMULA* IN IT!

RED, TAKE THESE TO *H.Q.* I'LL BE *RIGHT WITH YOU!*

YEAH, BOSS.

HUH? WHAT DOES HE MEAN? THIS *IS* BINGO POP H.Q.

OH, *I SEE!* HE'S GOT A *PERSONAL INTERPLANETARY DOOR.* BOY, THAT GUY IS *LOADED!*

C'MON, SULLEY, *MOVE IT.*

DAMN! HE'S *GETTING AWAY!*

TO *HECK* WITH THAT CONTRACT-- *LET'S GO!!*

262

WAK!

PRIVATE

BOOM!

RETURN RESET

CLIK!
CLIK!
CLIK!

EXIT

269

271

-- SO, ANYWAY, WE GOT ENOUGH ON HIM TO PUT HIM AWAY FOR *A FEW YEARS* AT LEAST.

'TIL HE *BREAKS OUT* AGAIN, Y'MEAN.

HEY, *ZACH!* DID THE *AD MONEY* COME IN YET?

WELL, ER, *YES AND NO,* DIGGER...

MEANING YOU CAN *FORGET* THE *CAR,* SHADES.

AWW...

ZOT, CAN I *TALK* TO YOU FOR A *MINUTE?*

UH, *SURE,* JEN. SEE YOU *LATER,* GUYS!

ZOT, *LISTEN.* I WANT YOU TO TELL ME *THE TRUTH,* ONCE AND FOR ALL!

DO YOU *LOVE ME?*

WELL, *SURE.* WHO WOULDN'T?

NO! NO! I MEAN, LIKE... Y'KNOW... DO YOU *LOVE* ME?!

OH, YOU MEAN, LIKE, *CAPITAL "L"* LOVE...

YES! THAT'S IT! *CAPITAL "L" LOVE!* DO YOU *CAPITAL "L" LOVE ME?!*

I--! I *DON'T KNOW!*

OH.

WHY? DO YOU LOVE *ME* THAT WAY?

UH... I GUESS I DON'T KNOW, *EITHER.*

WELL, WE'RE *OKAY,* THEN, *AREN'T WE?*

I GUESS... WHAT *IS* LOVE, ANYWAY?

YOU'RE ASKING *ME?*

I HEAR *SOME* PEOPLE SAY THE WORD SOMETIMES AND I DON'T LIKE THE *SOUND* OF IT...

...LIKE, WHAT THEY'RE *REALLY* SAYING IS "I *OWN* YOU."

MAYBE SOME PEOPLE *WANT* TO BE *OWNED,* ZOT,

MAYBE THEY THINK IT'S THE ONLY WAY TO BE *WORTH* SOMETHING.

NAW, THAT'S TOO WEIRD.

FOR *YOU,* MAYBE! *EVERYBODY* KNOWS THEY'RE WORTH SOMETHING ON THIS WORLD.

BUT WE'RE NEVER QUITE *SURE* ON MY PLANET.

WE'RE ALWAYS TRYING TO *PROVE* IT.

278

When I created *Zot!,* I wanted to highlight my characters' differences, both externally and internally. I'd noticed that writers who worked on a series long enough sometimes lost sight of those differences over time until their characters' voices became interchangeable. To avoid this, I looked for internal organizing ideas. For Zot, Jenny, Peabody, and Butch, I used Carl Jung's four functions of the human mind: Intuition, Feeling, Intellect, and Sensation. Jenny's orientation, Feeling, assigns value judgments, so she would be most likely to take offense at Zot's "selling out."

Some readers were annoyed that Zot would be so shallow as to endorse a product, but others were just annoyed that Jenny was such a nag about it. In my own clumsy way, I was trying to work out where my perfect hero was less than perfect.

Throughout these stories, I was wrestling with which of the two worlds I found more interesting, and at this point, our Earth was edging out Zot's universe. Stemming from my early fascination with Japanese comics, I had a strong interest in what I called "the beauty of the mundane." Drawing my hero rocketing, Astroboy-style, over a hyper-commercialized future city was fun and all, but a Burger King in the rain—now that was interesting!

When I'd created the Blotch some years earlier, I'd seen the future he represented, the future of capitalism run amok, as unlikely, so he was one of the "loud" villains (i.e., more impotent and boastful than, say, Zybox). But, by 1988, his future seemed a bit more relevant to the times we were living in, so he got a bit edgier. The scene where the Blotch erases Sulley's life savings is played as comedy, but I shuddered a bit when writing it.

Ivy and I struggled with money a lot in the late '80s. I can't count the number of times we'd run a utility payment in before 5:00 p.m. to avoid shut-offs during those years. The comics industry was going through a boom-and-bust cycle of black and white comics frantically trying to duplicate the success of the *Teenage Mutant Ninja Turtles*. I was neither lucky, clever, nor crass enough to reap the benefits of the boom, but the bust was taking its toll nonetheless.

We knew Kevin Eastman and Peter Laird, the Turtles' creators, two friendly, good-hearted young guys struggling to make sense of the millions of dollars thundering down upon them in nearby Northampton, Massachusetts. The scale of their success was almost unimaginable. Every station break brought another ad. Every kid in the country could name all four turtles. Whole aisles of Toys R Us were as green as the Barbie aisles were pink.

One Friday afternoon, around that time, Ivy and I were between checks yet again. Raiding the change jars and searching between the couch cushions, we'd managed to scrounge a little over ten dollars, enough to buy a long weekend's worth of groceries, provided we stuck to cheap stuff like pasta. Entering the local Stop and Shop, Ivy went off to buy milk, butter, and a couple of other items. I picked up some spaghetti and sauce, then arrived at the mac and cheese boxes. Doing the math, I figured we could get a couple of dinners out of the generic mac and cheese, or, if I felt confident that we'd get the next check by Monday, maybe we could afford to get the Kraft Dinner box for just one night.

Then I saw it: *Teenage Mutant Ninja Turtles Macaroni and Cheese.* I couldn't believe my eyes—Pete and Kevin had their very own brand of macaroni and cheese! I couldn't wait to show Ivy, knowing she'd get as big a kick out of it as I did. I picked up the box, ready to put it into the basket, when I happened to look at the price.

It was too much. I could not afford to buy that box of macaroni and cheese.

And all at once, I was looking down at myself from above—an instant frozen in time—and I knew that I would remember that moment for the rest of my life.

Three years later, Kevin Eastman, through his new publishing imprint Tundra, would bankroll the printing of my first book-length comics hit, *Understanding Comics*.

The Ghost in the Machine

First published in *Zot!* #23–25.

Lettering:
Bob Lappan

Original series editor:
cat yronwode

YOU MAY BE IN A CITY...

ON A FARM...

OR HIGH IN THE AIR...

BUT YOU CAN'T ESCAPE MY *GRASP.*

--OUTAGES DUE TO *INCREASED* USE OF *AIR-CONDITIONERS.*

NOW BACK TO MORE MUSIC-- WITH *VINNIE!*

THANKS, DAVE. HEY, I THOUGHT SUMMER WAS *OVER.*

WHEREVER YOU ARE, I *WILL* FIND YOU.

AND YOU'LL BE *MINE.*

WELL, WE *KNO-O-OW* WHERE WE'RE GOIN' BUT WE DON'T KNOW WHERE WE'VE *BEEN!*

AND WE *KNNNNN------!* -KKKKKK- WE'RE KNOWIN' BUT WE -KKKKKK-

5 53

-KKKK...-

AWW, JEEZ... NOT NOW.

HEY, *SIS!* C'MON *DOWN!* MOM'S ON THE PHONE!

IN A *MINUTE,* BUTCH!

284

AAH!!

GEEZ, ARE YOU *OKAY?*

BUTCH, *I SAW HIM!* I SAW *JACK!* TURN OFF THE POWER, *QUICK!*

AWW, *C'MON,* SIS. YOU'RE *IMAGINING* THINGS.

DO IT, BUTCH! TURN OFF THE FUSE BOX IN THE CELLAR!

HHH...

WOULD'A KILLED YA BY *NOW* IF HE *WANTED* TO...

KLAK!

THERE! IS THAT *BETTER?*

BUTCH, I *SWEAR* I SAW *HIM!*

OKAY, I BELIEVE YOU. BUT WHY WOULD JACK COME TO--?

HEY, YOUR *NECKLACE* THING IS GLOWING.

BUTCH, *LOOK!* IT'S ZOT!

ZOT, HE'S *HERE!* I SAW *HIM!*

9-JACK-9 IS ON *EARTH!*

ROLL 'EM!

TOK-TR-ROK!

HA! HA! MISSED!

HEY, WHOSE SIDE ARE YOU *ON?!*

NOBODY'S, RUBBER-DICK! I'M *CHAOTIC,* REMEMBER? I JUST WANT THE *JEWELS!*

--BUT IT'S SO *VIOLENT!* WHAT WAS WRONG WITH GAMES LIKE *CHUTES AND LADDERS?*

OH, I DUNNO... AT LEAST THEY'RE USING THEIR *IMAGINATIONS.*

DO YOU WANT TO *FIGHT IT OUT?*

NO, THEY *DON'T!* WE STILL HAVE AN *OGRE* TO KILL!

OKAY, I'LL STRETCH MY ARM AROUND AND *POKE 'IM* IN THE EYES.*

* RONNIE IS *MR. FANTASTIC.*

~ Yawn ~

I'LL LASSO HIM SO HE CAN'T MOVE.*

* ELIZABETH IS *WONDER WOMAN.*

I'LL *RIP HIS THROAT OPEN!* *

* BOB IS *WOLVERINE.*

I'LL BITE HIS *LEG* OFF.*

* GEORGE IS *MATTER-EATER LAD.*

OKAY, WONDER WOMAN HAS HIM TIED SO HE CAN'T MOVE... *OR* TELL A LIE, BUT I GUESS THAT DOESN'T MATTER...

OKAY, RON AND ROB, USE A D-20. ROLL 6 OR BETTER.

AH, *NO SWEAT!* HERE I GO-- *AAR!*

HA! HA! WATCH THIS-- *AAR!*

GEORGE.

OKAY, GEORGE BIT HIS *LEG OFF.* HE'S, UM...

WRITHING IN *AGONY.*

GREAT! NOW WE GO THROUGH THE DOOR--

NO, *WAIT,* I WANNA *TORTURE* HIM SOME!

HEY, *I'M TEAM LEADER!*

SAYS YOU!

THEN *I'LL* GO THROUGH *MYSELF!*

OKAY, SOMETHING BIG...*MUSHROOM-SHAPED* LURKS IN THE SHADOWS.

I'LL GO IN *FURTHER.*

IT'S *MAYOR McCHEESE.*

HUH?? WHAT KIND OF MENACE IS *MAYOR McCHEESE?!*

UM... OKAY. HE HAS A *MACHINE GUN.*

AWW, YOU'RE NOT TAKING THIS GAME *SERIOUSLY,* WOODY!

HEY, I *MADE UP* THIS GAME.

I'LL RUN FOR COVER.

I'LL KILL WONDER WOMAN.

WHAT?? WHAT DID *I* DO??

I JUST WANT TO *KILL* SOMEBODY.

UM... OKAY, BOB. GOING FOR THE *JUGULAR* AGAIN?

WOODY, IT'S PAST *SIX!* DIDN'T YOU HAVE A DATE WITH *JENNIFER?*

OH, NO! I BETTER *RUN!*

AW, NOT *NOW,* WOODY!

HEY, *WOODY! WAIT UP!*

Y'KNOW, RONNIE *DOES* HAVE A *POINT*, WOODY. YOU'RE NOT TAKING THE GAME TOO *SERIOUSLY* ANYMORE.

YEAH, WELL...I GUESS IT DOESN'T SEEM TOO *REAL* ANYMORE.

IF ZOT'S WORLD IS REALLY *OUT THERE*, THEN ALL THE REST IS JUST *FUNNY BOOKS*.

AND IT *IS* THERE, GEORGE! I SAW IT WITH MY OWN *EYES*!

I WISH *I* DID!

I DON'T KNOW WHY I KEEP CHASING JENNY. ANYONE COULD SEE THAT *ZOT* WILL GET HER IN THE END.

HEY, *SHE* ASKED *YOU* OUT *THIS* TIME, BUDDY! DON'T YOU *FORGET* THAT!

HMMM... WHY ARE ALL THE *LIGHTS* OUT?

Ding-Dong

HI, WOODY.

H--? WHAT'S *HE* DOING HERE?

JENNY, AREN'T WE GOING TO--?

NO, I'M *SORRY*, WOODY. SOMETHING'S *COME UP*. I'M GOING TO *ZOT'S* WORLD FOR THE EVENING.

UH... HI, WOODY.

HI, YOURSELF. JENNY, WHAT'S *GOING ON* HERE?! DON'T YOU SEE ENOUGH OF THIS GUY AS IT *IS*??

WOODY, *PLEASE*, IT'S NOT--

LOOK, *ENOUGH IS ENOUGH*, JEN! YOU CAN'T JUST *KEEP ME ON ICE FOREVER*, Y'KNOW!

WOODY, SOMEONE'S IN *DANGER*--

OH, *SURE*, THAT'S A *GOOD ONE*! GO ON! HAVE FUN *WITHOUT ME*! SEE IF *I* CARE!

WOODY, *TRUST* ME, IT'S--

SLAM!

Ding-Dong

IT'S *OPEN*.

I'M *SORRY*, JEN.

OF *COURSE* I TRUST YOU.

OH, WOODY, I'M SORRY *TOO*! I'LL SEE YOU *TOMORROW*, OKAY?

GOD... I SAY PUT 'EM *BOTH* OUTTA THEIR MISERY.

SHUT UP, BUTCH.

YUP. JENNY WAS *SMART* AND SHUT OFF THE POWER IN HER HOUSE.

SHE'S CLEAN, TOO. NO *WRIST-WATCHES* OR ANYTHING.

GOOD JOB! WE'RE ALMOST READY TO *ACTIVATE* THE *PORTAL.*

JENNY, THIS IS AN OLD FRIEND, DR. WALTER BISMARK.

GOOD MORNING, JENNIFER.

DOC BISMARK WAS SECRETARY OF STATE ON *ANTARES 3* BEFORE THE *COUP.*

"*COUP?*"

YES, IT WAS A *VIOLENT MILITARY TAKEOVER!*

DAMN BLOODY BUSINESS!

THOSE *ARMY OFFICERS* ARE THE ONES WHO'VE HIRED JACK.

THAT'S ALL I KNOW *SO FAR.*

THEN IT IS TIME YOU KNEW THE *REST...*

JACK WAS FIRST HIRED BY THE REBEL GENERALS TO *EXTERMINATE* PRESIDENT GALLO AND HIS *WIFE, SON,* AND *DAUGHTER.*

ONLY THE DAUGHTER ESCAPED. I FOUND A *PHOTOGRAPH* FOR YOU.

SUSAN TURNED *THIRTEEN* ON THAT *BLOODY DAY* TWO YEARS AGO...

SHE *ESCAPED* ONLY BY *SHEER CHANCE,* WHEN THE *VIOLENT CLASHES* OUTSIDE CAUSED A *BLACKOUT* IN THE *PRESIDENTIAL COMPLEX.*

THE *OFFICIAL LIE* HAS IT THAT THE GALLO FAMILY *BETRAYED* THEIR PEOPLE AND TOOK *THEIR OWN* LIVES.

I BROUGHT SUSAN TO OUR *"OTHER EARTH"* MYSELF, TO LIVE IN SAFETY.

NOW HER PRESENCE THERE HAS BEEN *DISCOVERED* AND 9-JACK-9 HAS BEEN HIRED ONCE MORE -- TO *FINISH THE JOB.*

IT'S UP TO YOU TO *ESCORT* SUSAN BACK TO THE *RESISTANCE* IN *SAFETY.*

WE REALIZE HOW *CLOSELY* SUSAN'S LOSS RESEMBLES *YOURS,* LAD. WE'LL *UNDERSTAND* IF YOU WISH TO *BACK OUT* NOW...

NO, I'LL DO IT.

THEN WE'LL *BEGIN!* OUR *SPECIALLY-CONSTRUCTED* GATEWAY HAS ENOUGH POWER TO REACH BOTH THE OTHER EARTH *AND* ANTARES--

--YET ITS MASSIVE VOLTAGE WILL SURELY ATTRACT JACK'S ATTENTION. YOU *MUST* BE SWIFT, ELSE HE'LL FIND AND KILL YOU *BOTH!*

I'M READY.

CLIK

SUSAN?

MAX, WHAT DO WE REALLY *KNOW* ABOUT JACK?

NOT MUCH, JENNY. JUST THAT HE RIDES ON *ELECTRICITY* AND *RADIO WAVES*... THAT HE CAN INHABIT ANY MACHINE LIKE A GHOST.

THEY SAY HE WAS FIRST SPOTTED ABOUT 50 YEARS AGO...

DAMN! WHY IS HE *TAKING* SO LONG?

MAX, *LOOK!*

SUSAN!

LORD, CHILD! YOU LOOK *DREADFUL!*

THEY'RE *THROUGH!* TURN IT *OFF*, TOM!

SHE DIDN'T WANT TO COME WITH ME, DOCTOR.

WHAT? DIDN'T YOU TELL HER OF THE *THREAT?*

YEAH, SHE KNOWS. SHE SAID JACK WOULD FIND HER NO MATTER *WHAT* WE DID...

...AND THAT EVEN IF SHE *COULD* GO ON LIVING--

--SHE DIDN'T *WANT* TO.

SHE *MUST* LIVE. SHE *MUST!*

ONCE THE *COORDINATES* ARE SET, THIS PORTAL WILL BRING SUSAN TO A SPECIAL CHAMBER *IMMUNE* TO JACK'S INFLUENCE.

HER *PRESENCE* WILL BE *INVALUABLE* TO THE MORALE OF OUR *RESISTANCE!*

TRY TO *UNDERSTAND* THE *SITUATION*, SUSAN, YOU--

LASS, WHAT *IS* THAT ON YOUR WRIST?

?

AWW, *NO!*

WHY DIDN'T I *NOTICE?!*

QUICK! GIVE ME *YOUR* HAND!

HUH? WHAT ARE YOU *DOING?*

STOP!

IT WAS A GIFT!!

BLAM!

YOU BASTARD!! IT'S NOT YOURS!!

DON'T YOU *SEE*, SUSAN? HE COULD HAVE *FOLLOWED* US IN *THAT!*

DADDY...

OH, PLEASE... *PLEASE* JUST LET ME *DIE...*

NO, SUSAN, I'M SORRY. I CAN'T.

I JUST CAN'T *DO* THAT.

297

HEY, *SARGE!* ISN'T IT TIME WE *CALLED BASE* TO SEE WHAT'S UP?

THEY'LL CALL *US*, WILLIE.

CAP'N SAID *RADIO SILENCE* AND HE *MEANT* IT, SO *SHUT UP* ALREADY.

COULD'A AT LEAST HAD SOME *MUSIC*...

OKAY, LET ME GET THIS *STRAIGHT.* WE GOT ONLY *NON-ELECTRIC* WEAPONS 'CAUSE THIS GUY JACK COULD, LIKE, *GET INSIDE* MACHINES AND *SCREW 'EM UP?*

SORTA.

WHAT HE DOES IS *CONTROL* 'EM, USE 'EM *AGAINST* YOU AND THEN JUMP FROM MACHINE TO MACHINE-- *FAST AS LIGHTNING!*

WOW...

ANYWAY, WE SHOULDN'T HAVE TO *FIGHT* HIM. WE'RE JUST HERE IF THEY NEED HELP GETTING *"GOLDILOCKS"* TO THE *SAFE HOUSE.* THEY WANNA *AVOID* JACK COMPLETELY.

WHO IS *"GOLDILOCKS,"* ANYWAY?

I DUNNO. SOME *DIPLOMAT,* I THINK.

BEEP! BEEP!

KLIK

SERGEANT CHOW.

WE'VE ACTIVATED THE *PORTAL,* SERGEANT. "GOLDILOCKS" IS COMING THROUGH!

WE SHOULDN'T NEED YOU TO... WAIT A MOMENT. WHAT? OH MY GOD, IS THAT--? WHAT IS--?

CRASH

CAPTAIN, WHAT IS IT?!

JACK IS HERE!! HE'S HERE!!

I'M ENDING *TRANSMISSION,* SERGEANT! *DESTROY YOUR RECEIVER IMMEDIATELY!*

BUT, CAP'N--!

DO IT! *NOW!!*

CLIK

DAMN!

CRAK!

SERGEANT? WHAT *HAPPENED?*

SARGE?

HE'S COMING.

I HAVE COME TO YOUR WORLD ONCE MORE TO *COMPLETE* THAT *ASSIGNMENT*-- AS I COMPLETE *ALL* MY ASSIGNMENTS.

AND-- WHILE I'M *AT IT*--TO INSTRUCT YOU IN THE *TRUE* MEANING--

--OF *FUTILITY.*

PLEASE CONSIDER THE FUTILITY OF YOUR *TACKY LITTLE REBELLION.* FOR *THREE YEARS* YOU HAVE FOUGHT IN VAIN AGAINST YOUR NEW RULING FORCES. SURRENDER *NOW* AND PERHAPS YOU WILL NOT END UP LIKE THIS CHILD.

MURDERER!! WE'LL NEVER GIVE UP THE FIGHT!

LONG LIVE THE REPUBLIC!

SO BE IT.

THE GIRL DIES *NOW.*

EEEE!!!

KKKKKKK!!

NO!!

THAT SURFACE! HIS REFLECTION!

EEEE!!

THE SWITCH!

KK KKK

IT *HAS* TO WORK!

?

KRAK!

305

WHAT HAPPENED?

I THINK I *SAW SOMETHING!* AN ARROW OR--

IT WAS AN *ARROW,* KID!

ONLY THAT *PARTICULAR* ARROW HAD MORE PUNCH THAN *MOST.*

WHO--?

SERGEANT CHOW, FIRST DIVISION.

HEY, SUZY.

LUCY?

LUCY!!

WELCOME *BACK,* LITTLE COUSIN.

ARE YOU *SURE* THERE WERE NO MACHINES BACK THERE?

NOT IN *THAT* AREA, NO. I CAN'T THINK OF ANYTHING JACK COULD HAVE *ESCAPED* INTO.

HE'LL BE BACK. I *KNOW* HE WILL.

DON'T *THINK* LIKE THAT, SUZY! YOU'VE GOT TO HAVE SOME *HOPE!*

307

"YEAHHH..."

IT'S RIGHT DOWN THE RAVINE AND OVER THAT HILL.

WHAT WAS THIS PLACE, LUCY?

OH, THIS *USED* TO BE AN *ARMY BARRACKS* BEFORE WE *BLEW UP* THE THING AND CLAIMED THIS SECTOR FOR THE *REBELLION!*

YOU GUY'S ARE REALLY INTO *BLOWING THINGS UP.* DOESN'T IT *BOTHER YOU* THAT SO MANY PEOPLE ARE GETTING *KILLED?*

NO.

THE TYRANTS WHO STOLE OUR LAND DON'T *DESERVE* TO LIVE. NEITHER DOES ANYONE WHO WORKS *FOR* THEM!

EVERYONE DESERVES TO *LIVE.*

REALLY? I'M SURPRISED YOU'D *SAY* THAT.

THEY *TOLD* ME ABOUT YOU, ZOT. YOU'RE NOT THAT *DIFFERENT* FROM SUZY. YOU *BOTH* SHOULD HATE *JACK.*

HEY, WHAT'S *THIS?*

SOME KIND OF *BOX.*

310

HEY, I THINK I SEE THE SHELTER!

JENNY, GET DOWN!

?!

UMPH!

OH MY GOD.

SARGE, WHAT--?

WEAPONS READY!

WHERE DID IT COME FROM?? DID ANYONE SEE?!

SEE WHAT, ZOT? WHAT'S WRONG??

STAY DOWN, JEN!

ZOT, WHERE'S SUZY?

SHE'S GONE, JEN.

WHAT?

LUCY, DID YOU SEE IT?! WHAT DIRECTION DID IT COME FROM?!

I--! I DON'T KNOW!

ZOT, WHAT DO YOU MEAN "GONE"? SHE WAS JUST HERE.

I'M SORRY, JEN.

ZOT, WHAT'S GOING ON?! SHE CAN'T BE GONE!

HE GOT TO HER, JEN. THAT'S IT.

DIDN'T ANYONE SEE?!

ZOT, SHE WAS JUST HERE! SHE WAS JUST HERE!!!

JENNY, I -- I'M SORRY.

BUT, SUZY--

OH, JESUS, ZOT. JESUS!!

MURDERER! THERE HE IS!

311

ZOT, WHY DID WE COME *HERE?*

I DON'T WANT YOU TO BE *ALONE.*

JENNY?

STAY WITH HER, WOODY.

WHAT *HAPPENED?*

SPLASH!

"DO YOU
REALLY
CARE
ABOUT ME
THAT
MUCH?"

"YEAHHH..."

MAX? ARE YOU *IN HERE?*

CHUF!

ZACH?

I FAILED...

YOU DID ALL YOU *COULD*...

MAX,...IS THERE ANY WAY TO STOP JACK FOR GOOD?

IS THERE ANY WAY AT ALL?

THERE IS.

I NEVER TOLD YOU BEFORE BECAUSE IT'S *EXTREMELY DANGEROUS* AND THERE'S NO GUARANTEE THAT YOU'LL *SUCCEED.*

I WANTED TO WAIT UNTIL YOU WERE *READY.*

I'M READY NOW.

ALL RIGHT, THEN...

...HAVE A SEAT.

WE *HAVE TO* DO IT, HARRY! THE REBELS WILL BE AT *THE PALACE GATES* IN MINUTES!

YOU'RE RIGHT. I'LL *KEY HIM IN*.

J9_

IS THAT ALL YOU HAVE TO DO-- TYPE HIS *NAME?*

J9AC_

AND *ENTER* IT. YES, THAT'S ALL.

J9AC9K_

WHEREVER HE IS, HE'LL *KNOW*.

HARRY, OLD SPORT! NEED ME AGAIN SO *SOON?*

DESPERATELY, JACK! THIS *"ZOT"* FELLOW IS ABOUT TO LEAD A SUCCESSFUL *COUNTER-REVOLUTION*.

OUR TROOPS CAN'T SEEM TO *DISPATCH* THE LAD. WE THOUGHT YOU MIGHT HAVE A *BETTER SHOT* AT IT.

KRAK!

HMMM...

ZOT WILL COST *THREE TIMES* WHAT THE GIRL DID, HARRY. CAN YOU AFFORD *MY PRICE?*

WE *HAVE* TO, JACK.

YOU SEE, WE'VE BECOME RATHER *ACCUSTOMED* TO RULING ANTARES. WE DON'T FANCY GIVING IT UP WITHOUT A *FIGHT*.

VERY WELL.

CONSIDER IT DONE.

I'M *HERE*, MAX! WHAT'S HAPPENING? IS ZOT *ALL RIGHT?*

C'MON IN, JENNY.

ZACH IS NEARING THE END OF HIS MISSION. WE HOPE HE'LL BE PASSING THROUGH *SOON.*

WE SHOULD KNOW BY *NIGHTFALL* IF HE SUCCEEDED OR NOT.

HE'S GONE AFTER *JACK, HASN'T HE?*

YEP... AND I *LET* HIM, LIKE A *FOOL.*

MAX, IS THAT--?

MY GOD! HE LEFT HIS *GUN! WHY??*

HE WAS AFRAID HE MIGHT HAVE TO *KILL* SOMEONE. HE DIDN'T WANT TO BE *FACED* WITH THAT CHOICE.

318

YOU SEE, THE ONLY WAY ZACH CAN *FIND* 9-JACK-9 IS BY GOADING SOMEONE WITH MONEY INTO *HIRING* JACK TO *KILL HIM.*

THAT'S WHY ZACH HAS JOINED THE REBELLION ON ANTARES III AND IS ABOUT TO HELP THEM WIN ONE OF THE *BLOODIEST WARS IN THE GALAXY.*

THE *FINAL ASSAULT* COULD START *ANY MINUTE* NOW. ANTARES' DICTATORS WILL *HAVE TO* HIRE JACK ONCE THEY CONCLUDE THAT ZACH IS *UNSTOPPABLE.*

BUT ZOT *ISN'T* UNSTOPPABLE, MAX*!*

NO, HE *ISN'T.* THAT'S TRUE.

"BUT HE DOES HAVE THIS KNACK FOR MAKING PEOPLE *THINK* HE IS*!*"

UNH*!*

THOK*!*

STOP HIM*!!* HE'S HEADING FOR THE PALACE GATES*!!*

"HOW CAN ZOT FIGHT IN A WAR WITHOUT *KILLING* ANYONE, MAX?"

"MOSTLY THROUGH ZACH'S UNIQUE STYLE OF *INFILTRATION*, JENNY. THE POWER OF THE *DICTATORSHIP* IS IN ITS *SUPERIOR WEAPONRY*-- ITS GIANT *BATTLESTATIONS* AND *LASER CANNONS*.

"THERE'S ALWAYS A WAY *INTO* SUCH GADGETS AND ZACH KNOWS HOW TO *FIND* IT.

"THERE WILL BE A LOT OF *BLOODSHED* -- ON *BOTH SIDES* -- ZACH CAN'T HOPE TO STOP THAT.

"BUT WITH ZACH'S *HELP*, THE KILLING COULD END AS SOON AS *TOMORROW*.

RRRIIP

"*WITHOUT* HIM, IT MIGHT HAVE LASTED FOR *YEARS*."

BOOM!

HE DID IT! ZOT BLEW OUT THE MAIN CANNON! THE PALACE IS *OURS*!

WE OUTNUMBER THE GUARDS EIGHT TO ONE! LET'S *GET 'EM*!

SORRY, JACK! WE'VE SEEN THAT TRICK *BEFORE!*

YOU DON'T MIND IF I--

--GET OUT OF *RANGE* THIS TIME?

I DIDN'T *THINK SO!*

OKAY, MAX.... I SURE HOPE THESE *SPECTRO-FILTERS* WORK!

AH!

I HAVE YOU *NOW*, JACK. AS LONG AS I CAN *SEE* YOUR *POWER BEACON*--

--I'LL BE ABLE TO FIND *ITS SOURCE!*

HE'S HEADING *DUE EAST*. JUST AS I THOUGHT. HE'S TRACING JACK TO *THE OLD HOUSE!*

WHAT HOUSE, MAX?

THE *BRITISH ESTATE* OF SIR JOHN SHEERS, JENNY, AN *OLD FRIEND* OF MINE. SIR JOHN IS JACK'S *HUMAN OPERATOR,* HIS *"ALTER-EGO,"* YOU MIGHT SAY.

WHAT-- *HOLD ON!*

MAX, YOU *KNOW* 9-JACK-9??

SURE. YOU'VE *MET* HIM, IN FACT. JOHNNY PLAYS FIDDLE WITH OUR LITTLE *THURSDAY NIGHT QUARTET.* HE'S ACTUALLY A FAIRLY NICE FELLOW... *ALL THINGS CONSIDERED...*

"JACK WASN'T *BORN* JOHN SHEERS... THE *REAL* SIR JOHN DIED *YEARS* AGO. JACK SIMPLY *ASSUMED* HIS IDENTITY THROUGH *PLASTIC SURGERY* AND ALTERED *COMPUTER RECORDS.*"

I DON'T KNOW WHAT JACK'S *TRUE FACE* LOOKED LIKE, OR HIS *TRUE NAME* OR WHO BUILT THE MACHINES. WE MAY *NEVER* KNOW THAT.

MAX, YOU COULD HAVE STOPPED HIM *BEFORE!*

NO.

"ONLY *ZACH* HAD ANY CHANCE OF *SUCCESS,* AND A *SLIM ONE* AT THAT. I COULDN'T SEND HIM UNTIL HE WAS *READY.*

"HE'S READY *NOW.*"

MAX, I'M *SCARED!* I WAS THERE WHEN JACK KILLED SUZY GALLO. I JUST LOOKED AWAY FOR A SECOND AND--

--AND SHE WAS JUST *GONE.*

ZACH WON'T BE QUITE SO *EASY.*

AH! THERE'S THE ESTATE!

THE CRUISER IS *TURNING AWAY!* HE WON'T FIRE ON HIS OWN HOUSE!

I MADE IT!

S M A S H!

SAYYY... I *LIKED* THAT WINDOW.

I ENJOYED IT *TOO!*

-*HMPH!*- ..SOME *"HERO."* I COULD HAVE YOU *ARRESTED!*

WELL, AS LONG AS YOU'RE HERE TO *STAY*, I MAY AS WELL SAVE YOU SOME *TIME.* IF YOU WANT MY *"DEN,"* JUST TURN LEFT AND OPEN THE FIRST DOOR ON THE *RIGHT.*

THANKS.

READY *OR NOT*, HERE I--

NOT THAT IT MATTERS.

THERE'LL BE NO *ESCAPE* THIS TIME, ZACHARY. IT'S ONLY A MATTER OF *TIME* NOW.

SO *TELL* ME, WHY *DID* YOU WAIT SO LONG TO *HAVE A GO* AT ME? NOT MUCH OF A *SON*, ARE YOU?

NO!

I *LOVED* THEM, YOU *BASTARD!*

WELL, THEN, YOU MUST *HATE* ME!

NO, I--

YOU WANT TO *KILL* ME, *DON'T* YOU? I'D SAY THAT QUALIFIES AS *HATRED.*

NO!! DAMN YOU, THAT WASN'T THE *IDEA!*

I WANTED TO *STOP* YOU, BUT--

"*STOP*" ME? "*STOP*" ME?? WHAT A *FEEBLE* THING TO SAY!

I SWORE I'D NEVER *KILL!*

KILL OR *BE* KILLED, Z--

AAAA

JACK! LOOK OUT!

Ping!

JACK?

NO, *C'MON!* YOU *CAN'T BE DEAD!* YOU *CAN'T BE!!*

NO PULSE.

ALL HAPPENED SO *FAST...*

JACK.

WHY CAN'T I *HATE* YOU?

PLEASE! I *BEG* OF YOU! AT LEAST TAKE THAT *TELEVISION* OUT OF HERE!

RELAX, *GENERAL*... 9-JACK-9 IS *DEAD.* HE WON'T TRY TO COLLECT FROM YOU.

OUR PAL *ZOT* GOT HIM *ONCE AND FOR ALL!*

ANYHOW, YOU'LL BE DEAD *SOON ENOUGH.* YOUR *"TRIAL"* STARTS AT NOON TOMORROW.

LISTEN. I DO HAVE *SOME MONEY!* CAN'T YOU GET ME *OUT* OF HERE?!

I'LL MAKE YOU *RICH!*

BUDDY, YOU DON'T HAVE A *THING*.

HA! HA! HA!

-*HMF*- BARBARIANS.

MIGHT AS WELL GET SOME *SLEEP*... PROBABLY MY *LAST CHANCE*...

DAMN *COT*... WHOLE PLACE STINKS... *WORSE THAN A MEAT PACKING PLANT DURING SUMMER...*

ZZZZZZZ...

HARRY, WAKE UP.

WHW? MRSHMRM!

HARRY, YOU DOLT, IT'S *ME*! WAKE UP!

HNH?

-*Gasp!*-

JACK! BUT YOU-- THEY SAID YOU WERE *DEAD*!

I *AM* DEAD, HARRY. DEAD AS A *DOORNAIL*, I'M AFRAID.

EVEN STAYED TO SEE THEM ZIP UP THE *BODY BAG*.

APPARENTLY THIS *ELECTRIC STAMP* UPON THE *ETHER* WAS A BIT MORE *PERMANENT* THAN MY *HUMAN SHELL*.

EVEN WITHOUT ITS *OPERATOR*, THE MATRIX KNOWN AS JACK *REMAINS*.

YOU'VE COME TO BE P-PAID, H-HAVEN'T YOU? JACK, I--I--

OH, *RELAX*, HARRY. I WON'T *HURT* YOU.

I WOULDN'T TRY TO *COLLECT* FOR A JOB I FAILED TO *COMPLETE*.

NO, I JUST CAME TO SAY HELLO.

I...UH...DON'T HAVE A LOT OF *FRIENDS*, HARRY...

JACK, *LISTEN*, I STILL HAVE THE *SIRUSIAN* MONEY! CAN YOU GET ME *OUT* OF HERE?

I'M SORRY, HARRY. THEY'VE IMPOUNDED THE SIRIUS ACCOUNTS. I CHECKED THEM ON MY WAY THROUGH *GALAC-NET*.

I SEE... WELL, THAT'S *IT* FOR *ME*, THEN.

SO... WHAT IS IT *LIKE*, JACK?

DEATH, I MEAN.

IT'S NOT TERRIBLY *DIFFERENT* IN *MY CASE*... I CAN STILL ROAM ABOUT THE GALAXY... STILL CONTROL THE MACHINES OF THE *LIVING*...

AND I STILL HAVE MY *PAINTINGS* TO LOOK AT... AND MOZART AND *CHOPIN*...

OF COURSE, I'LL HAVE TO FOREGO THE *WINES* I'D BEEN SAVING.

AND THERE WAS THIS LITTLE GIRL IN *PARIS*, BUT... WELL...

SHE CAN TAKE CARE OF HERSELF...

IT'S *ZOT'S FAULT*, JACK! *ZOT* DID THIS! CAN'T YOU JUST KILL HIM FOR *YOUR OWN* SAKE? *C'MON*, MAN! YOU DON'T NEED MONEY ANYMORE!

WHAT?? WORK FOR *FREE??* OH, HARRY!

HA! HA! HA!

MY GOOD FELLOW--

--I *NEVER* WORK FOR FREE.

Of all the *Zot!* stories, this is probably the darkest. Every major villain I created for the series represented a different potential future, and the level of credibility I assigned to that future determined the gravity of the character. 9-Jack-9 represented the most credible of all those futures—the very real possibility that technology, for all its benefits, would eventually do us all in.

Zot's unbeatable optimism referenced in issue #12 falls apart in one catastrophic, irreversible failure—this time on Zot's side of the portal. Unfortunately, to get the effect I was going for, I had to muddle the contrasts between Zot's universe and ours. That "ideal world" would never look quite the same again.

Jack also represented the bland apathy of death: the idea that death is simply going about its business, noticing you briefly when it's your time, forgetting you ever existed a moment later.

When I was a little kid, I used to watch old monster movies in the basement on our old black and white television set. One of them, a little Danish gem called *Reptilicus,* had a scene where the giant reptile tore the roof off a house in which a family had just sat down to dinner and ate one of the family members. Later, the hero sacrifices himself to defeat Reptilicus. It struck me at the time that I felt real compassion for the family, but very little for the hero. The hero's story had meaning, an audience, mourners and friends giving speeches, but that poor family was just sitting down to dinner. It wasn't even their story! Their loved one's death was meaningless and random and thus more disturbing.

When Suzy dies, it may have been less than random (and she certainly didn't go unmourned), but I wanted to capture at least a hint of that creepy feeling I got as a little kid, watching old monster movies in the basement and contemplating a violent, random, morally neutral universe for the first time.

A lot of readers couldn't buy the way Sir John Sheers (Get it? Get it? Mr. Subtlety, that's me!) was allowed to hang out in Max's company for so long, even though Max knew he was really Jack all along. His comment that Sir John was "a fairly nice fellow all things considered" certainly raised a few hackles. It's a weird bit, I'll admit. I think I understand where Max is coming from, but I'm not sure I could explain it to anyone else. Both Max and Zot are nonjudgmental in their dealings with others, but at times, like in this story, that quality may be hard to relate to.

Zot! officially went "monthly" with this story's first issue (#23), but I stumbled over my new deadlines almost immediately, despite cutting the page count from 24 to 18. Deadlines were always a problem for me and a prime source of our money troubles. It didn't help that my pages kept getting denser and more detailed. The splash page for this story took forever!

In Comics History: It was while working on the beginning of this story that I wrote the first draft of the *Bill of Rights for Comics Creators,* which I discuss in greater detail on scottmccloud.com and in my second book, *Reinventing Comics* (2000).

Ring in the New

First published in *Zot! #26–27*.

Lettering:

Bob Lappan

Original series editor:

cat yronwode

Plot assist:

Ivy Ratafia

Note: For over three years prior to this issue, there'd been a contest in the letters page to see which character readers would most enjoy seeing hit in the face with a pie. This odd little "story" is the result.

'HMF'-- ROBOTS WITH *DIGNITY*. WHAT A *STUPID CONCEPT*.

OH, NO, *LOOK!* WE FORGOT TO GIVE HIM THE PIE!

HA! HA! THAT'S OKAY. WE'LL JUST BRING IT WITH US.

YEAH, I GUESS... OH, *I* SEE NOW. IT'S JUST A PLAIN WHIPPED CREAM TOPPING. COULD BE *ANYTHING* UNDER HERE.

YUP. IT'S A *MYSTERY!*

WELL, *I* BET *CHOCOLATE CREAM*.

YOU'RE ON.

SURE.

HEY, ZOT, LET'S NOT TAKE THE BELT.

IT'S SUCH A *NICE SUNNY DAY*, I'D JUST AS SOON *WALK* TO CENTRAL.

JENNY, ARE YOU REALLY *SERIOUS* ABOUT MOVING HERE? REMEMBER, THIS WORLD HAS ITS TROUBLES, *TOO*.

"*TROUBLES*"? OH, ZOT, YOU'RE SO FUNNY. IF YOU ONLY KNEW WHAT MY EARTH GOES THROUGH EVERY--

VIC! WHAT'S UP?

HI, VIC.

HEY, ZACH!

GUYS, YOU'LL NEVER GUESS WHO JUST BROKE OUT OF JAIL AND IS *HEADED YOUR WAY!*

HMM... THE *BLOTCH?*

WE DON'T *KNOW* YET.

WHAT *KIND* OF DATE?

I HOPE IT'S *GERMAN CHOCOLATE*. OH, UM... YOU DON'T KNOW HER. WE MET LAST SUMMER IN *EGYPT*. SHE'S UP FOR THE WEEK.

WE'LL BE AT THE PARTY.

VIC, ARE YOU THE SAME AGE AS ZOT?

YEAH. ABOUT *TWO MONTHS* OFF. WHY?

I DUNNO. HERE, HAVE A SEAT.

YOU SEEM A LOT MORE *MATURE* THESE DAYS. I REMEMBER WHEN I FIRST MET YOU, YOU WERE ALWAYS GETTING INTO *TROUBLE*.

TRUE.

I GUESS I HAVE *MELLOWED OUT* IN THE LAST COUPLE OF YEARS. BUT THEN, WE *ALL* HAVE TO GROW UP *SOMETIME*.

HA! TELL ZOT THAT!

OH, RIGHT. I GUESS ZACH IS AN *EXCEPTION TO THE RULE*... HIM AND HIS UNCLE MAX.

YEAH, WELL, ON *MY* WORLD YOU *HAVE* TO GROW UP. THEY'LL *EAT YOU ALIVE* IF YOU DON'T.

DIE!!

OH, YOU *WACKY GUY.*

BOOM!

AND JUST THE *WORDS* "GROWING UP" MEAN SOMETHING UGLIER.

MY NEW, IMPROVED *FLYING JUGGERNAUT* HAS *SEIZED* YOUR *PUNY PISTOL!*

NOW, *BEHOLD,* AS MY *COAL TAR DISINTEGRATOR GUN--**

?

KLUNK!

THEY SAID THEY'D TRANSFER HIM TO *MAXIMUM SECURITY.*

GOOD! THAT GUY IS GETTING *DANGEROUS.*

CITY COURT

YOU KNOW I COULD'VE *BEAT* HIM, THOUGH.

WE KNOW.

THIS WAY, POPS.

FOOLS! CRETINS! DEATH TO YOU ALL!!

TRANSFER 9884

POL

GET IN THERE!

:HMF!!: HOW *DARE* THEY TREAT ME LIKE SOME *COMMON CRIMINAL!*

HEY, CHUM, YOU GOT SOMETHIN' AGAINST *CRIMINALS?*

EH? WHO--? EGADS!

SIDDOWN, GRAMPS. I GOT A *DEAL* FOR YOU.

Z212

I lifted Bellows' "Coal tar disintegrator gun" from one of Matt eazell's hilarious stick figure back-up stories in an earlier issue.

343

DIGGER!! GEEZ, WHAT THE HECK IS *WRONG* WITH YOU??

AWW, I'M SORRY, ZACH... YOU, TOO, JANEY... IT'S JUST THAT, WELL... DAD WON'T PAY FOR *DRIVING LESSONS* AND HE JUST WON'T TAKE THE TIME TO *TEACH* ME.

LOOK, DO YOU WANT *ME* TO TALK TO HIM, DIGGER? HE *ALWAYS* LISTENED TO *ME*.

WOULD YOU REALLY *DO THAT*, VIC? I SURE WOULD *APPRECIATE* IT...

C'MON, LET'S GO.

BYE, ZOT! JEN!

SEE YOU, VIC!

HERE, LET *ME* CARRY THAT FOR A WHILE, JEN.

OH, THANKS.

BOY, I WISH *MY* PROBLEMS WITH PARENTS WERE AS SIMPLE AS *DIGGER'S*.

OH! THAT *REMINDS ME!* I GOT THOSE CHIPS YOU LIKE SO MUCH, BUT I LEFT THEM IN *MY* WORLD.

WE CAN MAKE A QUICK *SIDE-TRIP*.

THERE! A FLICK OF THE OLD *WRIST* CONTROLS--

--AND YOU'RE *HOME!*

YEAH, "HOME." LET'S GET BACK OUT AS SOON AS *POSSIBLE*.

345

HERE ARE THE *CHIPS*. THE DIP IS IN THE FRIDGE.

DOWNSTAIRS?

YES-- *QUIETLY*.

BUTCH? WHAT ARE *YOU* DOING HERE? I THOUGHT YOU AND "BOOFA" WERE GOING TO THE *CONCERT*.

YEAH, WELL... WE *DIDN'T*.

HEY, IF YOU'RE *FREE*, BUTCH, HOW ABOUT COMING TO MAX'S *NEW YEAR'S* PARTY.

DON'T FEEL *OBLIGED*, BUTCH.

SURE, I'LL COME.

I WISH TERRY AND WOODY COULD COME TOO.

SURE, THEY CAN. WHY *NOT?*

HEY WHAT'S IN THE PIE?

WHUH?

TAP! TAP!

ZOT! HOW DID--?? OH, RIGHT. YOU CAN FLY.

HOW'S IT *GOING*, WOODY? WANT TO COME TO A *PARTY* WITH US?

C'MON, WOODY, IT'S ON *ZOT'S WORLD!* YOU'VE NEVER *BEEN!*

AW, *GEEZ*, I WISH I COULD, BUT I HAVE A *BIG TEST* TOMORROW. ANYWAY, MY FOLKS WOULDN'T LET ME OUT FOR MORE THAN *HALF AN HOUR*.

HEY, THAT'S *ALL YOU NEED!*

TIME IS KINDA *SCREWY* BETWEEN OUR EARTHS. YOU CAN SPEND A *WHOLE DAY* ON MY WORLD AND COME BACK *20 MINUTES LATER* IF YOU WANT.

A WHOLE *DAY?*

YOU'RE ON!

LEMME GUESS... *APPLE?*

WE DUNNO.

SO, TERRY NEXT?

WE CAN *TRY*.

NOPE. FORGET IT, JEN. *ONE* FLYING *SPACE CADET* IS WEIRD *ENOUGH*, THANKS. I DON'T HAVE TO SEE A WHOLE *PLANETFUL*.

AW, *C'MON*, TERRY! SURE, IT'S WEIRD. BUT IT'S *FUN* WEIRD, NOT *WEIRD* WEIRD.

ZACH, *C'MERE!* I NEED TO TALK TO YOU.

SURE, MAX.

LOOKS LIKE THIS WILL BE A REAL *SMASH*, HUH?

YES, WELL... PERHAPS IN MORE WAYS THAN *ONE*. WE'RE HAVING SOME *UNEXPECTED GUESTS*.

?

ZACH, I'VE JUST SPOKEN TO 9-JACK-9. HE'LL BE HERE IN A FEW MINUTES.

WHA-A-AT??

MAX, JACK IS *DEAD*. I SAW HIM DIE!

YES AND *NO*, ZACH.

SOMEHOW, THE *ELECTRIC MATRIX* THAT SIR JOHN PROJECTED HAS TAKEN ON A LIFE OF ITS OWN. THE BODY IS INDEED GONE, BUT JACK IS STILL WITH US.

I'M *SORRY*.

JACK, FOR HIS OWN REASONS, HAS ARRANGED FOR ARTHUR DEKKER TO BE RELEASED INTO MY CUSTODY. I AGREED, BUT ASKED THAT JACK'S VISIT BE A *SHORT* ONE.

I BETTER TELL *JEN*.

SO, HAVE YOU GUESSED WHAT *FLAVOR* YET?

YEAH, I'M GONNA GUESS PECA--

AAH!!! YOU'RE A MONKEY!!

TERRY, LOOK OUT!

OH, NO!

THE PIE!!

THINK OF ALL THESE *WITNESSES!*

I DON'T *CARE* WHO SEES ME, PUNK! ALL I KNOW IS MY FUNDS ARE LOW AND I GOTTA HAVE *CASH!*

DEATH TO YOU ALL!

AND WITH *GRANDPA* HERE, I CAN GET RICH *AND GET EVEN* ALL AT THE *SAME TIME!*

HMM... I THINK HE'S GETTING CLOSE TO A *"MELTDOWN."*

YOU *THINK* SO, MAX? THAT WOULD EXPLAIN A LOT!

LOOK AT HIS *HANDS.*

"SEE? ONLY *THREE FINGERS* AND THEY'RE LOOKING *SHAKY.*"

"YUP. IT'S A *MELT.*"

DIE!

NO, *WAIT!!*

GAAH! LOOK OUT!

BOOM!

NOT *YET,* STUPID!

EH?

FIRST YOU GET THE LOOT, *THEN* YOU KILL 'EM!

WHAT?? YOU *DARE* TO CRITICIZE THE GREAT *BELLOWS?!*

YEAH! WHEN THE GREAT BELLOWS *SCREWS UP,* YEAH!

WHY, YOU--!

358

I GUESS THIS WASN'T A GOOD NIGHT TO BRING TERRY AFTER ALL.

AT LEAST *YOU* STUCK AROUND, WOODY.

ARE YOU *KIDDING?* I WOULDN'T MISS THIS FOR THE *WORLD!*

I WISH I'D BROUGHT A *COAT*, THOUGH. ∹BRRRR!∹

SO WHERE'S THIS *"BIG CLOCK"* OF THEIRS?

UP *THERE.*

OH, *I* SEE IT...

HEY! THAT'S THE *MOON!!*

YEAH. ZOT SAYS IT'S ALL DONE WITH *LASERS* HERE ON *EARTH.*

WHAT HAPPENS WHEN IT HITS *MIDNIGHT?*

I DUNNO. I MISSED IT *LAST YEAR.*

"WELCOME '67." I GUESS.

2067?

NO, 1967. IT'S *WEIRD* HERE.

ALL I KNOW FOR *SURE* IS THAT IT WAS *1965* WHEN I FIRST CAME HERE EARLY LAST YEAR.

WOODY, YOU KNOW I WANT TO *MOVE* TO THIS WORLD.

YES, I CAN TELL.

YOU'LL *VISIT* ME, WON'T YOU?

EVERY DAY, IF THEY *LET* ME.

360

361

I'VE BEEN WORKING ON THE ASSUMPTION THAT *JENNY'S* EARTH IS AN *IMPERFECT REPLICA* OF OUR OWN.

I BELIEVE THAT.

COULD IT BE THE OTHER WAY AROUND, MAX?

POSSIBLY, WOODY.

I'D LIKE TO SEE *MORE* OF THIS WORLD, MAX. MAYBE I COULD HELP FIGURE OUT WHICH CAME *FIRST!*

YOU MIGHT INDEED, WOODY. ALL RIGHT, *TOMORROW,* THEN!

KNOCK! KNOCK!

WAKE UP, JEN! ZOT AND MAX ARE TAKING US ON THE GRAND TOUR.

HUH? OH, YOU GO AHEAD, WOODY.

IS BUTCH STILL HERE?

HE WENT HOME. IT'S JUST *YOU AND ME.* ARE YOU *SURE* YOU DON'T WANT TO COME?

NAW, I'VE SEEN IT *BEFORE*...

YAAAWNNNNn...

...I'LL SEE IT *AGAIN.*

THIS IS MY *NEW HOME.*

THIS *MILE HIGH TOWER* WAS DESIGNED BY--

FRANK LLOYD WRIGHT, I KNOW. IT'S JUST *DRAWINGS* ON *MY WORLD*

ALL THE *HEAVY TRAFFIC* IS *OVERHEAD* OR *UNDERGROUND* HERE IN THE CITY, SO THAT PEDESTRIANS CAN WALK *FREELY.*

OR *RIDE* THE *BELT.*

HOW ABOUT *DISNEY?*

JUST *THAWED HIM OUT* LAST MONTH!

THEY SAY HE MIGHT DO "A MIDSUMMER NIGHT'S DREAM."

WHAT DO YOU THINK OF IT ALL, WOODY?

IT...

IT'S *INCREDIBLE!*

ELECTROLINE

GOT ONE!

GOOD SHOOTING, WOODY.

...TECHNIQUES FIRST DEVELOPED IN *ETHIOPIA* AND *THE SAHARA*...

THIS WING OF THE MUSEUM IS ALL *PARTICIPATORY DIGITAL PAINTINGS* AND *HOLOGRAMS.*

HERE. TRY THE *COLOR WAND.*

...12 MILLION PEOPLE.

THAT MANY?

BUT IT SEEMS SO *SPACIOUS!*

YOU DON'T HAVE *C.D.'s?*

OH, THE *DISCS?* SURE! WE USE THOSE IN *JUKEBOXES.* EACH SIDE OF *"THE CUBE"* IS ABOUT A C.D. IN *PLAYING TIME.*

MAYBE MAX WAS RIGHT THE *FIRST* TIME.

MAYBE OUR WORLD IS THE COPY... THE *"IMPERFECT COPY."*

LIKE IT?

DELICIOUS!

IT'S *SEAWEED.*

--STILL *UNEXPLORED TERRITORY*--

--UNDERWATER CITIES NOW HOME TO--

THEN WHY CAN'T I SHAKE THIS FEELING THAT *SOMETHING* HERE IS *WRONG.*

SOMETHING DOESN'T MAKE *SENSE.*

WHAT *IS* IT??

WE BETTER *HEAD BACK,* WOODY.

WAIT A SEC, ZOT. I WANT TO *CHECK OUT* SOMETHING.

MR. DEKKER?

HI! WHAT ARE YOU *DRAWING?*

CAN *I SEE?*

CLIK

SORRY.

THIS PARTY'S BEEN GOING FOR *TWO DAYS,* ZOT. DOESN'T IT *EVER* END?

EXCUSE ME. WE'RE LOOKING FOR A *MAX McCLAREN...*

OH, IT *ALWAYS* WINDS DOWN *SOONER OR LATER.* I'D SAY *3 DAYS* MAXIMUM.

THAT'S *ME,* OFFICER. WHAT'S UP?

HI, WOODY.

JENNY, *LOOK AT THIS!*

I SAW A *WORKBOT* TAKING THIS DOWN AND ASKED IF I COULD *KEEP IT.*

"DECEMBER 22ND. FOLKFEST '64."

"WOODY AND ARLO GUTHRIE... LEADBELLY... TRACY CHAPMAN... THE WEAVERS..."

YEAH?

LOOK FURTHER DOWN... *SMALLER TYPE*...

"JESSE WINCHESTER... HIT SONG, 'YANKEE LADY.' " YEAH? SO?

JENNY, I *REMEMBER* THAT SONG! MOM USED TO PLAY IT ALL THE TIME.

IT'S ALL ABOUT A GUY WHO WENT TO CANADA TO AVOID GETTING DRAFTED DURING THE VIETNAM WAR.

OKAY, BUT WHAT--?

JENNY, ZOT'S WORLD NEVER *HAD* A VIETNAM WAR!

OH...

THAT'S *RIGHT!*

THERE'S STUFF LIKE THIS *ALL OVER THE PLACE*. YOU CAN FIND MOVIES LIKE *FULL METAL JACKET* OR *APOCALYPSE NOW*, BUT THEY'RE JUST *FANTASY FILMS* HERE!

EVEN *BRIDGE OVER THE RIVER KWAI*,...ZOT SAYS THERE *WAS* NO WORLD WAR TWO!

WE FIGURED ONCE WAS ENOUGH.

OUR EARTH *HAD* TO HAVE EXISTED BEFORE THIS ONE! TOO MANY THINGS ON THIS WORLD ARE BASED ON THINGS FROM *OUR* WORLD!

IT'S LIKE SOMEONE WENT RUMMAGING THROUGH OUR HISTORY AND JUST *TOOK OUT* ALL THE *BAD STUFF*. WHAT'S LEFT IS *NICE* ENOUGH, BUT IT DOESN'T ALWAYS MAKE SENSE!

WOW. I *FOLLOW* YOU...

SO MAYBE *THAT'S* WHY THE DATE DIDN'T *CHANGE!* IF YOU'RE GOING TO MAKE A WORLD WHERE HISTORY DOESN'T *WORK*--

--YOU MAKE A WORLD *WITHOUT* HISTORY.

I CAN'T BELIEVE I NEVER *THOUGHT* OF THIS.

WELL, IT'S JUST A *THEORY*, ANYWAY...

ZOT, YOU DID TELL ME YOU LEARNED ABOUT *WORLD WAR ONE*, RIGHT?

THE ONE IN *EUROPE?* SURE. ONLY HERE WE CALL IT *"THE WAR TO END ALL WARS."* I KNOW THEY TAUGHT US WHAT CAME *AFTER*, BUT I DON'T *REMEMBER* MUCH.

I'M NOT A REAL *HISTORY BUFF*.

READY, KIDS!

"READY?"

MAX AND ZOT ARE COMING TO *OUR* EARTH FOR A WHILE TO CHECK OUT MY THEORY.

IF OUR WORLD REALLY *IS* A COPY, THEN THE *BIG* QUESTION IS: WHO OR WHAT IS DOING THE *COPYING??*

SEE YOU AT THE PORTAL IN *5 MINUTES.*

WOODY, I KNOW THIS PLACE IS KIND OF *STRANGE* AND ALL, BUT DO YOU UNDERSTAND NOW WHY I'D WANT TO *LIVE HERE?*

SURE.

WHO *WOULDN'T* WANT TO LIVE ON A WORLD WITHOUT *WAR* OR *POVERTY* OR *DISEASE?*

NOT TO MENTION *HOMEWORK.*

∴UGH!∴ DON'T *REMIND* ME.

YOU KNOW, I THOUGHT *HIGH SCHOOL* MIGHT BE *BETTER* SOMEHOW, BUT IT'S NOT. IF ANYTHING, IT'S EVEN *WORSE.* EVERYONE'S SO *COLD* TO YOU UNLESS YOU'RE PART OF THEIR LITTLE *GROUP.*

YEAH, *TELL* ME ABOUT IT.

EVERYTHING IS FALLING APART ON OUR WORLD. EITHER IT'S THE *BIG STUFF* LIKE WARS AND CRAZY GUYS SHOOTING KIDS IN THE STREET OR IT'S JUST *PATHETIC* STUFF LIKE *MOM AND DAD.*

HOW *IS* THAT GOING, JEN?

THE USUAL.

I DUNNO, THEY MIGHT ACTUALLY *GO THROUGH WITH IT* THIS TIME. THEY HATE EACH OTHER SO MUCH THESE DAYS...GUESS THEY MIGHT AS WELL MAKE IT *OFFICIAL.*

DON'T GIVE UP *HOPE,* O.K.?

WOODY, IS THERE ANYTHING *WRONG* WITH WANTING TO LIVE IN A *BETTER WORLD?*

NO, I DON'T THINK SO.

OUR WORLD SURE NEEDS SOME FIXING...

C'MON, WE BETTER *GET GOING.*

HEY, THAT'S FUNNY.

VIC NEVER SHOWED UP FOR THE PARTY.

ZACH, WHY DON'T YOU EXPLAIN OUR LITTLE...ER... *PROBLEM* WHILE WE GET REVVED UP.

OH, YEAH, WELL, YOU SEE, THE FEDERATION'S FOUND OUT THAT WE'VE BEEN VISITING YOUR WORLD A LOT AND SORT OF TOLD US TO *CUT IT OUT.*

THEY DON'T LIKE *INTERDIMENSIONAL TRAVEL* -- THINK IT GETS REALITY ALL *KNOTTED UP.*

ANYWAY, SINCE WE'RE NOT SUPPOSED TO EVEN *HAVE* THE COORDINATES TO YOUR WORLD, MAX HAS HIDDEN THEM IN THE *REMOTE* HERE.

FEDERATION INSPECTORS MIGHT SEARCH THE *COMPUTER* FOR DESTINATION COORDINATES, BUT NOT THE *REMOTE.*

THIS WAY, WE CAN KEEP ON VISITING AND STUDYING YOUR EARTH, BUT WE'VE GOT TO KEEP IT *QUIET.*

CHECK.

-UNNH- WHAT'S IN THE CASE, ZOT? IT WEIGHS A *TON!*

I DUNNO. SOME KIND OF *SENSING* EQUIPMENT.

HERE, LET ME GIVE YOU A *HAND* WITH THAT

KNOCK! KNOCK!

OPEN UP! FEDERATION INSPECTOR!

UH-OH. BETTER *SHUT IT OFF,* ZACH.

ZOT, WHAT--?

INSPECTOR! GOTTA *COVER OUR TRACKS!*

CLIK

UH, ZOT, DO YOU THINK MAX KNEW YOU WERE ON *THIS* SIDE OF THE PORTAL WHEN HE SAID THAT?

OH.

WHOOPS.

WHAT'S *WRONG,* ZOT?

CLIK CLIK!

WE CAN'T OPEN THE PORTAL FROM THIS SIDE. THE SIGNAL WON'T CARRY.

CAN'T MAX COME AND *FIND* US?

NOT WITHOUT *THIS* GADGET. ALL THE INFO NEEDED TO *RETRIEVE US* IS IN *HERE.*

MAX DOESN'T *HAVE* ANY COPIES. THAT WAS *THE WHOLE POINT!*

I HAVE ONE IN MY *WRISTBAND,* BUT THAT'S *USELESS* WITHOUT THE BOX PLUGGED IN.

DIDN'T THEY HAVE PORTALS TO EARTH ON *SIRIUS* AND *ANTARES?*

THEY *DID.* MAX SAYS THE FEDERATION WIPED THOSE PROGRAMS ALREADY.

MAX HAD THE *LAST* ONE.

I DON'T THINK THERE *ARE* ANY OTHER WAYS TO GET HERE.

ZOT, ARE YOU TRYING TO SAY WHAT I *THINK* YOU'RE TRYING TO SAY?

UH... 'FRAID SO.

WE MIGHT BE *STRANDED FOR LIFE*.

YOU KNOW, I HAVEN'T EVEN *STARTED* STUDYING FOR THAT *MATH TEST*.

OUCH! AND YOU HAVE *BOYNTON* FOR THAT CLASS. *NOT* GOOD.

HEY, *LOOK!* SOMEBODY LEFT A *BAG OF CHIPS* BY THE TRACKS.

THEY'RE PROBABLY *POISONED*.

I CAN'T *BELIEVE* THIS! WE HAD A *PERFECT WORLD* RIGHT AT OUR *FINGERTIPS*. NOW WE MIGHT NEVER *SEE IT* AGAIN!

GOD, WHY DON'T THEY JUST *DROP THE BOMB* AND *GET IT OVER WITH?*

MM! THEY'RE STILL *FRESH*. THEY'RE GOOD CHIPS, TOO. *CAJUN* FLAVORED...

This is the last time you'll see any of my crazy supervillains in this collection. Starting with the next issue, *Zot!* became a very different sort of series, taking place entirely on our Earth, the only science fiction elements being Zot himself and the few gadgets he brought with him. Since all six villains appear in this story, I'd like to offer a bit more information about the hidden significance of the six primary characters in Zot's rogues' gallery.

Ever since Jules Verne, we've had hundreds of compelling visions for the future of technology and society, some good, some bad. In *Zot!*, I took the good ones and mashed them together to make a world. Then I took six of the bad ones and molded each into a character. Those six break down into two groups: the loud villains and the quiet villains.

The three loud villains were Bellows, the Blotch, and the De-Evolutionaries. All three were ultimately impotent, because the chances of their futures coming true seemed remote. Bellows' smoke-belching, clumsy, industrial revolutionary future, and the Blotch's hyper-capitalist nightmare, have both gotten a few new teeth in the intervening years, but at the time, I didn't see society heading full-speed in either direction—at least, not without a whole lot of people dedicating themselves to putting on the brakes. Meanwhile, the Devoes' hopes of putting the technological genie back in the bottle is as futile today as it ever was, hence they're the loudest and least serious of the lot.

The three quiet Villains were Dekko, Zybox, and 9-Jack-9. All three represented potent, credible futures when I created them in the '80s, and nothing has happened in the last twenty years to change my mind. I was particularly interested in the mirrored pair of Dekko and Zybox, the future in which we become our machines and the future in which our machines become us. Anyone following developments in artificial intelligence and the biomedical sciences knows that we may be in for a very weird century in which either of those scenarios could come to pass.

And finally there's Jack, the quietest and most powerful of the lot, the future of no future at all: the prospect that technology will simply wipe us out in the end. I had nuclear war in mind in the '80s, but any Armageddon will do. I wish I was as optimistic as my hero, but as of this writing, Jack still gets my vote for villain most likely to succeed.

As whimsical as it looked, there wasn't anything in Zot's world that technology couldn't eventually bring about. All those quaint old predictions for the future weren't dead ends, they just hadn't happened *yet*. The way I figured it, if our species screwed up in the end, then this was nothing more than a fond look in the rearview mirror. But if there was even a one in three chance of making our collective futures bright, then where better to focus our attention?

QUIET   LOUD

POTENT   IMPOTENT

Long before message boards and blogs took over fandom, letters pages provided a sense of shared community for fans and pros alike. *Zot!*'s letters page played host to a lively group of opinionated readers. Only a few issues before this one, we'd printed a letter from the legendary letter hack, the late "T. M. Maple," in which he'd signed his real name, Jim Burke, for the first time. He was celebrating his tenth anniversary of writing letters to comic books. By his count, that letter was number "three thousand one-hundred and twenty-eight."

We loved getting letters. Every time a new batch showed up in my post office box, Ivy would sit in my big green swivel chair and read them out loud while I drew (something she'd also do with trade magazines and the occasional novel). I couldn't listen to talking while writing or laying out a story, but tasks like inking went great with the sound track. We sincerely wished we could have printed them all—even the obnoxious ones—but space was limited. I often skewed in favor of the more critical letters for fear of feeling as if I were suppressing dissent(!), but the vast majority were supportive.

Sometimes we staged contests. One was a running vote tally for favorite character (fun fact: Digger was *nobody's* favorite character), and at the bottom of that chart was an invitation to vote for the character you'd most like to see get hit in the face with a pie. Unfortunately, when 9-Jack-9 won the contest, I had a bit of a quandary: I'd clearly established that Jack didn't really *have* a face. My solution, lame though it is, was to show the pie passing through Jack and hitting second-place "winner" Zot. Then, on the letters page, I included the graphics you see below and at right.

Note that a number of the characters shown in the, um . . . pie chart at right appeared only in the color issues. The contest had been running for a long time! There are also some odd in-jokes. I have no idea after all these years why comics writer Steve Gerber (creator of *Howard the Duck,* a great comic that became a bad movie through no fault of Steve's) received four votes.

I started listing Ivy as "plot assist" with this story since she helped me work out a lot of the pie's close encounters. In truth she'd been helping all along and would continue to give me ideas throughout the run. Maybe this big, fluffy meringue hardly deserves to be called a "story" at all, but at least we both had fun baking it.

RING IN THE NEW

PART TWO (OF TWO)

Part Two
The Earth Stories

Jenny's Day

First published in *Zot!* #28

Looking for Crime

First published in *Zot!* #29

Lettering:

Bob Lappan

Original series editor:

cat yronwode

Plot assist:

Ivy Ratafia

THE CITY COMES *ALIVE* IN AN *EXPLOSION* OF *MUSIC* AND *LIGHT*.

EVERYONE *SMILES* AS I SKIP PAST THEM ON THE *GOLDEN-TILED STREETS*.

I *DANCE* WHEN I *FEEL* LIKE IT, NO ONE *STOPS* ME, NO ONE *MAKES FUN* OF ME.

AT LONG LAST, THIS IS MY *HOME*.

YOU'RE *FREE*, JENNY! NO MORE *SCHOOL*, NO MORE *PARENTS ARGUING...*

YEAH! NO MORE *COLD SHOWERS* ON *MONDAY MORNING!*

BUT, *ZOT...* WILL THEY BE *OKAY* WITHOUT ME?

SURE, JENNY! YOUR MOM SAYS THAT THEY'RE GOING ON A *SECOND HONEYMOON!*

THEY'LL VISIT US *LATER*.

OH, ZOT, I'M SO HAPPY I FEEL LIKE *SINGING!*

PLEASE SING, JENNY! I *LOVE* TO HEAR YOU *SING!*

BRZZZ!!

~MROW!~

AH! AH! ~MNUH!~

BRZZZZ--

~MROW?~

OH, *NO...*

JENNY'S DAY

TWEET! TWEET!

1) Getting Up.

I *HATE* THIS PLANET.

TIME TO *GET UP*, JENNY!

JENNY?

COMING!!

-- MROW!!

GOTTA *HURRY*.

BEFORE BUTCH--

HA! HA! *BEAT YOU!*

SLAM!

MORNING, HONEY. *SLEEP WELL?*

WE STILL HAVE SOME *PANCAKES.*

UH... *PROBLEM,* JENNY?

FWSSH!!!

YEEOW!

OH, HONEY...

HE *DESERVES* IT.

380

YOU *TWO*...

DID DAD *LEAVE* ALREADY?

YES, HE SHOULD BE IN *SEATTLE* BY NOW.

HOW LONG WILL HE BE *GONE* FOR?

WE'VE DECIDED ON *SIX WEEKS*. THAT'LL GIVE US *BOTH* A CHANCE TO *THINK THINGS OVER*...

...DECIDE HOW WE REALLY *FEEL* ABOUT EACH OTHER.

"SIX WEEKS."

WSSSHH!

YESTERDAY, I WAS IN A WORLD FULL OF *HOPE* AND *PROMISE*. NOW, I MAY NEVER SEE IT AGAIN.

NOW, I'M JUST AN ORDINARY GIRL...

...IN AN ORDINARY LIFE.

AND NOW *HE'S* TRAPPED HERE WITH ME...

POOR ZOT...

381

ARE YOU *SURE* THIS *INVISIBILITY GADGET* IS GOING TO *WORK?*

ZOT BROUGHT SOME *EQUIPMENT* HERE BEFORE GETTING *STRANDED.*

SURE! I'M USING IT *RIGHT NOW.*

THE ONLY REASON *YOU* CAN SEE ME IS 'CAUSE YOU'RE WEARING *YOUR* PENDANT.

OH, *RIGHT.*

THERE'S *TERRY.*

HI, TER. *ALL SET?*

HI, JEN. NO *ZOT* THIS MORNING?

UH... NO, HE... *STAYED BEHIND.*

GOOD. I DON'T THINK I COULD *TAKE* HIM ON A MONDAY MORNING.

HE'S JUST SO--

-- GODDAMN *HAPPY* ALL THE--

SMEK!

WHO?

WEIRD.

LET'S GO.

3) Homeroom.

STOP TIME
FRANK CONROY

HEY, WOODY.

WHAT'S THE *BOOK* FOR, BERNSTEIN? *ENGLISH LIT?*

NO, JUST FOR *FUN.*

HUH?

OH, IT'S *DIRTY.*

NO, *JUST GOOD.*

IT'S ONE OF MY FATHER'S *FAVORITES.*

AND THIS MAKES YOU *WANT* TO READ IT??

OH, WOODY'S DAD IS *GREAT.* I HAD DINNER THERE THE OTHER NIGHT.

SO, WHAT *IS* IT WITH YOU TWO? ARE YOU, LIKE, *BOYFRIEND-GIRLFRIEND,* OR *WHAT?*

UH...

YEAH, JENNY. DO *YOU* WANT TO ANSWER THAT?

-AHEM-

SORRY I'M *LATE,* KIDS! NOW, LETS--

RRING!

4) English.

I'M IN LUCK. ALMOST *NO ONE* DID THE ASSIGNMENT.

SURPRISE QUIZ!

-GROAN-

I MAKE IT UP AS I GO ALONG.

① What does little Peter cry as he's rolled out of the room?

"Oh no! ..."

... does the ...

REVIEW:

SO!

HOW *DOES* THE YOUNG BLIND MUSICIAN TRY TO *KILL* HIMSELF?

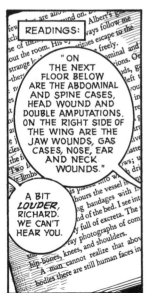

READINGS:

"ON THE NEXT FLOOR BELOW ARE THE ABDOMINAL AND SPINE CASES, HEAD WOUND AND DOUBLE AMPUTATIONS. ON THE RIGHT SIDE OF THE WING ARE THE JAW WOUNDS, GAS CASES, NOSE, EAR AND NECK WOUNDS."

A BIT *LOUDER*, RICHARD. WE CAN'T HEAR YOU.

-AHEM- "ON THE LEFT, THE BLIND AND THE LUNG WOUNDS, PELVIS WOUNDS, WOUNDS IN THE JOINTS, WOUNDS IN THE KIDNEYS, WOUNDS IN THE TESTICLES, WOUNDS IN THE INTESTINES."

LOUDER! SPEAK UP!

"TWO FELLOWS DIE OF TETANUS. THEIR SKIN TURNS PALE, THEIR LIMBS STIFFEN, AT LAST ONLY THEIR EYES LIVE..."

NEVER HAVE PANCAKES BEFORE ENGLISH.

"...THEIR SHATTERED LIMBS HANGING FREE IN THE AIR FROM GALLOWS; UNDERNEATH THE WOUND A BASIN IS PLACED INTO WHICH DRIPS THE PUS..."

386

5) Math.

YOU *STUDY?*

ME *NEITHER.*

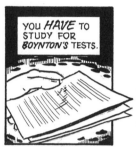

YOU *HAVE* TO STUDY FOR *BOYNTON'S* TESTS.

$4x^2 + y$

$-y^2 - 148 - 8y + 3$

$(x = 14x - 49)(y^2 +$

$\dfrac{(x-7)^2}{-4} \div \dfrac{(y+4)^2}{4}$

$\dfrac{(y+4)^2}{2} -$

WOODY STUDIED. HE *ALWAYS* STUDIES. I WOULDN'T DARE *COPY* HIM, THOUGH.

WOULD I?

Y'KNOW, *FAILING TESTS* WOULDN'T BE SO *BAD* IF YOU COULD ONLY KNOW *AHEAD OF TIME* THAT YOU WERE *GOING* TO FAIL. THEN AT LEAST YOU WOULDN'T HAVE TO *WORK* SO HARD.

Yawwn

OH, *LOOK* AT HIM.

I *WARNED* YOU, ZOT. SCHOOL IS *NO PICNIC* ON--

UH-OH.

I WISH HE WOULDN'T STAND SO *CLOSE.*

WHEW PASSED ME BY!

WHAT?

HEY! I WASN'T COPYING!

RRRIP!

AWW, *C'MON,* MR. B!

C'MON, I WASN'T COPYING!

OUT.

6) French.

I'VE HAD *SIX YEARS* OF FRENCH CLASS SO FAR.

EVERY FRENCH TEACHER I HAVE EVER HAD HAS BEEN *CHEERFUL, KIND, HELPFUL* AND *ENTHUSIASTIC.*

"VIALAT: MON É PAULE ME FAIT MAL..."

MONIQUE!

POLICIER: UN PEU DE PATIENCE. VOUS ALLEZ...

I'VE ALWAYS DONE THE ASSIGNMENTS JUST AS I WAS *TOLD* TO.

BIEN!

BIEN!

AND I'VE ALWAYS GOTTEN *A's* AND *B's*

stionaire

e presentent les
rt d'em avion?
quoi le policier
ce que les cha
ours bavards?
travail des pdi
ulier?

I *SWEAR TO GOD,* I DON'T KNOW A *WORD* OF FRENCH.

7) Lunch.

LUNCH I CAN *DEAL* WITH.

I'VE STARTED TO ACTUALLY MAKE SOME *FRIENDS* HERE. HIGH SCHOOL IS NEW TO *ALL* OF US, NOT JUST ME, LIKE IT WAS WHEN WE FIRST *MOVED* HERE.

Ding!

CHIPS
CHIPS
CHIPS

I'VE KNOWN *TERRY* THE LONGEST. SHE WAS MY FRIEND BACK WHEN NO ONE ELSE *CARED*. SHE ACTS *TOUGH* SOMETIMES, BUT I DON'T *BUY* IT.

HEY, DO ANY OF YOU *BRAINS* KNOW WHAT'S *IN* THIS STUFF?

WOODY, MY OTHER "*NOT-BOYFRIEND*." HE'S *NOTHING* LIKE *ZOT*, BUT STILL... OH, I WISH I COULD *MAKE UP MY MIND*.

C'MON, RONNIE, IT'S ONLY A *SEQUEL*.

GEORGE IS SMARTER THAN ANYBODY, BUT HE'S REALLY *LAZY*, SO HE KEEPS GETTING INTO SCHOOL TROUBLE. HE'S *COOL*, THOUGH. I *LIKE* HIM.

SOYBEANS AND PORK *BY-PRODUCTS*, I ASKED.

RONNIE TRIES HARD TO BE "*MATURE*," BUT HE ALSO WANTS TO WRITE *COMIC BOOKS*, SO HE'S OBVIOUSLY *DOOMED FROM THE START*.

NO, I THINK *ROBOCOP II* COULD BE A *SIGNIFICANT FILM*.

BRANDY IS RONNIE'S GIRLFRIEND, DON'T ASK ME WHY. SHE'S A REAL *DITZ*, BUT WE ALL LOVE HER *ANYWAY*.

OH, *CUT IT OUT*, SPIKE!

HA! HA!

GOD, I WISH I WAS THAT *SKINNY*.

HERE'S BOB. WE'VE STARTED CALLING HIM "*SPIKE*" FOR SOME REASON. HE'S THE OTHER *COMICS FAN*.

DIE! MEATLOAF FROM HELL!

STAB STAB

SPIKE'S SISTER *ELIZABETH* IS A BIG BLANK. I HAVE *NO* IDEA WHAT'S GOING ON IN *THAT* HEAD.

SLURP

MILK

AND NOW THERE'S *ZOT!*

HI, GUYS. SPACE FOR *TWO MORE?*

WE DON'T *HAVE* SCHOOL CAFETERIAS ON *MY* WORLD. WE JUST *GET OUT* AT LUNCH!

UN-HUH.

SO, HOW DID *MATH* GO, KIDDO?

-*HNF*-

I DON'T THINK JENNY *WANTS* TO TALK ABOUT MATH, TERRY.

SO, ZOT! WHERE ARE YOU *STAYING* NOW THAT YOU'RE MAROONED HERE?

THEY KNOW ALL ABOUT ZOT.

HEY, SPIKE, LET'S GET *ZOT* IN "THE BOOK." HE'S A SUPERHERO.

NO WAY, WHAT'RE HIS *POWERS?*

ACTUALLY, GEORGE, I'VE BEEN STAYING IN JENNY'S *BEDROOM.*

ZOT! SHH!

OOH!

WHAT??

IN A *BOX,* WOODY!!

IN A *GREAT BIG METAL BOX!!*

IN MY *CLOSET!!*

OKAY?!

OH! OH, *ALL RIGHT,* THEN.

I'M *GLAD* I HAVE YOUR *APPROVAL,* WOODY.

OH, *ZOT!* CAN I FEEL YOUR *HAIR?*

OOH, I LOVE IT. IT'S SO ZEN!

UH... I LIKE *YOUR* HAIR *TOO,* BRANDY.

-*AHEM*-

OH, I *HATE MY HAIR!* IT'S TOO *CURLY!*

SHE'S TRYING TO LOOK LIKE *EDIE BRICKELL.*

WHO?

I AM NOT!

HEH! HEH! **EDIE SUCKS!**

HEY, ISN'T ZOT'S WORLD SUPPOSED TO HAVE ALL THE BEST STUFF FROM *OUR* WORLD?

MAYBE EDIE ISN'T SO GOOD *AFTER ALL.*

RIP! RIP!

IS THAT *TRUE,* ZOT?

OH, DON'T *WORRY,* BRANDY. THE NAME JUST *SLIPPED MY MIND,* I'LL BET.

SHE *DOES* SOUND FAMILIAR.

SO, HOW DOES *ASTRO BOY* LIKE IT HERE IN *ALCATRAZ HIGH SCHOOL?*

YEAH, ZOT, THIS IS ALL PRETTY *NEW* TO YOU!

WELL, IT WAS...UH...

YEAH, *GO AHEAD,* ZOT. I'LL BET EVEN *YOU* CAN'T FIND SOMETHING NICE TO SAY ABOUT *THIS PLACE.*

GO AHEAD.

IT'S VERY *CLEAN.*

-GROAN-

IT IS *CLEAN.* THAT'S TRUE.

IT'S A VERY CLEAN SCHOOL.

GAK

AWRIGHT, SPIKE, WHAT DID YOU PUT IN ELIZABETH'S MILK?

I'LL *KILL* HIM.

RING!

I'M GOING TO *FLY AROUND* FOR A WHILE, OKAY, JEN?

UH, *SURE.*

ISN'T WOODY COMING?

NO, HE HAS *STUDY HALL* NEXT BLOCK.

8) Biology

GOD, THIS IS *SO GROSS*... THIS IS *SO* GROSS...

IT'LL BE OVER *SOON*, KIDDO.

HEY, IF *LAST* PERIOD WAS *LUNCH*, DOES THAT MAKE THIS *DESSERT*?

PISS OFF, SPIKE!

AT LEAST *ART* IS NEXT. I ACTUALLY *LIKE* ART CLASS.

ART CLASS D BLOCK CANCELLED

AW *RIGHT*!

YEH!

CANCELLED? GREAT!

I'M OUTTA HERE!

HI, ZOT. I'VE DECIDED TO SKIP *GYM* CLASS.

AW, YOU SHOULDN'T NEGLECT YOUR *PHYSICAL FITNESS*, JEN!

I *SAID* I'M SKIPPING GYM.

UM... OKAY.

CAN YOUR *INVISIBILITY* THING COVER US *BOTH*?

SURE, IF WE'RE *TOUCHING*.

9) Skipping Out.

HOME
AGAIN!

HOME?
I SUPPOSE.

10) Back to Bed.

HERE'S THE *BOX*. DID
I EXPLAIN THE *BOX*?

"*SPATIAL
DISTORTION
BOX*" IS
WHAT ZOT
CALLS IT...

...MEANING
IT'S BIGGER
INSIDE THAN
OUT. THIS
IS WHERE
ZOT *SLEEPS*.

OH! I DIDN'T NOTICE
THE *DOORS* BEFORE!

YEAH,
IT'S
COMFY.

ARE YOU SURE YOU HAVE
ENOUGH *SUPPLIES* AND STUFF
IN THERE?

WANT TO TAKE
A LOOK?

MAYBE *TOMORROW*. I'M
GOING TO SLEEP, SOON AS I
SAY GOODNIGHT TO MOM.

OKAY.

GOODNIGHT, ZOT.

SWEET DREAMS.

KLAK

YOU DON'T HAVE TO *YELL*, HORTON. LOOK, I'LL SEND IT-- WHAT? I *SAID*, I'LL SEND IT *TOMORROW, ALL RIGHT?*

LOOK, YOU COULD HAVE PACKED IT *YOURSELF!*

?

IS THAT *ALL? WHAT?* I KNOW, WELL, I *AM* MAD.

OH, *NO*, HONEY, I'D *LOVE* TO TRADE PLACES! *UNFORTUNATELY*, I DON'T *GET* A VACATION, NOW DO I?

NO, I'D BE *DELIGHTED* TO LET YOU STAY HERE, WORK *NINE TO SIX* IN THE CITY, TAKE CARE OF THE LITTLE *MONSTERS*--

AH--!

JENNY, *WAIT!* COME *BACK!* I DIDN'T *MEAN* THAT!

JENNY, *PLEASE* COME OUT OF THERE!

I'M BRUSHING MY *TEETH!*

JENNY, YOU *KNOW* THAT WE *LOVE* YOU!

YEAH. YEAH...

PLEASE... JUST *LEAVE* ME ALONE.

THE CITY *CALLS* TO ME IN *WARM BRIGHT COLORS*. MUSIC POURS FROM EVERY WINDOW.

NO MORE *SCHOOLDAYS*. NO MORE *BOOKS*. NO MORE *TEACHERS' DIRTY LOOKS*.

THIS IS MY HOME. *THIS* IS MY WORLD.

THIS IS MY LIFE AS LONG AS I *WANT* IT TO BE.

MAYBE, SOMEDAY, I'LL VISIT THE *OLD* HOME AGAIN...

MAYBE *SOMEDAY*...

LOOKING FOR CRIME

THANK YOU, ZOT. THAT WAS ONE OF THE NICEST BIRTHDAYS I'VE HAD.

HAPPY 15th.

WELL!
AHEM

GUESS IT'S ABOUT YOUR *BEDTIME*, HUH? IT'S BEEN A *LONG DAY*. WE'RE BOTH *SLEEPY*.

Sigh

I'LL GET THE *BOX*.

ARE YOU SURE YOU HAVE ENOUGH *ROOM* IN THIS THING?

YUP!

WANT TO TAKE A LOOK *INSIDE?*

MAYBE *TOMORROW.*

GOOD NIGHT, JEN.

KLAK

CLIK!

KLAK
KLAK
KLAK
KLAK

DINNER, SIR?

NO THANKS, CHARLIE. I ATE ALREADY.

JUST GOING TO RECORD SOME NOTES FOR *UNCLE MAX* AND GO TO BED.

DAY TWELVE: I'M SORRY I HAVEN'T KEPT TAKING NOTES *EVERY DAY,* MAX. I HAVEN'T FOUND MUCH WORTH REPORTING JUST YET.

I MUST ADMIT, I'M BEGINNING TO WONDER IF I'LL EVER SEE YOU AND OUR WORLD AGAIN, SO I'M LIKEWISE DOUBTFUL THAT THESE TAPES WILL BE OF MUCH USE.

NOT THAT I'M LETTING IT *GET ME DOWN* OR ANYTHING. LIFE IS STILL *FULL OF SURPRISES* AND THE COMPANY IS GOOD.

BEING *STRANDED* HERE HASN'T BEEN *TOO* BAD. EVERYTHING I NEED IS HERE IN THE BOX. AND IT'S SMALL ENOUGH ON THE *OUTSIDE* TO FIT IN JENNY'S *CLOSET.*

I HAD CHARLIE MAKE ME SOME REPLICAS OF THIS EARTH'S *MONEY.* JUST ENOUGH TO *GET AROUND* ON. I PROMISE NOT TO *OVERDO* IT...

"THINGS ARE GETTING KIND OF *SERIOUS* WITH ME AND JEN. I DON'T KNOW QUITE WHAT TO *DO* NEXT.

"EVERY NIGHT WE KISS AND SAY *GOOD NIGHT*. EVERY NIGHT SHE ASKS IF I HAVE ENOUGH ROOM IN HERE AND EVERY NIGHT I OFFER TO *SHOW* HER.

"MAYBE *TOMORROW*, SHE SAYS, AND CLOSES THE LID."

"IT'S NOT *EASY* WHEN THE LAST THING YOU SEE, *NIGHT AFTER NIGHT*, IS YOUR GIRLFRIEND'S *BELT BUCKLE*.

"AND YOU KNOW THAT THE FIRST THING SHE DOES WHEN--

KLAK

"WELL.

"ANYWAY.

"JENNY IS STILL GOING OUT WITH WOODY, SO IT'S NOT SIMPLE FOR HER EITHER. I'M DOING MY BEST NOT TO *PRESSURE* HER OR ANYTHING. WE'VE ALL GOTTA TAKE THINGS AT OUR OWN SPEED. *YOU* TAUGHT ME *THAT*.

"I *LIKE* WOODY, SO THAT HELPS."

JUST BETWEEN *YOU* AND *ME*, THOUGH, I DON'T THINK WOODY IS QUITE AS *PATIENT* AS *I* AM.

STAY TUNED.

"SO, HERE I SIT WITH ALL THESE *MACHINES* I HAVE *NO USE* FOR, LIKE THE *SPY-CAM* FOR SEEING WHAT'S GOING ON OUTSIDE THE BOX..."

OUTSIDE...

NO.

ANYWAY, THERE ARE *ONE OR TWO* BITS OF DATA I HAVE GATHERED RECENTLY, SO I DO HAVE *SOMETHING* TO REPORT.

Y'SEE, THE OTHER DAY--

401

"-- I RETURNED TO NEW YORK."

"*LAST TIME* I VISITED THIS WORLD'S PRIMITIVE REPLICA OF MANHATTAN, ALL I MANAGED TO DO WAS STOP A *PURSE-SNATCHING* AND GET *BEATEN UP.*"

"THIS TIME WAS GOING TO BE *DIFFERENT,* THOUGH."

"THIS TIME I WAS *LOOKING* FOR CRIME."

HELLO, NEW YORK!

MY NAME IS ZOT! I'M A CRIMEFIGHTER! ANYONE KNOW WHERE I CAN FIND SOME CRIME?

"A NUMBER OF PEOPLE *STARED,* BUT NO ONE *ANSWERED.*"

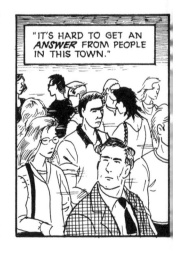

"IT'S HARD TO GET AN *ANSWER* FROM PEOPLE IN THIS TOWN."

SIR?

SIR?
MA'AM?

UH,
EXCUSE
ME.

MA'AM?

"I FINALLY SNAGGED THIS LITTLE *GROUP* -- TWO MEN, TWO WOMEN -- WHO WERE WILLING TO TALK."

AM I ON *T.V.?*

LOOKS LIKE *CAPTAIN MARVEL* OR SOMETHING.

"I EXPLAINED WHAT I WAS *LOOKING* FOR."

ANY *IDEAS?*

WELL, IF YOU GO *NORTH,* YOU'LL HIT *HARLEM,* AND EVENTUALLY THE *SOUTH BRONX.* PLENTY OF CRIME *THERE.*

WEST IS *HELL'S KITCHEN.* THAT'S A PRETTY BAD NEIGHBORHOOD.

IN BROOKLYN, Y'GOT *"BED-STUY."* THAT'S A GOOD BET FOR CRIMES. OR D'YA WANNA STICK TO *MANHATTAN?*

NAW, GO *SOUTH!* THE LOWER *EAST SIDE* IS THE *WORST!*

WOW, IT SOUNDS LIKE THIS CITY IS NOTHING *BUT* CRIME!

WHY DO YOU GUYS EVEN *LIVE* HERE??

OH, WE JUST NEVER *GO* INTO THE *BAD* PARTS.

BUT, IF YOU'VE NEVER *BEEN* IN THEM, HOW DO YOU KNOW THEY'RE SO *BAD?*

HEY, I'VE NEVER BEEN TO *BEIRUT* EITHER.

I HAVE! BEIRUT IS *BEAUTIFUL* THIS TIME OF YEAR!

HA! HA!

YOU LIKE *BEIRUT?*

YOU'LL *LOVE* NEW YORK!

KID'S CRAZY. LET'S GO.

"IT DIDN'T SEEM TO MATTER *WHICH* WAY I WENT, SO I CHOSE *NORTH*.

"I STAYED *INVISIBLE*-- GOOD GADGET, BY THE WAY-- SO I WOULDN'T ATTRACT TOO MUCH ATTENTION, EXCEPT WHEN I *WANTED* TO!"

"I WAS VERY *EXCITED*. I KNEW THERE WERE NO *SUPERVILLAINS* HERE, BUT I FIGURED *CAR THIEVES* AND *BANK ROBBERS* AND SUCH COULD BE JUST AS MUCH FUN!"

"JENNY TOLD ME THAT *CRUDDY-LOOKING* NEIGHBORHOODS ALWAYS HAVE THE MOST *CRIME*. SURE ENOUGH, THE BUILDINGS I PASSED WERE GROWING STEADILY OLDER AND MORE RUN-DOWN."

"WHEN IT LOOKED *BAD ENOUGH*, I BECAME VISIBLE AGAIN AND STARTED *WALKING*."

"I SAW SOME BOYS ABOUT MY AGE SITTING ON A STOOP."

HI, GUYS!

MY NAME'S *ZOT!* KNOW WHERE I CAN FIND SOME *CRIMES?*

HA! HA!

Y'KNOW, *BANK ROBBERIES, BREAK-INS,* THAT SORTA STUFF.

HA! HA! HA!

HA! HA! HA!

HE WANTS TO ROB A BANK!!

NO, NO, I WANT TO *PREVENT* CRIME!

-:SIGH:-

MIND IF I AKS YOU A *QUESTION?*

SHOOT.

WHAT *PLANET* ARE YOU FROM?

SAME AS *YOURS.*

UH-HUH.

DIFFERENT *DIMENSION,* THOUGH.

HA! HA! HA!

"I WAS ATTRACTING A CROWD."

HI, I'M ZOT. PLEASED TO *MEET* YOU.

YO, *SUPERMAN!*

ZOT.

YO, *ZOT!* WHAT ARE YOUR *POWERS?*

WELL, I CAN *FLY...*

OOH! HE CAN *FLY!* LET'S SEE YOU *FLY,* ZOT!

"I WAS *DEFINITELY* ATTRACTING A *CROWD*."

HONK!
HONK!

BET YOU DIDN'T *BELIEVE ME!*

"AFTER A WHILE, I STARTED GETTING SOME *USEFUL INFORMATION*."

SO IT'S MOSTLY LIKE...*WHAT--? MURDERS? RAPES?*

YEAH, THERE'S *GANG STUFF, DRUGS.*

MUGGINGS. LOTTA PEOPLE GETTIN' *MUGGED.*

HOW DO YOU *FIND* THEM?

BOY, THE WAY *YOU'RE* DRESSED, YOU AIN'T FINDING *NOBODY!*

GEE, I DIDN'T *BRING* A CHANGE OF *CLOTHES.*

AWW, HE'S *HOPELESS,* MAN!

NO, *HOLD IT.* IF HE CAN GET *INVISIBLE* AND STUFF, Y'KNOW, YOU CAN *DO THINGS* WITH THAT.

YO, GET IN THE *TRAINS,* MAN! THAT'S THE PLACE!

LISTEN, YOU WANT *CRIME,* BOY, YOU TALK TO *THIS* CROOK *HERE!* I SAW HIM--

SHUT UP, MA! I DIDN'T *HURT* ANYBODY!

CHUCK--IE!

HA! HA!

--GET HIMSELF KILLED--

--LANDLORD WON'T FIX--

--COPS GETTIN' *RICH* OFFA--

HOPELESS, MAN, HOPELESS.

...SOUTH BRONX-- TRAINS.

TRY *WALL STREET,* MAN.

YEAH! OR THE *WHITE HOUSE!* THAT'S *REAL CRIME!*

NO, THE *TRAINS!* START WITH THE *TRAINS.*

"THE *TRAINS*..."

"I SAT FOR MAYBE AN HOUR, *INVISIBLE*, WAITING FOR SOMETHING *BAD* TO HAPPEN.

"A LOT OF PEOPLE *AGREED* THAT THE SUBWAY WAS A GOOD PLACE TO START, BUT I WASN'T HAVING MUCH *LUCK*.

"AN OLD GUY SAT BY THE STAIRS, ANOTHER ONE *FURTHER DOWN* THE PLATFORM.

"THEY DIDN'T GET ON ANY OF THE TRAINS. I DON'T KNOW WHY.

"ORIGINALLY, I FIGURED I'D STOP A CRIME OR TWO FOR *CREDIBILITY* AND START WORKING WITH THE *POLICE*.

"MAYBE I SHOULD'VE TALKED TO THE POLICE *FIRST*, BUT THEY DON'T SEEM TO HAVE A GREAT *REPUTATION* HERE.

"Y'KNOW, MAX, I FIGURE WE HAVE *ONE HUNDREDTH* THE CRIME THAT *THIS* WORLD HAS. HOW COME IT'S SO MUCH EASIER TO *FIND* ON OURS?

"THE VILLAINS DON'T *ANNOUNCE* THEMSELVES HERE. THEY DON'T WEAR *COSTUMES*,

"EVENTUALLY, I GOT *ON* ONE OF THE TRAINS, HOPING TO SEE MORE *UP CLOSE*.

"I DIDN'T SEE ANY *CRIMES* COMMITED WHILE ON THE TRAIN, BUT NO ONE SEEMED PARTICULARLY *HAPPY* TO BE THERE."

"I STAYED *INVISIBLE*, BUT I'M NOT SURE THAT IT WAS *NECESSARY*. EVERYONE PRETTY MUCH *LOOKED THROUGH* EVERYONE ELSE. NO ONE *SAID* MUCH."

"ONE TIME A WOMAN BROUGHT HER *BABY* ON WITH HER. A COUPLE OF PEOPLE SMILED. THAT WAS ABOUT IT."

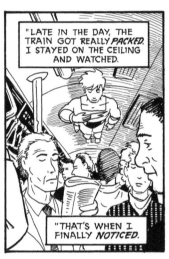

"LATE IN THE DAY, THE TRAIN GOT REALLY *PACKED*. I STAYED ON THE CEILING AND WATCHED."

"THAT'S WHEN I FINALLY *NOTICED*."

"WHENEVER THE TRAIN MADE CERTAIN STOPS, ALL THE *LIGHT*-SKINNED PEOPE *GOT OFF* AND ONLY *DARK*-SKINNED PEOPLE GOT *ON*."

"AT OTHER STOPS, JUST THE *REVERSE*."

"IT WAS THE *WEIRDEST THING!* OVER AND OVER *AGAIN*, LIKE SOME *CHANGING OF THE GUARD*."

"I THOUGHT BACK TO THAT *NEIGHBORHOOD*... SOME GUYS HAD CALLED ME '*WHITEY*' OR '*WHITE BOY*.' I FIGURED IT WAS JUST *SLANG*."

"THEY WERE TALKING ABOUT MY *SKIN COLOR!*"

"I STARTED *WALKING AROUND* AGAIN, PAYING *ATTENTION* THIS TIME."

"*SURE ENOUGH*, WHERE YOU LIVE APPARENTLY DEPENDS ON WHAT YOU *LOOK* LIKE."

"I THINK BEING 'WHITE' GIVES YOU AN *ADVANTAGE*."

"I ASKED THIS ONE OLD GUY ABOUT IT, BUT HE JUST GAVE ME THIS *AWFUL LOOK*, LIKE I'D SAID SOMETHING *PAINFULLY* WRONG..."

"I DIDN'T ASK AGAIN."

"ANYHOW, IT WAS GETTING *DARK* AND I'D HAD *NO LUCK AT ALL*. I WAS READY TO *PACK IT IN* WHEN SUDDENLY--"

HELP! POLICE!!

"A *YOUNG WOMAN'S* VOICE."

I'M COMING! WHERE ARE YOU?!

"IT WAS HARD TO TELL WHAT *DIRECTION* THE SCREAM HAD *COME FROM*."

"TOO MANY *BUILDINGS* IT COULD HAVE *BOUNCED OFF OF*."

MISS, WHERE ARE YOU?! HELP ME FIND YOU!

"I FLEW AROUND LIKE *CRAZY*, CALLING OUT TILL I WAS *HOARSE*."

HELP ME FIND YOU!

"WHERE DID THE VOICE COME FROM?"

PLEASE, HELP ME FIND YOU! PLEASE!

WHERE ARE YOU??

"I MUST HAVE COVERED THOSE FOUR OR FIVE BLOCKS OVER A *HUNDRED TIMES*, BUT I DIDN'T HEAR THE WOMAN'S VOICE AGAIN.

"JENNY TRIED TO TELL ME THAT THERE WAS SOMETHING... *WRONG* WITH HER WORLD, *'BROKEN.'* AS SHE PUT IT. *'CRIPPLED.'* LOOKING *DOWN* ON IT ALL THAT NIGHT, I WAS STARTING TO WONDER IF SHE WASN'T RIGHT *AFTER ALL*.

"*OUR* NEW YORK IS JUST AS BIG, MAYBE *BIGGER*. BUT I HAD BEEN IN *THIS* ONE FOR LESS THAN A DAY AND ALREADY I FELT *OVERWHELMED, LOST*...

"...AND UTTERLY *ALONE*.

"I'D REALLY THOUGHT I COULD JUST *WIPE OUT CRIME* HERE, JUST *MOP IT UP*.

"MAX, I CAN'T EVEN *FIND IT*!"

"BUT I KNOW, I JUST *KNOW*...

"IT'S *EVERYWHERE*.

"I DECIDED TO TAKE *ONE MORE RIDE* ON THE TRAIN AND GO HOME."

UNNH! SHIT! OH JESUS!

?

CONFUSION IS FUN!

FIGHT

"AN OLD GUY IN *RAGGED, SMELLY CLOTHES* WAS LYING BY THE STAIRS, OBVIOUSLY IN *PAIN*."

~*AGGHH*~

HELP ME! SOMEBODY!

"THERE WAS SOME *BLOOD* ON THE PAVEMENT. HE'D BEEN *STABBED!*"

HOLD ON, SIR! I'LL GET SOME *HELP!*

OH SHIT... OH GOD...

"I'D SEEN A HOSPITAL *TWO BLOCKS AWAY,* BUT TRAFFIC WAS STILL *HEAVY.* I COULD CARRY HIM, BUT I COULDN'T DO IT *ALONE.*"

MISTER, *C'MERE!* I NEED SOME *HELP!*

"HE DIDN'T *ANSWER.*"

MISTER, *C'MON!* A GUY IS *DYING!* YOU'VE GOTTA *HELP!*

SORRY. I'M IN A *HURRY.*

"IN A HURRY"?? WHAT ARE YOU *TALKING ABOUT??* C'MON!

I...OH, *ALL RIGHT.* WHAT *IS* IT?

OVER HERE.

WHAT, *HIM??* YOU'RE *JOKING, RIGHT?* THE GUY'S A *BUM!*

SO *WHAT?!* HE'S *HUMAN, ISN'T HE?!*

YEAH, YEAH. IT'S JUST--

HE'S DYING!! FOR *PITY'S SAKE,* ARE YOU GOING TO HELP ME OR *NOT?!*

AWRIIIGHT... AWRIIIGHT...

WHAT DO YOU *WANT* FROM ME?

411

"*WHEW!*– WHAT A *MESS* IN THERE, EH, MISTER? YOU'D THINK THEY COULD BE MORE *EFFICIENT.*"

EMERGEN

"WELL, AT LEAST YOUR FRIEND IS GONNA *MAKE IT.* YOU *HAPPY* NOW?"

"*SURE!* AREN'T *YOU?*"

"KID, THAT GUY IS GOING *RIGHT BACK DOWN THE TUBES* AS SOON AS HE'S *OUT.*"

"MAYBE."

"Y'KNOW, YOU REALLY SHOULDN'T *SMOKE.*"

"WHAT'RE *YOU,* MY *GUARDIAN ANGEL?*"

"SO, YOU'RE TELLING ME YOU DON'T EVEN CARE THAT YOU JUST SAVED A MAN'S *LIFE,* HUH?"

"UN-HUNH. COULDN'T CARE LESS."

:FLIK: FLIK:

"JUST A BIG, FAT *WASTE OF TIME.*"

THANKS *AGAIN*, MISTER.

"NOW, *I* *ASK* YOU, WHAT MAKES *ME* MORE OF A *HERO* THAN *HIM?*"

YEAH... YEAH...

SO THAT'S WHERE I LEFT OFF MY "STUDIES" IN NEW YORK. I'LL TRY AGAIN *TOMORROW.*

I DID CHECK UP ON OUR *STABBING VICTIM*. HE'S DOING OKAY. POOR GUY DIDN'T EVEN HAVE A *HOME,* BUT THEY MANAGED TO CONVINCE SOME *RELATIVE* TO COME OUT.

AS FOR WHY THE CITY IS ALL *SPLIT UP* BY SKIN COLOR, THAT'S STILL A BIG *MYSTERY.* BUT APPARENTLY IT'S A *WIDESPREAD PROBLEM.*

I FORGOT TO ASK *JENNY* ABOUT IT. SHE'S PRETTY GOOD WITH HISTORY AND SHOULD HAVE SOME IDEAS.

MAYBE THE SOUTH *WON*.

414

There are nine Earth Stories altogether, all of them 18 pages long except for the double-sized final issue. "Jenny's Day" isn't much more than introduction and exposition, but it gives a sense of the effects I was reaching for. Barely a decade out of high school myself, I had pretty fresh memories of the place and, if necessary, I could head over to Lexington High School for reference, living as we were by then in nearby Somerville, Massachusetts.

"Looking for Crime" is my attempt to counterbalance the more stereotypical comic book approach to street crime used in issue #11. When I look at it again, all these years later, I want to reach over and pat my younger self on the head and say: "Nice effort, but let's try sticking closer to home from now on, okay?" Fortunately, that's exactly what happened starting with the next issue. When *Zot!* fans tell me the Earth Stories were their favorites, it's almost always one or more of the next several stories they're thinking about. Some forget these first two even existed.

This was a strange, difficult time for us. Ivy and I had decided to start having children, but the process turned out to be a lot more difficult than we'd anticipated, and problems at work were getting Ivy down. Meanwhile, I was going quietly insane with frustration. Only one issue into the Earth Stories, I realized that what I really wanted—no, *needed*—was to be working on my massive, book-length comic book about the comics medium, a project I'd had in mind for years and which I suddenly realized I was finally ready for. I had to finish what I'd begun: I had to follow through on the Earth Stories, but the idea that I'd have to wait over a year even to *begin* a project that would, itself, take over a year to complete was maddening. I often wonder if the Earth Stories became what they did in spite of those external pressures and frustrations, or at least partially *because* of them.

My days at the drawing board were getting longer and longer as my pages were getting more and more detailed and my deadlines more and more battered. And my free hours started to get eaten up by a renewed obsession with chess, an affliction I'll always be grateful to Ivy for tolerating with such grace and understanding. I vividly remember working on "Looking for Crime" sixteen hours a day at the drawing board, while behind me, halfway across the room, a little computerized chess set I'd borrowed from our friend Clarence would ponder over its moves. Every several minutes, I'd hear a beep, turn around to look briefly at the board, make a move, then turn back to the drawing board.

Last minute note: As I'm getting ready to send this book out in 2008, I just heard some songs from a new album by Edie Brickell and Harper Simon (recording as The Heavy Circles). They sounded great! Brickell was a pretty new act when I wrote the bit on pages 390 and 391 way back in 1989. I liked her album but didn't know if she was going to turn out to be a flash in the pan or not. Apparently *not*.

Autumn

First published in *Zot! #30*.

Lettering:
Bob Lappan

Original series editor:
cat yronwode

Plot assist:
Ivy Ratafia

THIS USED TO BE MY *FAVORITE SEASON*.

THESE DAYS, I DON'T *HAVE* A FAVORITE. THE SEASONS PASS TOO *QUICKLY*.

THE TREES ARE PUTTING ON A NICE SHOW LIKE ALWAYS... BRIGHT *REDS, YELLOWS* AND *ORANGES*, EVERYWHERE YOU LOOK.

YET ALL I CAN THINK OF IS THE *DIRTY LAUNDRY* IN THE BASEMENT.

AND WHETHER TO TELL HARRY PETERSON I WANT TO GO *PART-TIME*.

AND WHEN DO I GET THE *TOYOTA* BACK FROM THE *SUNOCO STATION* SINCE HORTON WAS TOO CHEAP TO TAKE IT TO THE DEALER.

AND SHOULD WE GO AHEAD WITH THE DIVORCE.

AND WHEN DID LIFE BECOME SO *TRIVIAL*.

YOU TWO TAKE THE *SIDE*, I'LL FINISH UP BACK *HERE.*

OKAY, MOM.

THIS'LL BE DONE IN *NO TIME!*

JENNY IS *LUCKY* TO HAVE NICE FRIENDS LIKE ZOT AND HER OTHER "NOT-BOYFRIEND," WOODY, TO SPEND TIME WITH.

EN GARDE!

HA! HA!

SHE'S STILL SO *YOUNG.* BETTER ENJOY IT WHILE SHE *CAN.*

EEK! BURIED ALIVE!

LOOK AT THEM. JUST LIKE HORTON AND I USED TO BE...

...ABOUT *TWENTY YEARS* AGO.

HEE HEE! HONEY, *NO!* SOMEONE WILL *SEE* US!

C'MON, BABY. WE COULD SAY WE WERE GOING TO--

AHEM!

DON'T MIND ME!

MOM!

UH, *HI,* MRS. ALEXANDER! HELP YOU *CARRY THAT?*

DEAR *BOY!* NO, THANK YOU.

HOW DO YOU LIKE *NEW ENGLAND,* HORTON? BARBARA SAYS YOU'VE NEVER BEEN NORTH OF THE *MASON-DIXON!*

OH, IT'S *GORGEOUS,* MA'AM! WOULDN'T MIND *LIVING HERE* SOMEDAY.

OH, BABY, *COULD* WE?!

I SHOULD *WARN* YOU, HORTON, IT'S USUALLY NOT SO *WARM* AT *THANKSGIVING.* THIS IS JUST *INDIAN SUMMER.*

AN "INDIAN SUMMER" IS WHEN--

YEAH, I KNOW.

BURGERS, ANYONE? PLENTY MORE WHERE *THIS* CAME FROM.

WE'VE PLENTY *HERE,* DAN. SIT DOWN AND *EAT!*

DADDY--? ARE THOSE *LEAVES* IN THE TRASH BARRELS?

HMM? OH, YES.

SOME NEW ORDINANCE. THE TOWN DOESN'T WANT US *BURNING LEAVES* ANYMORE. RATHER WE TAKE 'EM TO THE *DUMP.*

BUT *WHY??*

FIRE *HAZARD,* I GUESS.

I THOUGHT IT WAS THE *SMOKE POLLUTION.*

WHATEVER. ANYWAY, IT'S FINE WITH ME. DAMNED SMOKE ALWAYS GOT IN MY EYES. AND THAT BLASTED SMELL...

I *LIKED* THAT SMELL, DADDY.

WELL, YOU WON'T BE DOING MUCH RAKING IF YOU TAKE THE APARTMENT IN *FLORIDA.*

SO, YOUNG MAN, I HEAR YOU'RE PLANNING TO *STEAL MY LITTLE GIRL* FROM ME.

YES, SIR.

WHAT DO YOU DO FOR A *LIVING*, SON? I TRUST YOU HAVE *SOME* PROSPECTS. I DON'T WANT MY DAUGHTER LIVING IN A *TRAILER PARK* SOMEWHERE.

HORTON IS GOING TO BE A *GREAT NEWSPAPER EDITOR* SOMEDAY, DADDY!

DANIEL, *REALLY!* "TRAILER PARK."

"*GOING TO BE*," EH? SO WHAT ARE YOU *NOW?* A *COPY BOY?*

OH, NO! I'M *WELL-PLACED* IN THE ORGANIZATION. IT'S JUST THAT WE'RE, UH...

WE'RE NOT...

YOU'RE NOT *MAKING MUCH*, ARE YOU, SON?

WE'RE A SMALL PAPER, SIR. WE'RE LOOKING AT THE *LONG TERM*.

IT TAKES TIME TO BUILD A *LOYAL READERSHIP*.

DID BARB TELL YOU I CAN GET YOU A BETTER JOB HERE AT THE STORE?

YES, SIR. I APPRECIATE THE OFFER, BUT--

BUT YOU'D RATHER BE A *NEWSPAPERMAN*. FINE.

I HAD MY DREAMS *TOO* WHEN I WAS YOUR AGE. I GUESS EVERY YOUNG BUCK HAS TO GET IT OUT OF HIS SYSTEM BEFORE HE SETTLES DOWN TO *REALITY*.

I'M SORRY IF MY GOALS SEEM *IMPRACTICAL*, SIR. I GUESS I JUST WANT MY LIFE TO *MEAN* SOMETHING.

ANYWAY, THAT'S THE *PATH* I'VE CHOSEN.

"I'VE GOT TO *FOLLOW IT THROUGH*."

EXCUSE ME, MRS. WEAVER. DO YOU WANT THESE BAGS *OUT FRONT?*

YOU CAN LEAVE THEM *HERE*, ZOT.

WHERE'S *JENNY?*

SHE WENT INSIDE TO CALL *WOODY*.

WE WERE PLANNING TO SEE THAT *NEW MOVIE* AT 5:00.

IF THAT'S *OKAY*.

422

SURE, I'LL GIVE YOU A *LIFT*... TELL ME, ZOT, WHAT DO YOU WANT TO DO WHEN YOU *GROW UP?*

OH, *I DUNNO.* SOME JOB *HELPING PEOPLE,* I GUESS.

THINK YOU CAN HELP PEOPLE AND STILL *MAKE A LIVING?*

SURE! YOU CAN DO *ANYTHING* IF YOU *PUT YOUR MIND TO IT!*

WELL, IT'S A *NOBLE AMBITION.* I HOPE YOU *SUCCEED.* I WOULDN'T WANT TO SEE YOU *DISAPPOINTED.*

HAVEN'T BEEN, *SO FAR.*

:YAAAWN!:

"MORNING." CAN I *BORROW THE CAR?*

NOT A CHANCE, YOUNG MAN! AFTER *LAST NIGHT,* YOU CAN JUST *FORGET* THE CAR FOR A *MONTH!*

UH...I'LL *FINISH UP* OUT FRONT.

AWWW, *COME ON !!*

LOOK, I HAD A FEW *BEERS,* OKAY? JEEZ, LIKE I'M THE ONLY ONE IN THE FRIGGIN' *GALAXY...*

HORTON, DON'T YOU *EVER, EVER* DRIVE HOME IN THAT CONDITION. *UNDERSTAND?*

UNDERSTAND?

HEY, WHAT I DO ON *MY TIME* WITH *MY FRIENDS* IS MY OWN *BUSINESS!*

NOT IF IT'S *MY CAR,* HORTON.

DON'T *CALL* ME THAT! YOU *KNOW* I HATE MY NAME!

OH? WELL, WHAT'S SO DISTINGUISHED ABOUT--?

BUTCH!! DID YOU EAT THE *LAST PIECE* OF ICE CREAM CAKE?!

YEAH, *SO?*

YOU *JERK!* YOU *KNOW* I WAS SAVING THAT!

BUTCH, YOU *DIDN'T!* JENNY'S *BIRTHDAY CAKE?!*

OH, WHAT DO *YOU* CARE?? YOU WEREN'T EVEN *HERE* FOR HER BIRTHDAY!

HELL, YOU *FORGOT* MINE !!

BUTCH, *CUT IT OUT!* YOU KNOW MOM AND DAD ARE GOING THROUGH *A LOT* RIGHT NOW!

BULL! THEY'VE *ALREADY* MADE UP THEIR MINDS. ALL THEY'VE GOTTA DO NOW IS THE *PAPERWORK* AND THEY CAN *DITCH* US BOTH FOR *GOOD!*

OH, HONEY, *PLEASE!* YOU KNOW I'D NEVER--

SAVE IT! I'VE HAD *ENOUGH* OF THIS CRAP. I'M GOING TO *EDDIE'S* HOUSE.

SEE YA IN A *YEAR* OR TWO.

MOM, DON'T LISTEN TO HIM. *I* KNOW YOU AND DAD CAN *WORK THINGS OUT.* I HAVE *FAITH* IN YOU!

OH, JENNY, I DON'T KNOW. I JUST DON'T KNOW...

I'M AFRAID HE MIGHT BE *RIGHT.*

HEY, ZOT.

HEY, WOODY.

WHERE'S THE *GODDESS OF BEAUTY?*

OUT BACK. TALKING TO HER *MOM.* I THINK THEY NEED SOME TIME *ALONE.*

RIGHT.

HAVE YOU SEEN THE NEW ADDITION TO THE *HOUSE*? IT'S REAL *PRETTY*.

KIND OF *DUMB* IF YOU ASK ME. BUY A NEW HOUSE JUST TO START *ADDING ON*.

WHY NOT JUST BUY A *BIGGER HOUSE* TO *START WITH*?

YOU CAN *TELL* THEY'RE GOING TO GET DIVORCED SOON WHEN THEY START DOING *DESPERATE STUFF* LIKE *THAT*.

I DON'T SEE A *CONNECTION*, WOODY. ANYHOW, I DOUBT THEY'LL GET A *DIVORCE*. THEY LOVE EACH OTHER *TOO MUCH* FOR THAT.

C'MON, ZOT, HOW WOULD *YOU* KNOW? YOU'VE ONLY MET THE OLD MAN *ONCE!*

JENNY *TOLD* ME ABOUT HIM.

YEAH, WELL...

MISS IMPARTIALITY.

I BELIEVE HER.

GREAT *TIME OF YEAR*, ISN'T IT? ALL THE *COLORS*.

OH, *YEAH*, AUTUMN IS *GREAT*, I THINK IT'S MY FAVORITE SEASON.

WHY?

SOMETHING ABOUT... I'M NOT SURE, *EXACTLY*.

IT JUST SEEMS MORE... *HONEST* THAN THE OTHERS.

"WE USED TO *BURN LEAVES* BY THE SIDE OF THE ROAD. I WAS ALWAYS *SPELLBOUND* WATCHING DADDY -- YOUR *GRANDFATHER* -- LIGHT A *SINGLE LEAF* AND DROP IT ON THE PILE."

"IT WASN'T VERY *EFFICIENT*. YOU'RE SUPPOSED TO LIGHT THE FIRE FROM *UNDERNEATH*. BUT THERE WAS A *CEREMONY* TO IT THAT I *LOVED*."

"I SAY 'CEREMONY.'"

"I'M SURE HE WAS JUST *TOO LAZY* TO *BEND OVER*."

"JUST THE SAME, IT FELT LIKE SOME SORT OF *SACRED RITUAL*.

"OR MAYBE SOMETHING *NOT SO SACRED*.

"MAYBE LIKE *BLACK MAGIC*.

"WE HAD A *BIG LAWN* SO THIS HAPPENED *A LOT* DURING AUTUMN."

MRS. EATON SAYS THAT THE UNIVERSE IS LONGER THAN *INFINITY*. THAT MEANS YOU CAN GO *FOREVER* AND NEVER REACH THE *END*.

UH-HUH.

I FIGURE IF YOU GO *FAR ENOUGH* YOU COULD FIND ANOTHER PLANET JUST LIKE *THIS* ONE AND ANOTHER *GIRL* WHO LOOKS JUST LIKE *ME*.

AND IF YOU GO FAR ENOUGH, A GIRL WHO LOOKS LIKE ME, LOOKING BACK, THINKING THE SAME THING AS *I AM*.

THINKING *"HI"* RIGHT *BACK* AT ME.

427

DINNERTIME!

C'MON, HONEY.

"AT DINNER, MY FATHER COMPLAINED THAT TEACHERS WERE FILLING HIS KID'S HEAD WITH *NONSENSE.*

"MOM *APPROVED* OF MY IMAGINATIVE THEORIES, HOWEVER, AND TOLD HIM TO STOP BEING SUCH AN OLD *CRAB APPLE.*

"AFTER DINNER, WE BURNED THE LAST TWO PILES. I SAT BY THE *SMOKING ASHES* FOR A WHILE AFTER DAD WENT INSIDE TO WATCH THE NEWS.

"WE HAD THIS *BIG HEAVY METAL FLASH- LIGHT.*

"THROUGH THE SMOKE YOU COULD SEE ITS BEACON... *STEADY* AND *STRAIGHT* LIKE A *LASER BEAM.*

"LEAPING INTO THE SKY AT 186,000 MILES PER SECOND.

"I PRETENDED THAT I KNEW *MORSE CODE* AND SIGNALLED TO MY FRIEND ON THE *OTHER WORLD*.

CLIK
CLIK

"WE SHARED ALL OF OUR *DEEPEST SECRETS*.

CLIK
CLIK

"AND WE BOTH PROMISED WE WOULDN'T MARRY ANYONE LIKE OUR *FATHERS*."

CLIK
CL'

OF COURSE, *I* DID ANYWAY.

THAT'S *LIFE*.

DAD IS STILL A *DREAMER*, MOM.

WELL.

HIS DREAMS AREN'T AS BIG AS THEY *USED* TO BE, I'M AFRAID.

REALLY? I ALWAYS FIGURED THE BIGGER I GET, THE BIGGER MY *DREAMS* GET.

NAH. YOU *START OUT* THINKING ABOUT *LIFE, THE UNIVERSE,* AND *THE EXISTENCE OF GOD*... NEXT THING YOU KNOW IT'S *PENSION FUNDS, LAUNDRY DETERGENT,* AND A *NEW MUFFLER*.

I CAN BELIEVE THAT.

I KNOW I USED TO THINK ABOUT ALL THE *BIG IMPORTANT STUFF* A LOT MORE THAN I DO *THESE DAYS*.

I'LL BET YOU DON'T THINK ABOUT THAT STUFF MUCH *EITHER*, ZOT.

ALL THE TIME.

OH, I BETTER GET YOU TO *THE THEATRE* IF YOU'RE GOING TO CATCH THAT *MOVIE*.

NICE BOYS. AND BOTH INTERESTED IN *JENNY*. I SHOULD BE *GRATEFUL*. LORD KNOWS SHE COULD DO *WORSE*.

ZOT IS TOO MUCH LIKE HER *FATHER*, THOUGH. ALL *VAGUE DREAMS* AND *EGO*, JUST *HEADING FOR A FALL*.

SHE *WANTS* THAT FANTASY, JUST LIKE *I* DID.

BUT SHE'D BE *SMARTER* TO FIND SOMEONE LIKE *WOODY*. YOU CAN TELL HE'S *ALREADY* BEEN HURT AND HE'S MUCH *STRONGER* FOR IT.

YOU CAN'T EXPECT *TOO MUCH* IN THIS LIFE. YOU'LL ONLY BE *DISAPPOINTED*.

I'LL PICK YOU UP HERE AT 7:00.

THANKS, MOM. *LOVE YOU*. BYE-BYE.

DAMN, I *FORGOT*. THE DUMP CLOSES AT *FIVE* ON SUNDAYS. IT'LL BE A *WEEK* BEFORE I'M HOME EARLY ENOUGH TO DROP THESE *OFF*.

CAR'S READY FOR THE *MORGUE*. I WISH THE *TOYOTA* WAS BACK FROM THE SHOP.

FINALLY. A *GREEN LIGHT*.

I TOOK THE *P.R.* JOB WITH *I.B.M.*

WHAT?

HORTON, *WHY??*

BARB, WE'VE BEEN MARRIED FOR *SIX YEARS* AND WE'RE STILL LIVING IN THIS *LOUSY APARTMENT*. I'VE GOT TO START PROVIDING FOR OUR *KIDS*.

WE *ARE* PROVIDING, HORTON!

NO.

"I WANT MY KIDS TO HAVE *MORE* THAN THIS.

"BUT, *HORTON*, YOU CAN'T JUST *THROW AWAY* YOUR DREAMS TO *DO IT!*

"DREAMS ARE FOR THE *YOUNG*, BARB. WE'VE GOT TO GROW UP *SOMETIMES*."

WELL, HORTON, WE'RE ALL *GROWN UP* NOW, JUST LIKE YOU WANTED.

WE HAVE THE *HOUSE* NOW. THE *TWO CARS*.

THE *INSURANCE POLICY*. THE *PENSIONS*. THE MONEY FOR *COLLEGE*. THE NEW *ADDITION*.

WE DID *GOOD*.

KEYS. HERE THEY ARE. SHOULD HAVE THOSE *FLAGSTONES* REPLACED. MAYBE PUT IN *CERAMIC*.

THE RAILINGS NEED A NEW *PAINT JOB*, TOO. SHOULDN'T TAKE *LONG*.

CLIK

HMM...

433

MATCHES. MATCHES.

WE COULD USE SOME NEW *FLATWARE*. WE KEEP LOSING *FORKS* IN THIS PLACE.

HERE.

"*OHIO BLUE TIPS*." SILLY. COULD GET THEM *FREE* AT THE 7-11. WE HARDLY *USE* THEM.

CHF!

LOOK AT THAT FLOOR. HASN'T BEEN MOPPED IN *AGES*. I SHOULD MAKE MY LOVING *HUSBAND* DO IT. WE *BOTH* WORK. THERE'S NO REASON I SHOULD DO ALL THE *CHORES*.

I GUESS I COULD GET THE LAUNDRY DONE BEFORE I PICK UP THE KIDS. THERE OUGHT TO BE ENOUGH TIME.

UNLESS WE'RE STILL OUT OF DETERGENT. I *THINK* I BOUGHT--

OH.

THAT SMELL...

"Autumn" was the first of five issues in a row in which I plucked a single supporting character and devoted a whole issue to his or her daily life. More tone poem than story, "Autumn" was about as far from a typical superhero story as anything I'd done to that point (with the exception of some weird little mini-comics). Looking back on it now, it's clearly a self-conscious attempt on a young genre writer's part to step up to "real" writing, while still clinging to his security blanket (the guy in the spandex costume). Somehow, though, the superhero elements don't seem all that out of place. There was always a bit of Peter Pan in Zot, ready to plug into whatever nostalgia metaphors his writer might take a fancy to.

Bill Loebs had recommended Sherwood Anderson's *Winesburg, Ohio* and I'm sure that Anderson's character portraits helped me visualize what I was going for. I also had observations from my own life to draw upon. As I neared thirty, I was a bit more attuned to the daily struggles of adult life, and it wasn't hard to imagine circumstances in which I might have to get a "real" job someday, especially if Ivy and I succeeded in having children while the U.S. comics market failed to enlarge its own family of readers. I could see life through either of Jenny's parents' eyes.

Most importantly, the artist in me rejoiced at the opportunity to draw some of the images I saw all around me. I loved New England, and found suburbia intensely beautiful and strange. One of my reference-taking missions took me on an hours-long walk after the rain through miles and miles of chilly, tree-lined streets in Arlington and Belmont, Massachusetts. Some of those images arrived intact—via about twenty miles of cross-hatching—in the big silent panels that punctuate this issue.

Jenny's house was my own mother's house in nearby Lexington, bought a few years before when our old family home seemed unnecessarily large following my father's death in 1982. The back porch on page 2 didn't exist when I drew it; I added it for visual interest. What I didn't know at the time was that my mother had indeed decided to add a porch to the

house, one that was eerily close to my drawn version. Neither of us had any idea what the other was up to. This was one of a handful of spooky coincidences that occurred around this time where my comics accidentally "predicted" real-life events.

Unfortunately for my long-suffering publisher, my usually slow pace of production became downright glacial as a result of the obsessive detail in this issue. Eclipse had wanted to promote both a collection of the first four issues and this issue together as a special promotion for the San Diego convention, and in the end neither one could ship in time. There had also been a well-meaning but ultimately doomed plan on their part to ship the issue with the scent of autumn leaves added. Pretty much everything that could go wrong did. Just speak the words "*Zot!* Month" to me at a convention if you want to see me cringe.

Clash of Titans

First published in *Zot! #31*.

Invincible

First published in *Zot! #32*.

Lettering:
Bob Lappan

Original series editor:
cat yronwode

Plot assist:
Ivy Ratafia

CLASH OF TITANS

THERE'S THIS *GUY*.

AND HE FALLS IN A VAT OF *RADIOACTIVE CHEMICALS* AND INSTEAD OF GETTING *SUPERPOWERS* LIKE YOU'D *EXPECT*, HE JUST *DIES*.

BUT THEN HE'S *UNDEAD* AND HE HAS ALL YOUR BASIC *VAMPIRE POWERS* EXCEPT HE ALSO HAS *CHEMICAL* POWERS!

AND THEN HE *FIGHTS CRIME*, OR MAYBE HE'S A *VILLAIN*, I HAVEN'T DECIDED. I'M STILL WORKING ON THE *NAME*.

MAYBE "*VLOTOX*."

YEAH. THAT'S A PRETTY GOOD NAME. I'LL WRITE IT DOWN IN *THE BOOK*.

OKAY, I'VE GOT ONE. IF *THOR'S HAMMER* IS UNSTOPPABLE AND *THE JUGGERNAUT* IS UNSTOPPABLE, WHAT HAPPENS IF THOR THROWS HIS HAMMER AT THE *JUGGERNAUT?*

THEY *DID* IT ALREADY. THE HAMMER JUST *STOPPED.*

BUT THAT *SUCKS!* THERE SHOULD BE A *BIG EXPLOSION* AND *EVERYBODY DIES* AND THE UNIVERSE IS *SET ON FIRE* AND EVERYBODY'S GUTS ARE *ALL OVER THE PLACE!*

NO, WHAT SHOULD HAPPEN IS THEY SHOULD BECOME *INTANGIBLE.* THAT WAY *NEITHER* IS STOPPED!

THOR'S HAMMER DOESN'T *BECOME INTANGIBLE!*

I *KNOW!* BUT IT *HAS* TO! SEE?

THE UNIVERSE COULD *SPLIT IN TWO.*

YEAH!

MAYBE MARVEL COULD USE IT IN *WHAT IF:* Y'KNOW, LIKE *WHAT IF: THOR'S HAMMER WAS REALLY AS STRONG AS EVERYBODY SAYS IT IS?*

GO FOR IT! WE'LL DO SOME *SAMPLES.*

SPIKE IS MY *ARTIST*.

FLAP!
FLAP!
FLAP!

THIS'LL BE MY *SEVENTH PREMISE* FOR "*WHAT IF:*" SO FAR. YOU NEED A LOT OF *PLOT IDEAS* IF YOU WANT TO *BREAK INTO* THE COMIC BOOK INDUSTRY.

I HAVE *MILLIONS*.

SOMEDAY SOON I'LL GO TO *NEW YORK* AND WALK RIGHT INTO *MARVEL COMICS* AND *SHOW THEM MY STUFF*.

I'LL HAVE SO MUCH THEY WON'T KNOW *WHAT* TO DO WITH IT ALL.

439

RRRIIING...!!

WRITING COMICS ISN'T *EASY.* IT REQUIRES *SPECIAL SKILLS.*

CAN ANYONE TELL ME WHO *SACCO* AND *VANZETTI* WERE?

MY SPECIALTY IS *CONTINUITY AND REALISM.*

CINDY?

TAKE THESE *VENETIAN BLINDS,* FOR EXAMPLE:

UM, *I* DUNNO. *BASEBALL PLAYERS?*

HEE HEE

IF *DAREDEVIL* JUMPED THROUGH THAT WINDOW, HE'D GET ALL *TANGLED* IN THOSE BLINDS, NOT TO MENTION *CUT UP* BY THE *GLASS.*

ORDINARY SCRIPTERS DON'T *CONSIDER* THESE THINGS, BUT *I* DO.

I'LL NEED LOTS OF *MATH* AND *SCIENCE* TRAINING TO BE ABLE TO WRITE THE STORIES IN MY HEAD... AND I'M *GETTING IT!*

ALMOST *STRAIGHT A's* IN THOSE *SO FAR.*

ENGLISH SUCKS, BUT THEN THE TEACHER'S *PREJUDICED.*

HEY, *SUPAH STUD!*

HE THINKS ALL *COMIC BOOKS* ARE *TRASH.*

HEY, *RONNIE!*

HI, WOODY.

HEY, GUYS.

WITH HER *STUNNING RED HAIR* SHE'S A *SHOO-IN* FOR PHOENIX IF THEY EVER DO AN *X-MEN MOVIE!* I CREATED A PHOENIX-LIKE CHARACTER FOR HER TO PLAY IN *WOODY'S WORLD*-- *THE CRIMSON FIREBIRD!*

SHE'S GETTING INTO COMICS *HERSELF* NOW, THOUGH SHE STILL NEEDS A LOT OF *GUIDANCE.* THE OTHER DAY I BROUGHT HER INTO THE *COMIC SHOP* TO BUY HER A COPY OF *BATMAN: YEAR ONE* AND SHE ALMOST BOUGHT A COPY OF THAT CARTOONY *BEAN* THING!

SOMEDAY, WHEN I'VE MADE MY *FIRST HUNDRED THOUSAND,* I'LL ASK HER TO *MARRY ME* AND--

DON'T *YOU* THINK SO, RONNIE DEAR?

HUH? OH, UH, UH...

SURE.

YOU *SEE,* WOODY?

OH, *C'MON,* RONNIE! HOW WOULD *YOU* LIKE IT IF *BRANDY* STARTED GOING OUT WITH *OTHER GUYS?!*

HE JUST *TOLD* YOU, WOODY! HE WOULDN'T MIND A BIT! ISN'T THAT *RIGHT,* DEAR?

HUH?

Y'SEE, WOODY? IF YOU *REALLY* LOVE ME, YOU'LL TRY NOT TO BE SO *POSSESSIVE!*

WHAT ABOUT *COMMITMENT?*

YOU CAN BE COMMITED TO TWO PEOPLE.

MAYBE *YOU* CAN...

OKAY, BRANDY, LET'S *YOU* AND *ME* GO OUT!

GREAT! I'D *LOVE* TO!

WHAT?!

444

WHERE'S *CAPTAIN VIRTUE?!* I *SPECIFICALLY SAID* I WANTED THE STINKBUG KILLED BY THE *CAPTAIN!*

AWW, HIS *COSTUME* IS TOO *COMPLICATED.*

AND WHAT THE HELL IS HAPPENING TO *ZOT* HERE?!

HEH! HEH! THAT'S WHERE *THE ALIEN* COMES *BURSTING* OUT OF HIS CHEST!

HEH! HEH!

SPIKE, I TOLD YOU A MILLION TIMES, WE DON'T HAVE THE RIGHTS TO THE ALIEN!!

AW, *SO WHAT?* IT'S JUST A *FANZINE.*

"JUST A FANZINE?!"

"JUST A FANZINE?!"

YEAH. GEEZ... *GROW UP,* WILLYA?

DROP DEAD! I'M GETTING A *NEW ARTIST...*

DRAW IT *YOURSELF,* WHY DON'T YOU?

HEY, C'MON, GUYS! EVERYBODY'S HERE!

THIS IS THE SETTING: YOU'RE IN A TWELVE-BY-TWELVE-BY-TWELVE FOOT SOLID STEEL ROOM LIT BY A SINGLE SYLVANIA FORTY-WATT LIGHTBULB IN THE CEILING. THERE'S A NORMAL-SIZED, TIGHT-FITTING STEEL DOOR ON EACH WALL.

THE DOORS ARE NUMBERED "ONE," "TWO," "THREE" AND "VANILLA." GEORGE, YOU'RE LEADER. YOU GO *FIRST.*

I'LL BITE! LET'S TRY THE DOOR MARKED "VANILLA."

AREN'T YOU *PLAYING,* JEN?

I'M NOT IN THE MOOD...

ELIZABETH IS *SHRINKING VIOLET* *

BRANDY IS THE *CRIMSON FIREBIRD* *

GEORGE IS THE *THING* *

I'LL *POSITION* MYSELF TO *ZAP* ANYTHING THAT *COMES THROUGH.*

ZOT IS PLAYING *"HIMSELF"*

SPIKE IS *WOLVERINE* *

I'M PLAYING *OPTIMAX* *

---

* THE *CRIMSON FIREBIRD* FLIES AND SHOOTS FLAME. *SHRINKING VIOLET* (DC COMICS) CAN GET SUPER-SMALL. *OPTIMAX* FIRES FORCE-BEAMS FROM HIS EYES. THE *THING* (MARVEL COMICS) IS A BIG ROCK-SKINNED STRONG DUDE. *WOLVERINE* (MARVEL COMICS) HAS BIG METAL CLAWS AND IS ANTI-SOCIAL.

--SCOTT

OKAY, GEORGE-- I MEAN, *THE THING* -- STARTS TO OPEN THE DOOR MARKED "VANILLA" AND AN IMMENSE WALL OF LIQUID--

I CLOSE IT! FAST!!

YOU'LL *TRY.*

ROLL A *D-12.* GET *FIVE* OR BETTER.

SIX! THE DOOR IS *CLOSED!*

-*PHEW!*-

THERE'S A FOOT AND A HALF OF *VANILLA EXTRACT* ON THE FLOOR.

"TRUTH IN ADVERTISING," I SHOULD'VE *KNOWN.*

HA! HA!

OKAY, ENOUGH *SILLY STUFF!* I'LL *BLAST THROUGH* DOOR NUMBER ONE!

NO SWEAT. *DOOR NUMBER ONE* IS BLOWN OFF ITS *HINGES.*

YOU SEE A *PATCH OF GREEN* AND SOME *LARGE OBJECTS* MOVING.

WE'LL GO THROUGH THE *DOOR.*

THE DOOR *VANISHES.*

YOU'RE ON A GIANT *POOL TABLE,* NEAR A *CORNER POCKET.* LIKE THIS, IT'S ABOUT *100 BY 200 YARDS.*

ALL FIFTEEN POOL BALLS-- TEN FEET HIGH-- ARE *RACKED UP* AT THE OTHER END OF THE TABLE. LIKE *THIS.*

ATOP EACH BALL IS A *DWARF,* DRESSED IN *ALUMINUM FOIL* WITH *FIERY GLOWING GREEN EYES.*

THEY DON'T MOVE, BUT THEIR EYES *WATCH* YOU.

THE SKY IS A SOLID *GREEN-GRAY CLOUD COVER,* VERY LOW. ON THE *HORIZON* IN EVERY DIRECTION YOU CAN SEE *TORNADOES,* THOUGH THE AIR AROUND YOU IS CALM AND *STALE...*

YOU'RE SO *CREATIVE,* WOODY.

THIS CAN'T BE *HAPPENING!* IT'S ALL A *BAD DREAM!*

AND ON THE *NEAR CORNER* OF THE TABLE, SITTING ON THE *RIM,* IS *JULIA CHILD,* EATING A *CAESAR SALAD* AND HUMMING *BEETHOVEN'S NINTH.*

I'LL ASK HER IF SHE'D LIKE TO *JOIN* OUR MISSION!

MISSION? *WHAT* MISSION?

Y'KNOW, PROTECT THE COMMON GOOD, UPHOLD THE LAW, HELP PEOPLE IN NEED, *THAT* SORT OF THING.

I'LL KILL JULIA CHILD.

NO!

HEY, *YOU* CAN'T ORDER ME AROUND. I'M *CHAOTIC.* *YOU* KNOW THAT.' ANYWAY, YOU'RE NOT EVEN THE *LEADER;* GEORGE IS!

SPIKE, *C'MON!* WHAT IF SHE HAS *IMPORTANT INFORMATION?!*

OKAY, I'LL *TORTURE* HER.

WE'LL ALL PREVENT WOLVERINE FROM TORTURING JULIA CHILD.

AWW, I *NEVER* HAVE ANY *FUN* ANYMORE.

FORGET IT...

OKAY, WOLVERINE *CALMS DOWN.*

ZOT ASKS HIS QUESTION, BUT SHE *IGNORES* HIM.

NEXT?

I'LL TAKE THE *CAESAR SALAD* AWAY FROM HER.

SHE *LETS* YOU.

THEN SHE LETS OUT A *BLOODCURDLING SCREAM* AND TOPPLES OFF THE EDGE OF THE TABLE AS A FIRE ALARM SOUNDS FROM OUT OF NOWHERE--

UH-OH.

-- AND THE *DWARVES* ON THE GIANT *POOL-BALLS* BEGIN TO *MOVE!*

OOOH!

I'LL TRY TO *TEAR OFF* THE *FELT* AND WRAP 'EM UP WITH IT.

I'LL GET MY *GUN* READY AND *FLY AROUND* TO THE *LEFT.*

I'LL HELP THE THING RIP THE FELT WITH MY *EYE-BEAMS.* I THINK HE HAS THE *RIGHT IDEA.*

I'LL *FLY OVERHEAD* AND ZAP THE ONE IN THE *REAR.*

I'LL *SHRINK DOWN* AND JUMP IN THE NEAREST DWARF'S *EAR.*

I'LL KILL *OPTIMAX.*

WHAT?! YOU TRAITOR!!

OKAY, WOLVERINE, ROLL A *D-20.* IF YOU GET *THIRTEEN* OR BETTER, YOU CAN GET TO HIM BEFORE ANYONE *SEES* YOU.

COOL.

I DON'T **BELIEVE** THIS!

NINETEEN!

AWRIGHT! I'LL GO FOR THE *JUGULAR.*

NO!! I QUIT! HE'S JUST PISSED OFF AT ME 'CAUSE I TOLD HIM HE COULDN'T USE THE ALIEN!

AWW, GO *STUFF* YOURSELF.

C'MON, RONNIE! SPIKE *ALWAYS* TRIES TO KILL *SOMEONE.* IT'S HIS STYLE.

HA! WHY SHOULD I LISTEN TO *YOU,* WOODY?

YOU--

YOU--

-- GIRLFRIEND STEALER!

WHAT? OH, COME ON!

GOOD RIDDANCE.

RONNIE, *PLEASE* DON'T GO!

RONNIE!

TO HELL WITH *ALL* OF THEM! *THEY'LL SEE!*

SOMEDAY, I'LL *CHANGE THE WHOLE WORLD* AND *THEN* THEY'LL SEE.

THEN THEY'LL SEE.

BAD DAY, HUH?

NOBODY *UNDERSTANDS* ME, MOM.

I'VE GOT ALL THESE *IDEAS* IN MY HEAD. ALL THESE *GREAT THINGS*...

BUT THEY NEVER *COME OUT* RIGHT! SOMETHING ALWAYS *RUINS* IT.

I WANT *SO MUCH* TO BE A *WRITER.*

YOU *CAN* BE, RONNIE! BUT YOU HAVE TO WRITE WHAT YOU *KNOW.* YOUR OWN LIFE MIGHT NOT SEEM AS EXCITING AS SOME *SUPERHERO'S,* BUT IT *CAN* BE. IF YOU WEREN'T SO *CLOSE* TO IT, YOU'D SEE WHAT A FASCINATING LIFE YOU LEAD.

OH, *MOM...*

...THAT'S SUCH AN *ENGLISH TEACHER* THING TO SAY.

WELL, *EXCUSE ME...*

IT *IS* MY JOB.

ANYWAY, WHO THE HELL WOULD WANT TO READ ABOUT *ME?*

CLIK

BRANDY BOUGHT ME THIS CHAIR AT A *YARDSALE.* SAID IT COULD BE MY *THINKING CHAIR.*

NEED SOME *MUSIC.*

WAGNER
SELECTED OVERTURES

KLIK

SONY

HOW *EVER* DID WE COME TO THIS *DESOLATE, WAR-RAVAGED PLANET?!*

SO *FAR FROM HOME!* PERHAPS TO *DIE* HERE!

AND PERHAPS *NOT!* PERHAPS TO *KILL?!*

POWER TO SEND THE HEAVENS CRASHING DOWN UPON US!!

KLIK

IT'S TIME FOR *DINNER,* HON'.

I'LL BE DOWN IN A *MINUTE.*

-SIGH-

BUMP!

invincible

THAT ONE!

SNAP!

THERE!

WRF?

WHAT DO YOU THINK?

GEE, I'M *SORRY*, MR. GIBSON, YOU JUST *MISSED HER!* CAN I GIVE HER A *MESSAGE* FOR YOU?

WELL... ER...

YOU KNOW, THE RENT IS STILL--

OH, *THAT!* THAT'S *COMPLETELY* UNDER CONTROL NOW, MR. GIBSON. DON'T WORRY A *BIT* ABOUT *THAT!*

WE'LL HAVE IT FOR YOU *TUESDAY,* AT THE *LATEST.*

"IT"? DO YOU MEAN *BOTH MONTHS?*

"BOTH"?

WE STILL HAVEN'T GOTTEN *NOVEMBER'S* RENT, BRANDY. I'M AFRAID YOU'RE NEARLY *TWO MONTHS OVERDUE.*

I THINK WE'LL BE PAYING *DECEMBER'S* RENT!

THEN YOU'RE PAYING FOR *BOTH*...

NO, JUST *DECEMBER'S.* BUT WE'LL PAY FOR *NOVEMBER'S* AS SOON AS WE CAN!

GOTTA STAY *CURRENT,* Y'KNOW?

BUT, THAT DOESN'T--

SORRY! I'VE GOTTA *RUN!* TAKE *CARE!*

BUT--

SAY "HI" TO MRS. GIBSON FOR ME! *BYE-BYE!*

HERE'S HOW TO ALWAYS BE HAPPY:

NUMBER ONE: REMEMBER THAT *EVERY MISTAKE* YOU MAKE *TEACHES* YOU SOMETHING *IMPORTANT*, SO IT MUST BE *WORTHWHILE*.

THEREFORE, YOU CAN NEVER REALLY *MAKE* ANY MISTAKES! IT'S *LOGICALLY IMPOSSIBLE!*

NUMBER TWO: ONCE YOU MAKE A *FRIEND*, MAKE SURE YOU *STAY FRIENDS FOREVER!*

DID YOU *SEE* WHAT *BRANDY* IS WEARING?? *GHOD!!*

BET SHE MADE IT *HERSELF.*

YEAH, *NO KIDDING!* HA! HA!

BRANDY! WAIT UP!

HM?

OH, *HI,* GORDIE!

BRANDY, THIS IS MY *BEST FRIEND, CHRIS!*

HI, BRANDY! GORDIE HAS TOLD ME *SO MUCH* ABOUT YOU!

HE *HAS?*

YEAH. I *LOVE* YOUR *NAME!* HOW DID YOUR MOM *COME UP* WITH IT?

HA! HA! IF YOU KNEW HER *MOM*, YOU WOULDN'T HAVE TO *ASK!*

HA!

HA!

POW!

OH, GORDIE! ARE YOU OKAY?!

HERE, I'LL HELP YOU UP...

... I'M SO *SORRY!* SOMETIMES, IT'S JUST -- Y'KNOW-- KIND OF A *REFLEX!*

...

LET ME *MAKE IT UP TO YOU!* WHAT ARE YOU DOING *SATURDAY?* WANT TO TAKE ME TO A *MOVIE?*

NUMBER THREE: THE LONGER YOUR *BAD LUCK* LASTS, THE MORE *GOOD LUCK* YOU *ACCUMULATE.*

HMM...

ACTUALLY, *NUMBER TWO* SHOULD PROBABLY COME *LAST,* 'CAUSE THAT'S THE MOST *IMPORTANT.*

BRANDY! IS THAT ALL YOU'RE HAVING FOR *LUNCH?*

HERE LET ME *GET* THAT FOR YOU.

HI, BRANDY!

GREAT *OUTFIT,* BRANDY!

LET ME BUY YOU A *SANDWICH,* AT *LEAST!*

OH, *THANKS,* RONNIE! YOU'RE A *SWEETHEART!*

THERE HE *IS.*

MILK

DO YOU HAVE ANY MORE OF THOSE LITTLE *CATSUP POUCHES?*

IF ONLY JENNY WOULD GIVE HIM UP FOR JUST *ONE DATE...*

HERE YOU GO! HAM AND CHEESE, YOUR *FAVORITE!*

THANK YOU, *RONNIE.*

SO, *TELL* ME, ARE YOU STILL GOING OUT WITH MY SO-CALLED *FRIEND,* TONIGHT?

OH, NOW, *STOP IT,* RONNIE! WOODY HAS AS MUCH RIGHT TO *ASK ME OUT* AS *ANYBODY.* EVEN *YOU.*

YEAH, I'M *SORRY,* RONNIE, BUT I'M *TIRED* OF ALL THE GIRLS TELLING ME I'M TOO POSSESSIVE ABOUT *JENNY.*

I FIGURE IT'S *YOUR* TURN.

"TURN"?? WHO'S TALKING "*TURNS*"?! BRANDY, I *LOVE YOU!* YOU'RE MY *GIRL!*

I LOVE YOU, *TOO,* RONNIE, BUT I DON'T *BELONG* TO *ANYBODY!*

I BELONG TO *ME!*

OH, WHY NOT JUST *GO OUT WITH EVERYBODY,* THEN? SEE IF *I* CARE...

GREAT IDEA, RONNIE! OKAY, WHO WANTS TO GO OUT WITH ME TONIGHT?!

HUH?

ME!

ME!

LET'S SEE... *SPIKE,* YOU CAN HAVE ME AFTER SCHOOL UNTIL 4:00. *GEORGE,* YOU'LL TAKE THE 4:00-5:30 SHIFT. *WOODY* GETS ME FOR DINNER AS ORIGINALLY PLANNED.

ZOT, YOU'LL MEET ME OUTSIDE THE MAIN OFFICE AT *7:30*--

I'M SORRY, I WASN'T *LISTENING.*

YOU'RE *TAKING ME OUT* TONIGHT!

OH, OKAY.

HEY, *WAIT A MINUTE*--!

AND *RONNIE*, SINCE YOU'RE SO DETERMINED TO PROVE HOW MUCH YOU *LOVE ME*, *YOU* CAN HAVE ME *LAST!*

IS *9:00* OKAY?

FINE.

GREAT!

OH! OH! AND THIS IS MY *FAVORITE PART!* CHECK OUT HOW HIS BRAINS DON'T SO MUCH *EXPLODE* AS KIND OF *GUSH!*

I'LL PUT IT IN *SLO-MO*...

CLIK!

RRING!!

OH, *EXCUSE ME!* PHONE!

HI, WOODY! YEAH, SHE'S STILL *HERE*. NAH, GEORGE NEVER *SHOWED*...

HM? NO, WE HAD A *GREAT TIME!* I SHOWED HER ALL THE BEST PARTS OF *HELLRAISER II, BASKET CASE, DAWN OF THE D--*

NO, *REALLY!* SHE *LOVED IT!*

SO, IS IT YOUR TURN *ALREADY?* WOW... *HOW TIME FLIES*, HUH? OKAY, DO YOU WANT TO PICK HER UP *HERE* OR--

OH, OKAY. HOLD ON A SEC.

BLEAAGGH!

IT'S *WOODY!* WANT TO TALK TO HIM?

IN A MINUTE...

FEEL ANY *BETTER?*

YEAH, *THANKS.*

I'M SORRY I DIDN'T HAVE THAT MUCH OF AN *APPETITE,* WOODY...

S'OKAY.

Y'KNOW, BRANDY... I REALIZE THAT TONIGHT STARTED OUT AS KIND OF A *JOKE,* BUT I, UM... Y'KNOW... IF YOU EVER ARE, UM... LOOKING FOR SOMEONE... WELL, I WANT YOU TO KNOW I...

I REALLY DO *LIKE* YOU.

I LIKE YOU *TOO,* WOODY.

SO, WHY DO YOU THINK *GEORGE* NEVER SHOWED UP?

I DUNNO. TO TELL YOU THE *TRUTH,* I WAS KIND OF SURPRISED THAT HE VOLUNTEERED IN THE *FIRST PLACE.*

I DON'T THINK HE REALIZED THAT YOU WERE REALLY GOING TO *GO THROUGH* WITH THIS.

GEE, MAYBE HE DOESN'T LIKE GIRLS! I HOPE I DIDN'T *PUT HIM ON THE SPOT* OR ANYTHING.

YEAH, WELL...

LOOKS LIKE ZOT ISN'T HERE YET.

WOULD YOU WAIT HERE WITH ME, WOODY? IT'S SO *DARK.*

SURE.

NICE NIGHT OUT, HUH?

YEAH.

WOODY, WHY ARE PEOPLE SO *UPTIGHT* ABOUT *SEX?*

UH... *COME AGAIN?*

465

I'M *IMPRESSED*, BRANDY! I DIDN'T THINK *ANYONE* COULD FIT THROUGH THAT WINDOW!

YEAH. BEING SKINNY AS A *BEANPOLE* DOES HAVE ITS *ADVANTAGES*.

SO, NOW THAT WE'RE *IN HERE*, WHAT DO YOU WANT TO *DO?*

I'VE GOT TO TELL YOU, THE *SCHOOL GYM* WASN'T QUITE WHAT I WAS EXPECTING WHEN YOU *ASKED ME OUT.*

ACTUALLY, I HAVE A *FAVOR* TO ASK.

SURE, WHAT IS IT?

FLY FOR ME, ZOT.

OKAY.

466

I *KNEW* IT! IT'S *TRUE!* IT'S ALL *TRUE!* EVERY *WORD* OF IT!

SORRY, CAN'T *HEAR* YOU!

ZOT, YOUR *WORLD*...IS IT AS *BEAUTIFUL* AS JENNY SAYS? IS IT REALLY LIKE *HEAVEN ON EARTH?*

MORE OR *LESS,* YEAH.

IS EVERYONE *FREE* ON YOUR WORLD? ARE THE CITIES *SAFE?* ARE HUNGRY PEOPLE *FED?* IS THERE NO MORE *WAR* OR *POVERTY* OR *PREJUDICE?* IS EVERY BIG PROBLEM FINALLY *SOLVED* THERE?

MOSTLY, YEAH. I GUESS YOU COULD SAY THAT.

ZOT... IF YOU EVER *GET BACK* THERE, I HAVE A MESSAGE FOR YOUR *WORLD.*

SURE.

GO AHEAD.

ZOT, I WANT THEM TO KNOW THAT NOT *EVERYONE* ON OUR WORLD IS LIKE JENNY. SOME OF US LIKE THIS WORLD *JUST FINE* AND HAVE *NO INTENTIONS* OF *LEAVING IT.*

MAYBE IT'S NOT *PERFECT,* BUT I WOULDN'T TRADE THIS WORLD FOR *ANYTHING!*

PERFECTION IS *BORING!* GIVE ME *IMPERFECTION* ANY OLD DAY!

I *AGREE.*

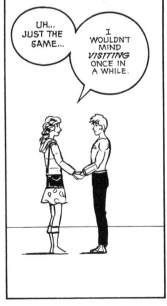

UH... JUST THE SAME...

I WOULDN'T MIND *VISITING* ONCE IN A WHILE.

MAYBE WE BETTER *SIT DOWN*...

UH...

ARE YOU *OKAY?*

HEY,... HEY, YOU,... BE *HAPPY*, WILL YA?

I GOT *ICE CREAM*.

CHOCOLATE?

UH-*HUH*.

I'LL BE *RIGHT BACK*.

C'MON!

I CAN'T *BELIEVE* YOU'VE NEVER *BEEN* HERE, RONNIE! ESPECIALLY WHEN YOU LIVE SO *CLOSE!*

DO YOU KNOW, THEY BUILT THIS PLAYGROUND IN JUST *ONE DAY?!*

ISN'T IT *BEAUTIFUL?*

THE WAY *I* HEARD IT, THERE'S THESE PEOPLE WHO COME INTO TOWN AND HELP *PLAN* IT ALL.

THEN THEY GET ALL THE LUMBER AND STUFF FROM *LOCAL BUSINESSES* AND THE WHOLE *TOWN* COMES OUT TO HELP PUT IT *TOGETHER!*

CAREFUL...

HEY, RONNIE, WHY IS IT THAT WHEN YOU SEE PICTURES OF *OLD PEOPLE* FROM WHEN THEY WERE *YOUNG* THAT THEY DON'T REALLY *LOOK* YOUNG? THEY STILL LOOK KINDA *OLD?*

HOW DID *THIS* COME UP?

OH, I WAS LOOKING AT SOME OF YOUR PARENTS' *WEDDING PICTURES* EARLIER TONIGHT. HOW OLD *WERE* THEY BACK THEN?

UM...PRETTY *YOUNG*, I THINK... *EIGHTEEN* MAYBE.

WEEE!

RONNIE! THAT'S ONLY *THREE YEARS AWAY* FOR US!

WOW.

I was riding on a bus to Harvard Square one day when a slightly shifty-looking older man walked past me and asked a girl with a young voice directly behind me if he could take the seat next to her. He began asking her questions, some of which seemed a bit overly probing to me, though she didn't seem to mind. She was chatty and volunteered a lot of information about herself. I dutifully eavesdropped (following the advice of all good writing teachers), and at a certain point the conversation turned to her physical appearance. He said she looked younger than her stated age. "I think I'll always look young," she said, "I know I always have." I stole the line and gave it to Brandy, pulling together a moment I now like as much as anything in the series.

Ronnie and Brandy's stories have aged pretty well, I think. Apart from my usual reservations about the art—and wondering occasionally why there's some guy in a superhero costume hanging around—I can look through these pages without shuddering much. I have real affection for the characters and wish them success on the long, bumpy road ahead of them.

Needless to say, Ronnie and his friends weren't much of a stretch for a card-carrying nerd like me. I still have my own three-ring binder, filled with superhero ideas from high school. (In fact, Kurt Busiek and I may yet collaborate on one idea we worked on together back in the day that's kind of cool.)

Woody's role-playing universe is a lot like the kind I created for our circle of friends. I wasn't interested in the official rule books and such, so my "dungeons" were informal pencil-and-paper creations that included characters from comics, TV, movies, and literature. It wasn't unusual to find a hero like Ultra Boy* fighting Rover (the big white balloon from the classic BBC show *The Prisoner*) while dodging those stilt-legged Apple Bonker guys from *Yellow Submarine*.

Creating Brandy was a mental excursion that took me a bit further from home than Ronnie, but I had many of the parts close at hand, including Ivy's bohemian flourishes and

fearless affection for those around her, our daily money struggles, and that same third floor walk-up in Somerville, Massachusetts (complete with an equally reasonable landlord). Happily, Brandy's alcoholic mother was pure invention; neither of us had that kind of addiction in our family.

When I imagine them growing up, I have trouble deciding how life will go for Brandy, but I firmly believe that Ronnie will break into comics someday and that he will grow as a writer over time. I have to believe it about him because I have to believe it about myself.

In Comics History: It was while working on these stories that I took time out to try drawing a complete 24-page comics story in a single day as a challenge to my friend Steve Bissette, and as therapy for my chronic slowness at the drawing board. Steve did likewise a few days later. He sent copies to Dave Sim, Rick Veitch, and Neil Gaiman, each of whom made their own such comics. In the eighteen years since, thousands have taken the 24 Hour Comics Challenge, culminating in the annual international 24 Hour Comics Day (now in its fifth year) and inspiring several spin-offs, including the 24 Hour Plays phenomenon. For more information on the 24 Hour Comics, check out 24hourcomics.com.

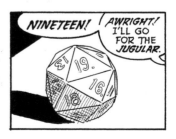

*Dude, Ultra Boy has all of Superboy's powers, but can only use them *one at a time*. How cool is that?!

473

Normal

First published in *Zot! #33*.

Lettering:
Bob Lappan

Original series editor:
cat yronwode

Plot assist:
Ivy Ratafia

Harvey Award Nominee 1991:
"Best Single Issue"

479

NO, NO... I'M SORRY.

LOOK, I'M JUST KIND OF *GROUCHY* TODAY...

IT'S OKAY, TER. WE LOVE YOU ANYWAY.

C'MON, HAVE LUNCH WITH THE *DWEEBS.*

YEAH, *C'MON,* TERRY!

WHOSE *TURN* WAS IT?

BRANDY'S LOOKING REAL GOOD TODAY. HOW DOES SHE STAY SO *THIN?*

GOD, I WISH I *KNEW!* I'D GIVE *ANYTHING* TO LOOK LIKE HER. SHE'S SO MUCH *PRETTIER* THAN I AM.

DON'T SAY THAT, JENNY! *I* THINK *YOU'RE* PRETTY! YOU'RE ONE OF THE PRETTIEST GIRLS I *KNOW!*

YOU'RE NOT A *BOY.*

MY BROTHER *HECTOR* THINKS YOU'RE PRETTY!

HEY, *SPEAKING* OF WHICH, I FOUND SOME OLD *PLAYBOYS* IN THE BACK OF HECTOR'S CAR THE OTHER DAY.

HAVE YOU EVER *LOOKED* AT THOSE THINGS?

YEAH, I FOUND SOME OF *BUTCH'S* ONCE.

AREN'T THEY *GROSS?* I'LL NEVER KNOW WHAT GUYS *SEE* IN THAT STUFF.

YEAH.

ME NEITHER.

ROOM FOR ONE MORE?

TERRY!

HI, TERRY! HERE, YOU CAN SIT BETWEEN JENNY AND ME.

SO I STILL NEED THAT SKETCH OF THE SHE-HULK, RIGHT? BUT ALL THE GOOD ARTISTS ARE BUSY. SO I GO UP TO SOME BLACK-AND-WHITE GUY--

HEY, WHAT ABOUT SPIDER-MAN? DIDN'T YOU GET SPIDER-MAN?!

RONNIE, DO YOU WANT ANY MORE OF THAT MEATLOAF?

YOU CAN HAVE MINE, BRANDY.

WHAT HAPPENED TO YOU, ZOT?!

OH, JUST A SPRAINED WRIST. I TRIED TO STOP A MUGGING IN THE CITY LAST NIGHT.

TRIED TO--?! HE DID STOP IT! IT WAS IN ALL THE PAPERS!

Panel 1:
IT'S *TRUE*, TERRY! HE ACTUALLY MANAGED TO TAKE THIS GUY'S *GUN* AWAY!

WOW!

IF YOU KEEP THIS UP, ZOT, PEOPLE WILL START TO THINK YOU REALLY *ARE* A SUPERHERO!

RONNIE, HE *IS* A SUPERHERO! WHY WON'T YOU *BELIEVE* US?!

IT'S *TRUE*, RONNIE! I'VE BEEN TO HIS *WORLD!*

EVEN *I'VE* BEEN THERE, FANBOY. IT'S *REAL*, ALL RIGHT.

I'D *TAKE* YOU THERE, RONNIE, BUT I'M STILL MAROONED HERE ON *THIS* EARTH.

OH, *CUT IT OUT*, YOU GUYS! HA! HA!

Y'KNOW, ZOT, YOU OUGHTTA BE *CAREFUL* IN THE CITY. YOU COULD GET REALLY *HURT* SOMEDAY!

HE HAS A *POINT* THERE, BLONDIE.

OH, I WON'T DO ANYTHING *CARELESS*. ANYWAY, THE CITY ISN'T ALL *THAT* BAD.

I MEAN, *NO* PLACE IS *COMPLETELY* SAFE.

THAT'S FOR SURE. LOOK AT POOR *HARRY SINGER*.

YEAH, THOSE *BASTARDS*... I'D LIKE TO STICK A FIRECRACKER IN *THEIR* EAR!

HEY, THAT'S *IT!*

HUH? WHAT'S "IT"?

WOODY, YOU *CAN* DO SOMETHING ABOUT HARRY! YOU'RE *ON* THE SCHOOL PAPER!

YOU COULD DO A WHOLE BIG THING ON *HEMOPHILIA!*

EH... YOU MEAN *HOMOPHOBIA*, JEN.

ANYWAY, THE ANSWER IS *NO*.

WHY?! WHY *NOT?!* C'MON, IT'D BE *GREAT!* YOU COULD REALLY MAKE A *NAME* FOR YOURSELF!

THAT'S FOR SURE.

JENNY'S *RIGHT,* WOODY! YOU COULD BE A *CRUSADER FOR SOCIAL JUSTICE!* RAH! RAH!

NO THANKS.

C'MON, WOODY! GIVE ME *ONE GOOD REASON* IT WOULDN'T *WORK,* HUH? JUST GIVE ME *ONE!*

I...

YEAH, WOODY!

LOOK, GUYS, YOU KNOW WHAT HAPPENED TO HARRY... I'M NO HERO. I DON'T *NEED* THAT KIND OF TROUBLE.

BUT THAT'S *DUMB,* WOODY! THOSE JERKS THOUGHT HARRY *WAS* GAY! YOU'D JUST BE--

...

THAT'S *IT,* ISN'T IT? YOU FIGURE THAT IF YOU *WRITE* ABOUT--

CAN WE JUST *DROP IT,* JEN? *PLEEEZ?!*

WOODY, I'M *AMAZED* AT YOU! *ZOT BREAKS HIS ARM* STOPPING A *CRIME* AND YOU WON'T EVEN LIFT A *FINGER*--

AW, LEAVE HIM BE, JEN.

JEN, I'M NOT *LIKE* ZOT. I TRY TO *AVOID* THAT KIND OF STUFF. I WANT TO *STAY IN ONE PIECE.*

YEAH, WELL, IT'S THAT KIND OF ATTITUDE THAT PUT HARRY IN A *WHEELCHAIR* FOR THE REST OF HIS *GODDAMN LIFE!*

IF YOU CAN'T STAND UP FOR WHAT YOU BELIEVE IN, YOU'RE JUST A *HYPOCRITE!*

JENNY, WHY ARE YOU *DOING* THIS?!

JENNY, YOU DON'T *UNDERSTAND!* IT'S *DIFFERENT* FOR GUYS. IT'S *DANGEROUS*--

WOODY, YOU'D JUST BE *WRITING* ABOUT IT! C'MON! IT'S *EASY!*

IS ANYONE *LOOKING* AT ME?

YEAH? THEN WHY DON'T *YOU* WRITE IT, JENNY? *I* COULD GET YOU IN!

I CAN'T *WRITE.*

I FEEL SICK.

SURE YOU CAN, JENNY! I'LL *HELP* YOU! I DON'T SUPPOSE YOU'LL MIND IF *EVERYBODY* THINKS YOU'RE A *LESBIAN?*

STOP IT! *STOP IT,* PLEASE!

WOODY, I WOULDN'T GIVE A *SH*--

I--!

I'VE GOTTA GO!!

TERRY?

OH, GOD!

OH, GOD!

485

WHAT WILL I DO *NOW?!?* WHO CAN I *TALK* TO?? I WON'T HAVE *ANYONE!* THEY'LL THINK I'M A *FREAK!*

I *AM* A FREAK!

OH, *GOD.*

THEY'LL ALL *KNOW!*

THEY'RE ALL GOING TO *KNOW!*

TERRY! THERE YOU ARE! JENNY HAS BEEN LOOKING ALL *OVER* FOR YOU.

OH.

HELLO, ZOT.

YOU SHOULDN'T BE OUT HERE IN THIS *WEATHER,* Y'KNOW. YOU COULD CATCH *PNEUMONIA* OR SOMETHING!

GREAT. MAYBE I'LL *DIE SOONER.*

AT LEAST TAKE MY *COAT.* HERE. DO YOU WANT SOMETHING TO *EAT?* I'VE GOT A BAG OF *PEANUTS...*

I DON'T NEED YOUR HELP, ZOT.

I DON'T NEED *ANYONE.*

JUST *LEAVE ME ALONE,* OKAY?

JENNY'S VERY *BEAUTIFUL*, ISN'T SHE?

I DON'T THINK ANYONE *KNOWS*.

YOU KNEW.

I'VE SPENT A LOT OF *TIME* AROUND YOU AND JEN. I'VE SEEN THE WAY YOU *LOOK* AT HER, HOW YOU *ACT* AROUND HER.

OH, BUT SHE'S NOT...

IT'S NOT JEN. I MEAN--

SHE'S NOT *THE ONE*, HUH?

WELL, I DUNNO...

SHE IS *STRAIGHT*, ISN'T SHE?

YEAH, I *THINK* SO.

I MEAN, I SUPPOSE *AT FIRST* I...

WELL, THERE'S *SOMEONE ELSE NOW*...

SOMEONE I'VE LET MYSELF *LOSE TOUCH* WITH AND...

...AND MAYBE I *SHOULDN'T* HAVE.

YOU HEARD ABOUT *HARRY SINGER*, RIGHT?

YEAH, I HEARD. THAT WAS REALLY *SICK*.

THOSE GUYS WHO DID THAT TO *HARRY*...

DO YOU HAVE PEOPLE LIKE THAT ON *YOUR* WORLD, ZOT?

YEAH, I GUESS... HERE AND THERE.

THEY JUST AREN'T *RUNNING THE PLACE*, THAT'S ALL.

ZOT...

ON YOUR WORLD...

WOULD I BE *NORMAL?*

HA! HA!

TERRY, YOU *ARE* NORMAL!

ZOT, I MEAN IT! PLEASE, TELL ME! WOULD THEY THINK I WAS *NORMAL?!*

YES, OF COURSE.

OF *COURSE* THEY WOULD.

TSK.

OH, *LOOK* AT YOU.

LOOK WHAT THEY'VE DONE TO YOU.

YOU *DIDN'T!*

UH-HUH.! AND THEN I SAID, *"LOOK, BUSTER,* IF YOU THINK YOU CAN *FEEL ME UP* AFTER JUST ONE BOX OF *CANDY--"*

YEAH, AND THEY WEREN'T THAT GOOD EITHER.

I SAID, "YOU'VE GOT ANOTHER 'THINK' *COMING!'*"

YEAH, *PUT YOUR MONEY WHERE YOUR MOUTH IS,* I SAY!

WOW, YOU GUYS HAVE A LOT MORE *GUTS* THAN ME.

AW, *YOU* CAN HANDLE IT, TER. I STILL SAY YOU OUGHTA *COME UP* WITH US SOME TIME.

YEAH, WELL... MAYBE *SOME-TIME.*

OH, THAT *REMINDS* ME! VINNIE'S BROTHER IS *DEFINITELY OUT-OF-THEEE-PICTURE!*

HE WAS UP THERE WITH SOME *SLUT* NAMED *MARYBETH* AND--

UH, SOMETHING *WRONG,* TERRY?

OH, *WATCHOUT,* GUYS, HERE COMES *PAM-A-LEZ.*

EU. SHE GIVES ME THE *CREEPS.*

UH, I GOTTA *GO* NOW.

SEE YA, TERRY. CAREFUL YOU DON'T GET *RAPED* ON THE WAY TO *BIOLOGY.*

HA! HA! YEAH.

Whatever its virtues or flaws as a story, "Normal" is the issue that left the most lasting impression on *Zot!*'s readers, many of whom have told me their own experiences in the intervening years and the ways in which Terry connected to them. Reaction was mostly positive at the time; I was preaching to the converted in the progressive independent comics scene. One of the exceptions, a longtime reader with religious objections to homosexuality, wrote an earnest, strongly worded objection to the story, but then kept reading the series and commenting, which I thought was awfully charitable of him.

The climate in 1990 for such a story was mixed. On the one hand, underground and erotic comics had dealt with sexual identity issues long before I entered the fray, and magazines and newspaper with gay and lesbian readerships regularly showcased great comics from significant talents like Howard Cruse and Alison Bechdel. On the other hand, the popular mainstream publishers Marvel and DC that dominated comics stores and subscribed to the rigid Comics Code Authority had a zero tolerance policy for openly gay heroes (at least for another two years, though that's another story).

Zot! was a different animal entirely, however—neither fish nor fowl. As part of the ground-level independent comics wing, featuring a superhero in the title role, it was allowed to share the shelves with more mainstream fare and wasn't hidden behind an "over 18" curtain or banished entirely. This meant that for a young reader questioning his or her sexuality in 1990, *Zot!* #33 stood a decent chance of being their earliest encounter with such themes in a comic book. For those readers, I'm grateful for the opportunity to have been there and told them that they had nothing to be ashamed of, and of all the moments from "Normal" I've heard repeated back to me across the years, I think Zot's remark "Look what they've done to you" is the one that readers remember most vividly.

That, and the trick ending.

When originally laying out issue #33, I planned to end Terry's story with the downbeat missed opportunity seen on the previous spread. It seemed the more plausible real-world ending to a situation of that kind, at least in the average American high school. In the end, though, I decided that even though I'd sidelined the guy in the red suit, this was still a *Zot!* story, and that meant that in close contests between hope and disillusionment, hope should at least win the coin toss.

Adding the nineteenth page seen here provided an interesting challenge though. It was customary to end all *Zot!* stories on the left-hand page, allowing the letters pages to start on the facing right hand page. If we had just added the extra page, it would have thrown off that tradition, so I placed the new last page after the first letters page, hiding it from view in much the same way I did here, and providing a welcome surprise for most readers (at least those who hadn't peeked ahead to see if their letter had been printed).

Years later, I discovered that a few readers were so upset by the grim first ending that they put the issue down and wouldn't look at it again, unaware of the second ending for hours or even days. I wonder sometimes if there isn't a disgruntled 32-year-old former *Zot!* fan somewhere out there who gave up with issue #33, page 18, and still has no idea that Terry ever turned around.

Compared to a modern multilayered graphic novel with sexual themes like Bechdel's *Fun Home,* such a short, simple story may seem no more substantial than the comics equivalent of an old CBS after-school special or public service announcement. But even if that's true, I still have no regrets about the story. Even baby steps serve a purpose if they're in the right direction, and I'd like to think that's where I was heading.

As I write this in 2008, our local news in southern California is reporting from a middle school in nearby Oxnard, where an openly gay student named Lawrence King had actually dared to wear feminine clothes to school and apparently ruffled a few feathers in the process.

As Lawrence sat in computer class last Tuesday, one of his classmates walked up to him, pulled out a handgun, and shot the him in the head.

Sometimes, a Direction...

First published in *Zot! #34*.

Lettering:
Bob Lappan

Original series editor:
cat yronwode

Plot assist:
Ivy Ratafia

Sometimes a Direction...

498

"FEELS PRETTY *GOOD*, DOESN'T IT--? DOING WHAT YOU KNOW IS *RIGHT*."

"I DON'T KNOW, DAD. IT FELT GOOD SHOWING JENNY THE *ARTICLE*. I DON'T KNOW HOW GOOD IT'LL FEEL WHEN DOUGIE ALEXANDER AND HIS PALS KNOCK MY *TEETH* OUT."

DID YOU NAME *NAMES* IN THE ARTICLE?

NO, IT'S JUST ABOUT *GAY-BASHING* IN GENERAL, BUT EVERYONE KNOWS IT WAS *DOUGIE* AND HIS FRIENDS WHO DID IT TO HARRY SINGER.

THE GUY'S BEEN BRAGGING ABOUT IT TO EVERY KID HE KNOWS.

WHY HAVEN'T THEY *ARRESTED* THE LITTLE SCHMUCK?

DA-A-A-AD! I SAID EVERYONE *KNOWS*. THAT DOESN'T MEAN ANYONE IS *TALKING*!

I'M THE ONLY ONE DUMB ENOUGH TO ACTUALLY *SAY* ANYTHING.

I MEAN, I KNOW IT WAS *RIGHT*, LIKE YOU SAID, BUT RIGHT NOW IT DOESN'T SEEM LIKE IT WAS PARTICULARLY *SMART*.

WELCOME TO THE *REAL WORLD*, WOODY.

PRETTY SOON, YOU'LL HAVE TO DECIDE JUST WHAT *DIRECTION* YOU WANT YOUR LIFE TO TAKE.

LIKE SEEING A *LIGHTHOUSE* ON THE *HORIZON* AND *SAILING* FOR IT.

THIS IS WHAT *MY* FATHER SAID...

MEMORIZE WHERE THAT LIGHTHOUSE IS AS SOON AS YOU SEE IT, WOODY, BECAUSE THERE'LL BE TIMES IN YOUR LIFE WHEN YOU CAN BARELY MAKE IT OUT FOR ALL THE SNOW AND FOG AND RAIN.

"LIFE WILL ONLY GET *MORE* COMPLICATED AS YOU GET OLDER, NOT *LESS.*"

WOW, THIS IS SOME *HEAVY STUFF,* WOODY. HOW DID YOU GET IT PAST MISTER *KRUPER?*

AH, *KRUPER'S* ALL RIGHT. HE SAID THE SCHOOL PAPER *NEEDED* A LITTLE CONTROVERSY.

YOU SURE *GAVE* IT TO 'EM, WOODY!

I DON'T KNOW IF *CLUNE* * IS GOING TO LIKE THIS. YOU REALLY LAY INTO THE STAFF FOR *LOOKING THE OTHER WAY.*

THAT'S WHAT'S SO *GREAT* ABOUT IT, GEORGE! WOODY ISN'T AFRAID TO OFFEND *ANYBODY!* RIGHT, RONNIE?

YEAH, IT'S...

IT'S REAL *WELL WRITTEN,* WOODY.

YOU *BET* IT IS!

I HOPE I DID THE RIGHT THING. I COULD GET IN A LOT OF *TROUBLE.*

WE'LL STAND BY YOU, WOODY! AND *OF COURSE* YOU DID THE RIGHT THING.

DON'T YOU THINK SO, ZOT?

SURE.

WELCOME TO THE *HERO* BUSINESS, WOODY.

DR. BERNARD F. CLUNE, PRINCIPAL.

HEY, *FAGGOT!*

YOU TALKING TO *ME?*

YEAH, I'M TALKING TO YOU, BERNSTEIN! JUST THOUGHT YOU'D LIKE TO KNOW THAT AFTER SCHOOL WE'RE GONNA *RIP YOUR DICK OFF* WITH A *RUSTY CHAINSAW* AND STUFF IT DOWN YOUR *FAGGOT THROAT* UNTIL YOU CHOKE AND *DIE!!*

AH, YOU'VE... READ THE *ARTICLE,* I TAKE IT.

NAWWW... A LITTLE *BIRDIE* TOLD ME!

LISTEN, TURD! I'M NOT *SCREWING AROUND* HERE! YOU BETTER START MAKING OUT A *WILL,* 'CAUSE BY *TOMORROW* YOUR *FAGGOT ASS* IS GONNA BE *SIX FEET UNDER* AND *CRAWLING* WITH *MAGGOTS!*

YOU AND ALL YOUR *FAG* FRIENDS!

GET LOST, CREEP! YOU DON'T EVEN KNOW WHAT YOU'RE *TALKING ABOUT!* WOODY IS *TWICE* THE MAN YOU ARE!

YEAH! BET *YOU* CAN'T EVEN *GET IT UP* LIMP-DICK!!

LOOK, I DON'T WANT ANY *TROUBLE,* DOUGIE--

TOO BAD! YOU *GOT IT,* JEW-BOY.

501

PAM, *WAIT!* ARE YOU, UM...LIKE, ARE YOU *SEEING* ANYONE? I MEAN, IF NOT, WANNA *HAVE LUNCH* WITH ME OR SOMETHING?

OH, UH...

I DON'T MEAN TO BE TOO *FORWARD*, BUT--

--I MEAN, IT ISN'T EVERY DAY I GET KISSED BY A BEAUTIFUL *STRANGER* AND I--

WAIT! WAIT. HOLD ON, WOODY.

LOOK, I *APPRECIATE* IT, BUT, Y'SEE HARRY *ISN'T*...

...I AM.

OH.

"YOU WERE *RIGHT*, DAD."

WHA--

TERRY?

"LIFE IS *DEFINITELY* GETTING MORE *COMPLICATED*."

YOU *TOLD* HIM?

"SO, WOODY, HAVE YOU HAD ANY MORE TROUBLE WITH THAT *BULLY?*"

"NO, NOT *YET*. I'M SURE IT'S JUST A MATTER OF *TIME* NOW."

YOU KNOW, IF IT GETS BAD, YOU COULD ALWAYS CALL THE *POLICE*. JUST BECAUSE HE'S A JUVENILE DOESN'T MEAN HE CAN'T BE *ARRESTED*.

SOMEHOW, DAD, I DON'T THINK THAT WOULD SOLVE ALL MY PROBLEMS.

PHONE CALL, JACOB!

IT'S *DAN PHILIPS* AT THE *BULLETIN*. I'LL KEEP MY *FINGERS* CROSSED!

MOM, COULD YOU STAY HERE FOR A SEC?

SURE, HONEY. WHAT'S UP?

I NEED SOME *ADVICE*.

O-KAY.

MOM, I DON'T SEEM TO BE MAKING MUCH *PROGRESS* WITH JEN. I MEAN, I'VE GOT HER *RESPECT* AND ALL, BUT AS LONG AS SHE'S STILL GOING OUT WITH ZOT, I FEEL LIKE I'M JUST--

--WELL... *LEFTOVERS*.

I'VE TRIED SEEING OTHER GIRLS, BUT IT NEVER SEEMS TO WORK OUT.

WELL, TOOTS, I *WOULD* SAY "BE PATIENT," BUT I GUESS YOU *HAVE* BEEN FOR A *WHILE* NOW.

ELEVEN MONTHS.

MAYBE IT'S TIME TO *MOVE ON*.

IF SHE REALLY LOVES YOU, SHE'LL COME AROUND. JUST DON'T BURN ANY BRIDGES BEHIND YOU.

WHAT IF I FORCE A DECISION?

YOU DON'T *HAVE* TO. TELL HER YOU'D RATHER NOT CONTINUE LIKE THIS. SHE'LL KNOW IT'S IN HER HANDS.

YEAH.

504

MOM, HOW DID DAD EVER WIN *YOU?*

GRADUALLY...PATIENTLY...

I WAS GOING OUT WITH THE *CAPTAIN OF THE FOOTBALL TEAM* AND YOUR DAD WAS JUST THIS BOOKISH LITTLE *SOPHOMORE.* HE HAD TO WORK *OVERTIME* JUST TO GET ME TO *NOTICE* HIM.

BUT, I GUESS, AFTER A WHILE I REALIZED THAT TO YOUR *FATHER* I WAS SOMEONE *IMPORTANT,* SOMEONE TO SHARE IDEAS WITH, TO ASK ADVICE...

TO THE *OTHER* GUY, I WAS JUST A *PROP.*

I DON'T EVEN REMEMBER HIS *NAME* NOW.

UNCLE HARRY SAYS DAD COULD HAVE BEEN *SECRETARY OF STATE* IF HE'D PLAYED HIS *CARDS* RIGHT. IS THAT *TRUE?*

WAS IT REALLY JUST SOME LITTLE THING THAT GOT HIM DEMOTED?

YES, IT *WAS,* HONEY. IT WAS JUST ONE *LITTLE THING.*

HE TOLD SOMEONE VERY POWERFUL THAT HE WOULD NEVER *LIE* FOR HIM.

IT'S MY TURN TO MAKE DINNER; I BETTER GET *STARTED.*

HOLD IT, LOUISE! NO COOKING FOR YOU TONIGHT! WE'RE GOING *OUT* FOR DINNER! DAN SAYS HE'S RUNNING MY PIECE ON *CZECH INDEPENDENCE!*

CONGRATULATIONS, DEAR!

AAAH, HE JUST WANTS TO GET OUT OF DOING *DISHES!*

505

ANY *TROUBLE* YESTERDAY?

NO, BUT ZOT IS *MEETING* ME AGAIN, JUST IN CASE.

Y'KNOW, WOODY, I REALLY APPRECIATE THE ARTICLE... JUST THE SAME, I ALMOST WISH YOU *HADN'T*...

YOU AND ME *BOTH*, PAL.

I'M REALLY *NERVOUS* ABOUT WHAT HAPPENS NEXT.

I MEAN, AT LEAST YOU *ARE* STRAIGHT.

SOME BIG TOUGH GUY CALLS *ME* A "FAGGOT", I DON'T KNOW *WHAT* I'D SAY. PROBABLY I'D JUST TURN WHITE.

MAYBE I'D *THROW UP.*

YOUR SECRET'S SAFE WITH *ME*, GEORGE.

I KNOW, WOODY. THANKS.

SEE YOU AROUND.

506

WHERE *IS* HE??

HI, WOODY! SORRY I'M *LATE.*

ZOT?

WHERE--?

I'M *INVISIBLE,* WOODY.

INVISIBLE?!!

SHSH! DOUGIE IS COMING THIS WAY. I'VE BEEN *FOLLOWING* HIM ALL AFTERNOON.

IF HE *HITS* YOU, TRY TO HIT HIM BACK. I'LL DO THE REST.

I WAS HOPING NOT TO HAVE TO GET HIT *AT ALL.*

THERE HE IS.

SORRY. CAN'T THROW THE FIRST *PUNCH.* IT'S AGAINST MY *PRINCIPLES.*

NOW YOU TELL ME...

H-HI, DOUGIE, UH... LOOK, COULDN'T WE *TALK THIS OVER* FIRST?

I MEAN, *LOOK,* I DIDN'T NAME YOU IN THE ARTICLE. THERE'S NO REASON YOU SHOULD TAKE THIS THING *PERSONALLY.*

IF WE JUST TALK ABOU--

QUEER!

HEY, **MISTER!** COULD YOU HELP ME? MY BROTHER THREW MY **BASEBALL CAP** ON THE ROOF AND I CAN'T **REACH** IT!

SURE, I'LL GET IT.

WE HAVE A **RAKE** IN THE GARAGE.

NO, I CAN JUST **CLIMB UP.**

I HAD TO GET MY *SNEAKERS* DOWN A LOT WHEN I WAS YOUR AGE.

"SO *TELL* ME, DAD...

"DID *YOU* EVER REACH *YOUR* LIGHTHOUSE?"

"NO. NOT *REALLY.*

"BUT AT LEAST I NEVER TURNED *BACK.*"

THANKS, MISTER! THAT WAS REALLY *NICE* OF YOU!

NO SWEAT.

BYE!

SEE YOU!

"SOMETIMES, A DIRECTION IS A DESTINATION.

"FOR *SOME* OF US, IT'S *ENOUGH.*"

GOD, *LOOK* AT ALL THESE *GLASSES!* I KEEP BRINGING THEM *UP* HERE AND THEN FORGETTING TO TAKE THEM BACK *DOWN.*

NO WONDER THERE WEREN'T ENOUGH FOR THE PARTY.

THE RIDDLE-CUPS WERE FUN.

OH, *ZOT!*

I *LOVE* WOODY, I REALLY *DO,* BUT NOW THAT HE'S *GONE* I SUDDENLY FEEL SO *FREE!*

WOODY'S A NICE GUY. I HOPE HE *FINDS SOMEONE.*

ME, *TOO...* HERE, I'LL BE RIGHT BACK. I SHOULD AT LEAST BRING SOME OF THESE *GLASSES* DOWNSTAIRS.

SURE.

Y'KNOW, JEN, I DIDN'T WANT TO *PRESSURE* YOU, BUT I AM *GRATEFUL* YOU CHOSE ME, EVEN IF IT MEANT THAT WOODY HAD TO LOSE OUT.

IT SURE MAKES THINGS A LOT *SIMPLER,* DOESN'T IT?

YEAH.

WANT TO HAVE SEX?

As noted up front, I made changes to the bully Dougie's dialogue in this story. In the original version, his language was so strong that even regular readers were taken aback and yanked out of the story to some degree. Many of us who grew up on mainstream superhero comics where strong language of any sort was prohibited were still exercising our new freedom, seeing how far we could take it. Terry's story had been a successful bit of limit-testing, I think, but looking back on Woody's issue a few years after the fact I found myself agreeing with readers who'd written in to complain that Dougie's over-the-top swearing didn't fit the tone of the series ("a turd in the punch bowl" as one reader put it). When we were planning the collection, I volunteered without prompting to trim back some of Dougie's excesses. It's still some pretty menacing stuff as it stands, but hopefully more in keeping with the stories that surround it.

A related problem that's too late to fix was the fact that I'd demonized this fictionalized real-world bully more than the assassins, crooks, megalomaniacs, and dictators that populated the rest of the series. I remember thinking myself justified (and maybe a bit clever) to have made my worst villain an ordinary school yard bully. Now I realize, looking back, that I was simply getting my own symbolic revenge on a handful of aggressive kids I had to deal with in my own grade school years, particularly elementary school. I had an emotional agenda, and it distorted what, up until then, had been an underlying current of understanding and acceptance of the fact that everyone is a hero in their own mind.

Real-world parallels abound during these issues. Spike's comics in Ronnie's story were inspired the lunchroom doodles of our friend Rob Morrison, and Clune was indeed the last name of our principal at Lexington High School during the years 1978–1982. Kurt and I thought "Clune!" made a great sound effect and put it into a comic we were working on at the time. I also did a short silent comic where "Dr. Clune"—a giant plastic levitating version of our principal—battled Brian Dewan's

character "The Incredible Indestructible Floating Fool." Yeah … It's a wonder I ever got a date before college.

Some readers guessed that Woody was a thinly fictionalized version of me, and there's plenty of evidence to support the theory. Looking at my old high school peers though, I saw Woody as a bit more like the kids in my class whose families were more politically engaged: the ones writing for the school newspaper or running for class president; nerds to a degree, perhaps, but more adult somehow, more engaged with the outside world. These were the children of journalists and Harvard law professors rather than my crowd, the geeky kids of engineers and computer scientists.

The art was unraveling even more than usual in these pages. An odd tendency to draw my characters as long, stiff shampoo bottles was starting to creep in here and there, and you can tell I was rushed in places. Figure drawing was always my Achilles' heel, but as the stories focused more on ordinary teenagers having ordinary conversations, my artistic limitations were increasingly getting in the way of the intended effects.

The Conversation

First published in *Zot! #35*.

Lettering:
Bob Lappan

Original series editor:
cat yronwode

Plot assist:
Ivy Ratafia

Eisner Award Nominee 1991:
"Best Single Issue"

HIYA.

IF THIS ISN'T A *GOOD TIME*, JEN--

NOOOO, ZOT. NOW IS AS GOOD A TIME AS ANY.

I DON'T THINK THIS IS THE KIND OF THING YOU CAN JUST *PUT OFF.*

OKAY, THEN...UM... WHAT DO YOU THINK? WANT TO HAVE *SEX?*

Z-HOHHT!!!

I--Y--YOU DON'T JUST--

JUST--

BH--

MBH--

...

ZOT, YEH--
EH--RR--

....

ZOT, YOU NEVER
EVEN SAID YOU
LOVE ME!

I LOVE YOU.

WELL, IT'S THE WRONG ORDER.

I LOVE YOU, TOO.

MR. *PERFECT TIMING.*

SO YOU WANT US TO M-MAKE LOVE, HUH?

IF YOU'D *LIKE* TO, YEAH.

I DON'T KNOW, ZOT. I REALLY WASN'T *EXPECTING* THIS FROM YOU. I MEAN, FROM *WOODY*, SURE.

HELL, I HAD AN ANSWER *ALL READY* FOR WOODY, BUT HE NEVER ASKED.

WOODY SURE DESERVES *SOMEBODY*, DOESN'T HE?

YES.

YES, HE DOES.

ZOT, WHAT *HAPPENED* TO YOU? I THOUGHT YOU WERE SO...SO *INNOCENT*. AND THEN YOU JUST...OUT OF THE BLUE...

WHY *NOW?*

WOODY'S GONE. I FIGURED IT'D BE LESS *COMPLICATED.*

AND WE'RE *ALONE.*

BUT THE *WAY* YOU SAY IT-- LIKE YOU WERE ASKING ME OUT *BOWLING* OR SOMETHING...

ZOT, HAVE YOU...?

HAVE YOU HAD ANY KIND OF, LIKE... Y'KNOW-- *EXPERIENCE?*

NO, NOT REALLY...

... I MEAN, UNLESS YOU COUNT MASTURB--

NO.

NO, WE WON'T COUNT THAT, ZOT.

ZOT, YOU *DO* UNDERSTAND WHY I'M KINDA *UPSET,* DON'T YOU?

ZOT, WHAT WERE YOU *EXPECTING* ME TO SAY?!

I DON'T KNOW, *EXACTLY,* JEN.

I GUESS EITHER YES, YOU'D *LIKE* TO--

OR--OR NO, YOU'D RATHER NOT--

OR *MAYBE,* AND, UH...

AND L-LET'S *TALK* ABOUT IT.

ZOT, I DON'T KNOW ABOUT *YOUR* WORLD, BUT SEX IS PRETTY *COMPLICATED* ON *THIS* ONE.

IF WE DID--I'M NOT SAYING WE *MIGHT*--BUT IF WE DID... I MEAN, DO YOU EVEN HAVE A *CONDOM* OR SOMETHING?

YEAH, OF *COURSE.*

I MAY BE *INEXPERIENCED,* BUT I'M NOT *STUPID.*

OKAY, GOOD. ACTUALLY, I DID... HAVE SOME... IN CASE YOU DIDN'T.

MOM GAVE THEM TO ME, JUST IN CASE I DIDN'T *WAIT* LIKE SHE...

...LIKE SHE SAID SHE HOPED I WOULD.

WELL, IF YOU THINK YOUR PARENTS WOULD BE *UPSET*--

OH, *NO,* I'M SURE THEY'D BE JUST *THRILLED* TO FIND OUT I'D LOST MY *VIRGINITY!*

OH, THAT'S A RELIEF.

I WAS BEING *SARCASTIC,* ZOT.

SORRY, I DON'T UNDERSTAND SARCASM.

ANYWAY, WHAT ABOUT *AIDS,* HUH?

WE'RE BOTH *VIRGINS.*

OH. RIGHT.

HUNH.

PRETTY *CASUAL* FOR A VIRGIN, IF YOU ASK ME.

...

OH--!

I TRUST YOU! I TRUST YOU!

BIG
BEAR.

THIS IS *MARVIN*.

DIDN'T I EVER
INTRODUCE
YOU?

NOPE.

I'M SORRY. ZOT,
THIS IS MARVIN.
MARVIN, THIS IS
ZOT.

HI,
MARVIN.

I GOT MARVIN ON MY FIFTH
BIRTHDAY. WE WERE MOVING FOR
THE FIRST TIME THAT WEEK. THE
IDEA WAS I'D HAVE AT LEAST ONE
FRIEND I COULD TAKE WITH ME.

I MADE 'EM PROMISE TO LET
MARVIN COME WITH US IN THE CAR,
INSTEAD OF WITH THE MOVERS.

EVERY TIME WE'VE MOVED SINCE, HE'S COME WITH US, ALL STRAPPED IN BESIDE ME.

ALL EXCEPT THIS *LAST* TIME 'CAUSE WE TOOK THE *PLANE*. THEY SAID HE WAS *TOO BIG* TO *CARRY* ON.

SO THEY *STUFFED* HIM IN A *CRATE*. AND PUT HIM IN THE *LUGGAGE COMPARTMENT*.

I WAS SO *PISSED OFF.*

HE WAS THE ONLY FRIEND I HAD LEFT.

'TIL *YOU*, ANYWAY.

I'M SO *MESSED UP.*

I DON'T EVEN KNOW WHY YOU *WANT* ME.

YOU DESERVE SOMEBODY AS PERFECT AS *YOU* ARE.

I'M NOT PERFECT, JENNY.

HNH.

PERFECT ANSWER.

527

ZOT.

YEAH?

I'M *SCARED*. I FEEL LIKE I *HAVE* TO DO IT AND I'M JUST NOT *READY*.

YOU DON'T HAVE TO DO THIS, JEN. YOU DON'T HAVE TO DO *ANYTHING* IF YOU DON'T WANT TO.

I KNOW, ZOT. AND... AND YOU'RE A *SWEETHEART*, BUT...

BUT SOMETIMES I FEEL LIKE I MUST BE THE ONLY GIRL IN THE *UNIVERSE* THAT HASN'T DONE IT YET.

Y'KNOW TERRY'S FRIEND JUDY--? SHE SAYS SHE'S *DONE IT* WITH *FOUR DIFFERENT GUYS* ALREADY. AND SHE'S JUST A *SOPHOMORE*.

SHE *SAYS* SHE HAS...

DO YOU THINK SHE'S *LYING?*

WELL, I WOULDN'T WANT TO SAY, BUT I KNOW THAT TERRY ASKED HER IF THEY USE A CONDOM...

YEAH--?

AND JUDY SAID, "NO, RICKY'S NOT *INTO* REAL ESTATE."

REALLY??

WOW.

SO, YOU...

YOU REALLY THINK OF ME THAT WAY, HUH?

I MEAN,... SEXUALLY.

SURE.

WHAT

UM...

WHAT EXACTLY IS IT THAT... UM, Y'KNOW... *EXCITES* YOU?

I DUNNO. *EVERYTHING,* I GUESS

AW, *C'MON!* WHAT *IS* IT, ZOT? WHAT ABOUT ME *TURNS YOU ON?*

WELL, I, UH...

IS IT MY *HAIR?* IS *THAT* IT?

SURE, IT'S NICE HAIR.

AH, BUT YOU SAID *"NICE"!* YOU SAID *"NICE"* HAIR!

HAIR ISN'T *IMPORTANT,* IS IT?!

NNNNN...

NO. NOT REALLY.

PLEASE, ZOT, *PLEASE!* JUST NAME *ONE THING.* I'M *DYING* TO KNOW!

WELL, THERE IS THAT, UM...

UH, *THIS,* UM...

WHAT DO YOU CALL IT?

THIS. HERE.

WHAT, THIS? I KNOW WHAT YOU MEAN. THIS LITTLE *BONE* THING, RIGHT?

I DON'T KNOW WHAT IT'S CALLED EITHER.

YOU REALLY LIKE THAT? *WEIRD.*

SO, IS THAT THE SEXIEST THING ABOUT ME?

WELL... NOT THE *MOST* SEXY.

SO, WHAT *IS* IT? WHAT DO YOU THINK ABOUT THE *MOST?*

OH.

SORRY.

THAT'S OKAY. WHY SHOULD *YOU* BE ANY DIFFERENT?

YOU WANTED THIS SO MUCH.

I'VE LASTED SIXTEEN YEARS *WITHOUT* HAVING SEX, JEN. I'M SURE I CAN LAST A FEW MORE.

HNH...

SOMEHOW, ZOT, I DON'T THINK YOU'LL HAVE TO WAIT QUITE *THAT* LONG.

ZOT, I WISH YOU'D SAY *"MAKE LOVE"* INSTEAD OF *"HAVE SEX."* IT SOUNDS SO MUCH *BETTER.*

MUCH MORE *ROMANTIC.*

YEAH, I GUESS...

I DON'T KNOW WHY I SAY IT THAT WAY.

I KNOW THAT SEX *WITHOUT* LOVE IS A BAD IDEA.

MAYBE I JUST DON'T WANT TO GET THE TWO *CONFUSED.*

OH, WELL,

GUESS IT'S TIME FOR BED.

What a strange artifact this story is! It was nominated for an Eisner Award, so *someone* must have liked it. It was an unusual exercise for its day and it was worth trying in principle. I can even live with the script; the dialogue may induce cringes, but they're mostly in the right places. No, all that's fine.

The *art,* however, has always bugged me. Somehow, I managed to create the perfect showcase for everything awkward and embarrassing about my drawing style. Worst of all, I remember how earnestly I was trying to get it right, even as I could see it slipping through my fingers. Throughout this collection, I've made a few adjustments where possible, but the only way I could truly fix this one eighteen years later is by drawing it over from scratch, and in that way lies madness.

A big problem in this particular instance was the need not only to create natural, convincing poses and expressions for Zot and Jenny (hard enough for me on a good day) but then to repeat them with only minimal variations throughout dozens of subsequent panels. In my attempt to keep those rows rigidly consistent, any life I might have been able to breathe into a single image was choked out of its various clones.

Consistency is a big problem for cartoonists with formalist tendencies like me. We get bored easily and want to change gears and try new things constantly. Character designs waver, inking styles shift. But consistency is indispensable for creating the illusion of life from panel to panel and issue to issue. Without it, the fact that the reader is just looking at lines on paper reasserts itself.

I'm not always so negative about my art. I like the varied visual designs of most of my characters. I like the crazy abstractions of Dekko. I like the compositions and effects I found in ordinary objects like school desks and buses. And my perspective and environments were solid for the most part.

I just couldn't draw *people* yet. And people have a way of turning up.

As for the ending, yes, I deliberately left it open to interpretation. It was important to assert Zot's basic decency in the way he accepted Jenny's wish to wait, but I didn't have a lot of strong opinions about what teenagers should do with each other in interdimensional suitcases, provided they took appropriate precautions.

Again, now I'm the parent of a teenager myself, so *ha ha,* the joke's on me. (Jenny is, for the record, a couple of years older by this issue.)

I won't tell you what I think happened next, but I will tell you that my editor thinks they did and Ivy thinks they didn't. Readers were similarly split.

The Great Escape

First published in *Zot! #36.*

Lettering:
Bob Lappan

Original series editor:
cat yronwode

Plot assist:
Ivy Ratafia

I'LL TELL YOU A *SECRET.*

I'M ACTUALLY A LOT SMARTER THAN EVERYONE *THINKS.*

THIS WILL BE THE *SECOND SEMESTER* IN A ROW THAT I'VE RECEIVED A *D* IN EVERY SINGLE CLASS.

NO *A*'s. NO *B*'s. NO *C*'s. NO *F*'s. JUST *D*'s.

BUT THE *TRUTH* IS I ACTUALLY KNOW MY SUBJECTS BETTER THAN ANY OTHER KID IN SCHOOL.

I *COULD* GET *STRAIGHT A*'s IF I *WANTED* TO.

THAT'S WHAT *THEY* WANT ME TO DO. THAT'S WHAT THEY *EXPECT* ME TO DO.

BUT I'M NOT *LIKE* THEIR *OTHER* CHILDREN. I DON'T *WANT* TO BE LIKE THEM. THAT'S TOO EASY.

ANY HARDWORKING STUDENT CAN GET *STRAIGHT A*'s.

AH, BUT STRAIGHT *D*'s...WITHOUT EVEN A *PLUS* OR A *MINUS*...

...NOW *THAT* WOULD BE AN *ACCOMPLISHMENT!*

ANYWAY, THAT'S MY SECRET.

ONE OF THEM.

THE GREAT ESCAPE

Betsy knew that the heat of the MotherShip's primary boosters would obliterate the school and everyone in it,

but in her heart, she felt that Xxyzizor was right, that this was the only way.

The pressures of the acceleration bore down on her like an immense pillar of lead,

yet still she found the stength to turn her head toward the rear monitor

and watched numbly as the flames consumed the surrounding neighborhood

ELIZABETH!

ELIZABETH!! IS YOUR LIGHT STILL ON? PUT THAT BOOK DOWN *THIS INSTANT* AND GET TO *BED!*

ELIZABETH!

DO YOU HEAR ME?!

and her parents' house with it.

ZOT, PLEASE DON'T GO.

I *HAVE* TO, JEN.

THERE'S THIS GUY.

AND HE HAS THE POWER TO ESCAPE FROM *ANYTHING*.

HE *TELEPORTS*...

OR NO, HE HAS A *CAPE* OR SOMETHING.

AND HE CAN JUST *STEP THROUGH* THE *CAPE* AND BE *ANYWHERE ELSE*.

IF HE DOESN'T LIKE WHERE HE IS, HE CAN JUST STEP THROUGH THE CAPE.

AND BE *FAR, FAR AWAY*...

THAT'S A *GOOD* ONE, I SHOULD WRITE THAT DOWN IN *THE BOOK.*

IT'S OKAY, ZOE, MY MOMMY DIDN'T MEAN TO HIT YOU.

WRUF!

YE-ES, DEAR. I KNOW. I KNOW.

MOMMY WILL BE OKAY, ZOE. JUST YOU *WAIT AND SEE.*

HEY, DO YOU KNOW HOW TO MAKE EVERYTHING GET BETTER?

YOU JUST *CLOSE YOUR EYES* AND THINK OF EXACTLY HOW YOU WANT LIFE TO BE.

IF YOU DO THIS *OFTEN ENOUGH*, YOU'LL JUST *WAKE UP* ONE DAY AND *THERE YOU'LL BE.*

NO ONE HAD TO *TELL ME THIS!* I KNEW IT *INSTINCTIVELY!*

HE SAID THEY'D *UNDERSTAND* ME ON HIS WORLD.

IS IT *POSSIBLE?*

WHAT IF HE FINDS HIS WAY *BACK THERE* SOMEDAY?

WOULD I WANT TO GO TOO? WOULD *SHE?*

MAYBE NOT *FOREVER,* BUT...

BUT, JUST FOR A WHILE...

TO ESCAPE...

CLEK

ZOT?!

HELLO... MOM HOME?

BUTCH!

UH... MOM'S NOT COMING HOME 'TIL *TOMORROW NIGHT*, REMEMBER?

WHICH WAY'S THE BATHROOM? I GOTTA THROW UP...

BUTCH, YOU'VE GOT TO *HELP ME!* ZOT'S IN *TROUBLE*, I'M *SURE* OF IT!

NGUH... GOTTA GO SLEEP... NO... GODDA THROW UP, THEN GO SLEEP...

BUTCH, *LISTEN!!*

ZOT DIDN'T *COME BACK* LAST NIGHT! WE'VE GOT TO GO INTO THE CITY AND *FIND HIM!!*

WHEN DID HE SAY HE'D BE BACK?

SIX A.M. HAVE YOU BEEN *DRINKING?*

I'M GOING TO BED NOW.

AFTER I THROW UP.

BUTCH, *PLEASE!*

PLEASE...

LOOK...

...IF HE'S NOT BACK IN AN HOUR, COME AND *GET* ME, OKAY?

OKAY, BUTCH. ONE HOUR.

THANKS.

DONE!

HAVE A *GOOD SUMMER,* WOODY!

THANKS, MR. J. YOU TOO!

HI, GEORGE. ARE RONNIE AND SPIKE STILL IN THERE?

YEAH. HOW DID *FRENCH* GO?

DAMN! SOMEBODY *PICK UP!*

HI, WOODY!

TERRY, *WAIT UP!*

DAMN.

CLIK!

JENNY DIDN'T SHOW UP FOR HER *FINAL* THIS MORNING.

WOW, THAT'S NOT *LIKE* HER!

HAVE YOU *TALKED* TO HER?

NOT SINCE *SATURDAY.*

YOU HEARD THE *NEWS,* RIGHT?

ABOUT THE DIVORCE. YEAH.

I HOPE SHE'S *ALL RIGHT,* WOODY.

ME TOO.

549

LOOK, BUTCH! SEE THE WAY THE *PENDANT* IS GLOWING? THAT MEANS ZOT IS *NEAR* HERE!

BUT I DON'T GET IT. IF HE WAS IN ONE OF THESE BUILDINGS, WHY DIDN'T HE JUST *CALL?*

YEAH, I KNOW WHAT YOU MEAN, SIS. THIS ISN'T EXACTLY *"CRIME CENTRAL."* I FIGURED HE WAS IN A GUTTER IN *HARLEM* OR SOMETHING.

RIGHT, THANKS FOR THE *MORAL SUPPORT.*

AW, *YOU* KNOW WHAT I MEAN!

YEAH. YEAH.

LOOK, I THINK IT'S LEADING US *THIS* WAY.

OKAY, I'LL USE MY *EYE-BEAMS* TO--

Ding-Dong!

PIZZA! YEAH!

OKAY, *HOLD ON!* I'LL GET IT!

RRIING!

OH, UM...OH, SHIT, UH... HERE, RONNIE, YOU GET THE PIZZAS!

MONEY.

RING!! RING!!

HERE.

HELLO? JENNY?

IT *IS!* BOY, AM I GLAD *YOU* CALLED, I WAS--

HUH? WHAT?

OH, MY GOD.

OH MY *GOD!* IS HE--?!

UH-HUH.

LESSEE-- TEN, TWENTY, THERE YOU GO.

KEEP THE CHANGE.

THANKS.

UH, NO, I THINK TERRY'S AT *HOME*. I COULD *CALL* HER FOR YOU.

JEN, HOW--?

OH, WOODY. THEY *SHOT HIM!* HE WAS ONLY TRYING TO *HELP* AND THEY *SHOT* HIM!

NO, NO. THE *POLICE*.

NO, THEY DIDN'T *MEAN* TO...

OH, IT'S SO *STUPID*, WOODY... THEY WERE RAIDING SOME *CRACK HOUSE* OR SOMETHING. THERE WAS A LOT OF *SHOOTING*...

AND...AND...

HE THOUGHT HE COULD *TALK* TO THEM. *JESUS!*

OKAY, *WAIT*, HOLD IT. TALK TO *WHO?*

THE *POLICE?*

NO, THE UM..., THE GUYS, THE *ADDICTS*. AND *THEY* CLAIM THEY WERE JUST MAKING *FUN* OF HIM, BUT... BUT I DON'T... AND THEN THE *SHOOTING* AND...

AND THE POLICE THOUGHT...

OH, WOODY, HE'S LOST A *LOT* OF BLOOD AND HE... HE...

HE'S NOT *WAKING UP*.

THEY ALREADY OPERATED *ONCE*; NOW THEY'RE TALKING ABOUT--WAIT, THE *DOCTOR'S* COMING BACK. I BETTER *GO*. WOODY, I KNOW IT'S A LOT TO ASK, BUT--

I'M ON MY WAY.

THANKS, WOODY. I... THANKS.

I'M AFRAID WE'LL HAVE TO GO IN AGAIN.

STEP BACK, PLEASE.

CLIK

HERE THEY ARE! I GAVE HIM--

HEY, WHAT'S WRONG?

THANKS FOR GIVING US A *RIDE*, DAD.

YEAH, *THANKS*, MR. B.

NO PROBLEM.

I'D RATHER *THIS* THAN HAVE YOU GO IN BY *YOURSELVES*. SEEMS THE CITY'S GOTTEN *WORSE* SINCE LOUISE AND I HAD THE APARTMENT.

JUST LIKE EVERYWHERE ELSE, I SUPPOSE... YOU'VE GOT TO *LOOK OUT* FOR YOURSELF THESE DAYS.

THERE THEY ARE.

HOW IS HE, BUTCH? IS HE GOING TO *MAKE* IT?

YEAH, HE'LL BE OKAY. THEY GOT HIM PRETTY *DOPED UP*, THOUGH. HE MIGHT NOT BE AWAKE FOR A WHILE.

HOW IS JENNY DOING?

HOW DO YOU *THINK?*

LOOK, UH...WHY DON'T I SHOW YOU GUYS WHERE THE *ROOM* IS? YOU STAY *HERE*, BERNSTEIN.

SURE, BUTCH.

WOODY?

I'M HERE NOW, JEN. ARE YOU OKAY?

CAN I GET YOU ANYTHING?

JEN?

WOODY, I *HATE* THIS PLACE.

I KNOW, JEN. HOSPITALS ARE JUST SO--

WOODY--

I'M NOT TALKING ABOUT THE HOSPITAL.

YEAH, I'LL BE FINE. WHAT DID *MOM* HAVE TO SAY?

SHE SAID SHE'D BE BACK AROUND SEVEN TOMORROW NIGHT. I DON'T THINK SHE'S GOING AWAY AGAIN FOR A WHILE.

I DIDN'T TELL HER ABOUT ZOT.

HOW DID SHE SOUND?

SHE SOUNDED PRETTY *BAD*. I DON'T THINK HAVING YOU *MAD* AT HER IS *HELPING* ANY.

YOU COULD'VE AT LEAST *TALKED* TO HER.

YEAH, I... YOU'RE RIGHT, I... I SHOULD'VE...

I GUESS...

IT'S JUST...

I DUNNO...

GET SOME *SLEEP*, WILLYA? YOU SOUND LIKE A *ZOMBIE*.

BUTCH?

I'M HERE.

LIFE *SUCKS*, RIGHT? I MEAN, EVERYTHING JUST TOTALLY *SUCKS*, RIGHT?

YEAH, PRETTY MUCH.

OKAY, THANKS.

JUST CHECKING.

GOODNIGHT, JEN.

GOODNIGHT.

...WANT TO PUT IT THAT WAY, LARRY... BUT IF THE CONGRESS DOESN'T BG SOME?...

WE'LL BE *RIGHT BACK* AFTER THESE IMPORTANT MESSAGES... ♪ DOUBLE YOUR PLEASURE! ♪ DOUBLE YOUR FUN! WITH DOUBLE MINT DOUBLE M DOUBLE DOU

JENNY, WAKE UP.

NO, ZOT... PLEASE DON'T MAKE ME WAKE UP.

WHY, JENNY? DON'T YOU WANT TO *SEE* ME?

I DON'T WANT TO SEE THEM *HURT* YOU *EVER AGAIN.* PLEASE LET ME STAY HERE. DON'T MAKE ME GO BACK THERE.

BUT THERE'S SO MUCH TO *SEE,* JEN. DON'T YOU WANT TO *SEE* LIFE?

NO, I'VE SEEN *ENOUGH.* IT'S *COLD* OUT THERE, ZOT. CAN'T I JUST STAY IN HERE WHERE IT'S *WARM?*

IT'S WARM OUT HERE *TOO.* C'MON, JEN. OPEN YOUR EYES.

IT'S *MORNING.*

YOU *DID* IT.

SO, HOW'D YOU GET *FIXED UP* SO *FAST,* BLONDIE?

ACTUALLY, BUTCH, IT TOOK ME ABOUT *THREE WEEKS* ON *MY* WORLD, BUT SINCE TIME *FLOWS DIFFERENTLY* BETWEEN OUR DIMENSIONS, I WAS ABLE TO COME BACK *HERE* JUST A FEW HOURS *LATER.*

-*TSK*- I FIGURED *THAT* OUT.

WHAT *I* WANT TO KNOW IS HOW DID YOU FINALLY *FIND* US HERE, MAX? I THOUGHT THE ONLY COPY OF MY WORLD'S COORDINATES CAME WITH *US!*

ALMOST! FORTUNATELY, I REMEMBERED SCRIBBLING DOWN THE DATA WHEN WE SENT YOU HOME THAT FIRST TIME. HAD TO CLEAN OUT THE LAB TO FIND THE DAMN PIECE OF PAPER, THOUGH.

TOOK *WEEKS.*

WAIT A MINUTE! IF TIME "*FLOWS*" SO DIFFERENTLY, HOW COME YOU GOT HERE *A WHOLE YEAR LATE?!*

YES, WELL...

I'M AFRAID MY *HANDWRITING* ISN'T ALL THAT GOOD... SORRY.

AWW, MAX, *WE* FORGIVE YOU!

WE HAVE *MORE* GOOD NEWS, JEN. MAX AND I FINALLY CONVINCED THE *SCIENCE COUNCIL* TO APPROVE *INTERDIMENSIONAL TRAVEL* AS *SAFE!*

GREAT! SO WHEN CAN I COME *VISIT* AGAIN?

WELL, I WANTED TO SHOW MAX AROUND THE *CITY* TODAY. WHY DON'T WE MEET HERE IN THE BACK YARD AROUND EIGHT? YOU CAN INVITE *THE WHOLE GANG* IF YOU WANT.

IT'S A *DATE!*

IS THAT ALL WE HAVE TO DO? JUST *STEP THROUGH* IT?

YUP. THAT'S ALL.

WILL IT *HURT?*

IT'LL *TINGLE* A LITTLE. NOTHING *SERIOUS.*

WILL WE BE...*WELCOME* HERE, MAX?

EVERYONE IS WELCOME HERE. C'MON IN.

WHERE DID *JENNY* GO?

THIS ISN'T *REAL*, RIGHT? I MEAN, THIS IS ALL SOME KIND OF *TRICK*, ISN'T IT?

OH, RONNIE, I *LOVE* YOU, BUT YOU ARE SO *DENSE!*

AND THIS IS *PEABODY*, ZOT'S ROBOT BUTLER.

PLEASED TO MEET YOU.

A *ROBOT?* A *REAL* ROBOT?!

I think it was my editor at Eclipse, cat yronwode, who described the ending of this story as my attempt at a defense of fiction, or at least the escapist variety that *Zot!* grew out of. A cartoonist I know said it came across more like a case for taking drugs (whoops!). If I had to hazard a guess, I think that on some level, I may have been trying to justify the very existence of comics like *Zot!* to myself.

Understanding Comics was already taking shape on my drawing board by the time this issue hit the stands. I was on fire with the conviction that comics were a medium, not a genre. I saw comics as a blank slate, capable of accommodating any style, any technique, any subject matter. I was inspired by the depth and beauty of the great European masters, by the dizzying variety of the huge manga industry (long before it conquered the U.S. market), and by the aggressive experimentation of Art Spiegelman and his allies. I knew that making better comics was about so much more than just making better superhero comics, even though the spandex set still comprised the vast majority of the comics market in America despite all our advances to that point.

What then was I to make of that first six years of my career? Was I part of the problem? Was the entire superhero genre just one big dead horse I'd been trying to find new ways to beat?

As it turns out, I wasn't so much struggling to correct an imbalance in the marketplace as I was trying to correct an imbalance in myself. Creating a book like *Understanding Comics* satisfied that need perfectly as I plunged into a prolonged formalist adventure, but it led eventually to a different kind of imbalance that I'm only now beginning to correct after seventeen years as I prepare to head back into fiction.

Revisiting these stories, rediscovering what I loved about comics in those early days, and the ways in which my own skills served or hampered my goals, has been enormously valuable for me. Other work by talented writers and artists from this period is still sadly out of print, so I'm grateful for the opportunity.

When we announced this collection, one online journalist familiar with my later career remarked that it was unusual to see me turning my attention to the past after such a consistent focus on the future of comics. He had a point. Looking back was never my strong point.

But this is *Zot!*, after all, a world where looking back and looking forward are one and the same. The far-flung future, the distant past, and every moment in between.

Life After Zot

As soon as the final pages of *Zot!* were sent off, I dove head-long into writing and drawing the 215 pages of *Understanding Comics*. During the fifteen months it took to complete the book, we finally succeeded at conceiving, with a little help from Boston IVF, and our first daughter was born only a few weeks before the book was published. We had been trying to have a baby for four years by that point. Those nine months of Ivy reading to me in the green swivel chair while both our little "projects" grew was one of the most gratifying periods of our lives.

When *Understanding Comics* hit the stands in May 1993, fans saw it as a book about comics by the guy who did *Zot!*, but within a few months, *Zot!* was demoted to "that series McCloud did before *Understanding Comics.*" *U.C.* has since been translated into sixteen languages and presumably read by twenty times as many people as ever read *Zot!* in its original incarnation. Many readers who have come to recognize me for my little cartoon avatar had no idea why the little guy was wearing a T-shirt with a lightning bolt on it.

Still, a loyal group of fans at conventions would frequently ask me when *Zot!* was coming back. I always told them that I wanted to bring *Zot!* back "in a year or two," but that I had a few projects to get out of the way first. I always meant it, but somehow the date kept getting pushed back and the list of projects kept growing. There were too many other possibilities to pursue.

For the rest of the '90s and the early part of this decade, computers and the Web became a full-time obsession. Unlike my earlier obsession with chess, comics and digital media didn't have to compete for my attention, since they combined quite naturally. I became closely associated with the webcomics movement, though a lot of my aesthetic and economic theories about where we could go got me in hot water with others in the fast-growing field, especially when many of those ideas saw print in my second, more controversial book, *Reinventing Comics,* in 2000.

That same year, *Zot!* did return briefly in the form of an experimental webcomic. It was a Dekko story in sixteen "chapters," each of which were laid out in long rows of panels, connected by the linking lines I call "trails." The art is a bit raw, drawn clumsily on a small Wacom tablet at 72 dots per inch to make it impossible for me to "repurpose" it for print (yes the Dekko in me won over the Max in that instance). Still, it has some nice moments. If 559 story pages of *Zot!* aren't enough for you, feel free to check it out.

The future was no longer some abstract fictional concept as it was in *Zot!* Talking about strategies for the future of comics became a daily concern. I found myself lecturing at computer

My avatar, complete with Zot! T-shirt.

companies, conferences, and universities with increasing frequency (a good thing too, since I was giving away the webcomics for the most part, and my royalties on the books, as good as they were, were hardly enough to live on exclusively all these years). I also took on the occasional interesting side job, doing comics features for magazines like *Wired, Computer Gaming World,* and *Nickelodeon,* as well as writing some *Superman* titles for DC Comics.

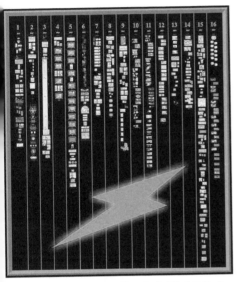

Graphic novel at-a-glance: A "long shot" of Zot! *Online's 440 panels, available at scottmccloud.com.*

Some of my hopes for webcomics have yet to pan out, but I'm optimistic that the thousands of creators making them and the hundreds of thousands of readers who enjoy them will continue searching for new ways improve the experience on both sides of the monitor. Meanwhile, I get to take a few years off from rolling that particular boulder up the hill, because as of now, I have a *new* obsession.

Since 2002, I've been teaching seminars in the art of making comics, starting at the Minneapolis College of Art and Design, then moving on to destinations as diverse as M.I.T., a Boston arts high school, and a Barcelona getaway for the writers of Danish Disney duck comics. Teaching how to tell stories in comics form awakened my desire to tell one of my own; an idea I'd had since the *Zot!* days that I realized could make a great graphic novel.

In 2006, my third book, *Making Comics,* gave me the opportunity to sharpen my ideas on storytelling and teach myself enough about the subject that I could do my new story justice. If all goes well, I hope to start work on that graphic novel shortly.

I feel like Halley's Comet, returning to fiction after all these years. The pull of its gravity gets stronger every day. Now that I've passed back through *Zot!'s* old orbit, I'm more at peace with all the mistakes the younger me made, and better able to appreciate the spots where I got it right. I'm also more at peace with the role that genre fiction, including superhero fiction, plays in the greater ecology of the narrative arts.

I think that at the heart of most genres is the desire to escape to a new world every bit as convincing as this one, yet safely removed from this one's daily pain, while at the heart of most progressive narrative movements is the desire to meaningfully reconnect with that pain, or to strip away the illusion entirely and rethink the nature of the creative act itself.

I jumped to that third option in 1993 and have rarely looked back since, but I've also continued to enjoy genre fiction in other media. I've seen what a powerful effect it's had on my family and I can appreciate the deeper truths such stories can unearth while still entertaining us. Meanwhile, though, that middle option has tantalized me from afar as modern masters like Ware, Bechdel, and Spiegelman have given us a much more honest document of the world we live in than anything comics in America could offer in its first hundred years—a revolution in content to offset the revolution in form that's kept me excited all these years.

I don't know exactly where I'll next land on that expanding creative landscape, but I can't wait to find out.

www.scottmccloud.com